ON THE T

'If I am to have suspicions, what should they be about?'

Artunian took a long time replying. He put the tips of his fingers together and examined them carefully. He threw his head back and looked out towards the Louvre. A *bateau-mouche* hooted briefly as it approached the Carrousel bridge.

'If I wanted to harbour ungenerous suspicions about André Marchand – ' the words were spoken so softly that I had to strain to hear them above the traffic ' – if I wanted to do that, I think I would finally ask myself the subversive question that none of us has any right to ask about colleagues of the Resistance. And that question is: *why did he survive the war?*'

I waited, but clearly there was to be nothing more.

Also by Derek Kartun in Sphere Books:

BEAVER TO FOX

Flittermouse

DEREK KARTUN

SPHERE BOOKS LIMITED
London and Sydney

First published in Great Britain by
Century Publishing Co. Ltd, 1984

Published by Sphere Books Ltd 1985
30–32 Gray's Inn Road, London WC1X 8JL

For my Mother

TRADE
MARK

Printed and bound in Great Britain by
Cox & Wyman Ltd, Reading

CHAPTER 1

André Marchand

On the corner of the rue La Fayette and the rue Cadet there stands a *boulangerie-patisserie* with an annual turnover which a knowledgable client once estimated at something over 1,500 million francs: say for convenience a figure in the $300 million range. It will surprise no one to learn that all this cash isn't derived from the *croissants* and *cafés-crèmes*, served by a sharp-faced lady of uncertain provenance and dressed all in black. As a matter of fact, as *boulangeries* go, it is nothing special. And the impressive turnover is achieved not by the shop but by its customers. For here on any weekday can be found shrewd-looking men in dark suits conducting business in twos and threes at the little round marble-topped tables. Most of them are Jewish and those who are not Jews look Jewish and are in fact Armenians. They all wear waistcoats, summer and winter, and they all have security pockets in the inside lining of their waistcoats. These pockets contain twenty-centimetre squares of tissue paper folded inwards to form secure envelopes. And in these envelopes they carry precious stones, usually diamonds. The address of the *boulangerie* is No. 51 rue La Fayette and it has been there since 1911. It is almost opposite the Diamond Club and it probably sees more business done than the Club itself.

'You'll find this man Artunian at number fifty-one most mornings between ten and twelve,' Andrew Pabjoy had said. 'It's the only place to contact him because like most *courtiers* – they're diamond brokers – he hasn't got an office. He's very big in emeralds. And well clued up, though he hasn't worked directly for the DST* for the last ten years. But he keeps in touch with his friends.'

'He knew Marchand?'

'He must have known a good deal *about* him. Marchand was Minister of the Interior for a couple of years while Artunian was on the DST payroll. The DST keeps a very close watch on its boss.'

'Will he talk to us?'

'He owes me a favour.'

'But what exactly am I supposed to be looking for when I get over there?'

'Don't really know till you begin to find out, do you? Talk to Arti. You'll get insights, leads, fresh avenues to explore. New horizons opening up. You could use a new horizon, Carey. Hell, how should I know what you're looking for?'

Pabjoy was good at distancing himself slightly but usefully from a project. He would set something up, fold someone into it like a cook folding eggs into the batter and then take a 'your party, not mine' position which enabled him to show a clean pair of heels in the event of disaster. But disaster was rare because he was skilled in steering it away from the Section. It was why he had demonstrated what he would call survival capability in a post where the professional mortality rate was high. It was why the Section itself was still there.

'Let us consider a scenario,' Pabjoy said. He liked to affect the clichés of the American business world. At that time they were always writing scenarios. Or structuring their options. Though for Pabjoy this hip talk was not a substitute for thought. He stole the phrases but left their soporific purpose behind.

'What have we?' Pabjoy pulled one of his special yellow pads towards him and picked a pencil from among a dozen which Penny kept viciously sharpened in a holder on the immaculate

*Défense et Sécurité du Territoire: the service responsible for counter-espionage on French soil. Heads to the Minister of the Interior.

desk. The pads he got by the dozen whenever he was in the States. They were a sickly buttercup yellow with green feint lines, in an inconvenient page size which fitted no known European envelope. He always kept four of them – not three or five, but four – in a perfectly trimmed pile on his desk.

'What have we?' The sharp 2H drew neat squares on the yellow page as he enumerated his propositions, and from squares they developed sides and tops to become cubes, and inner corners to become empty boxes with, ultimately, open lids.

'We have a suicide which is, on the face of it, implausible, but which Wavre persists in dismissing as *sans signification*.'

First box completed. Pabjoy's French accent, acquired during a distant posting to the Paris Station, was passable and he liked to air it.

'We have implausibility in the sense that Marchand no doubt *took* his overdose, but has no record of depression. Also, he had no visible troubles which he couldn't cope with, unless you classify, as I concede some would, the Common Agricultural Policy as a matter for suicide. Also, I simply do not believe that members of Government who are still *compos mentis* ever commit suicide, just as they never give up office, unless there's one hell of a good reason.'

Second, larger box hovering above the first one.

'So he must have *in*visible trouble. And when a Minister – a man who has been in and out of Government for over thirty years – has the kind of trouble which leads him to take twenty Nembutal at Claridges and leave a patently improbable note behind, then we begin to have a *situation*.'

Third box. Pabjoy divided life into 'situations' and 'non-starters'. Situations were what he was there to clear up. Non-starters were fake situations, designed to trap the unwary into wasting Government manpower and money. Frugal by nature, he did not like waste.

It seemed to me there were more exciting tasks than proving out a hunch that the French Minister for Foreign Affairs had a skeleton in his cupboard. Everyone knew the cupboards of French Governments concealed a veritable Golgotha of skulls and tibias. And the French never really mind. The search for truth, as a distinguished Frenchman once pointed out, is not a French passion.

Pabjoy was working on his fourth box.

'Then we have a quite surprising – I would even say an astonishing – interest from the Foreign Secretary. All right, no one likes to have an official French corpse, in rigor and with an empty pill bottle, on the second floor of Claridges, with Parliament sitting and HMG in one of its Common Market spasms. No one likes it, I'll grant you that. And one would expect the Foreign Secretary to like it least of all. But is that a reason, Carey,' and here Pabjoy put rapid lids onto all his boxes, 'is that a reason for the little Welsh runt himself to call me at the unearthly hour of eight am to tell me he'll see me in his office at eight forty-five sharp?'

'It isn't,' I said.

'You're damn right it isn't.' Much of Pabjoy's slang was obsolete. 'Anyway, the Sûreté and the Yard are swarming all over the entire business and neither need, request nor want any help from the Section.'

'What did he tell you?' I asked.

'It's none of your damn business what he told me,' Pabjoy said amiably.

'But I'll tell you this. He had Matthews there from the War House. And that shit Killigrew from Special Branch. And one of his own security people. I didn't know him. Chap with a withered arm and to all appearances a deaf mute. So what does all that suggest to you, Carey?'

'A degree of inter-departmental co-operation which I simply don't believe.'

'Neither do I. But I do see a very unusual degree of inter-departmental *interest* or *concern*, or even *panic*. I see a big *situation*.'

Pabjoy put powerful emphasis on certain words. He was

inclined to use italics when he talked. New boxes were being added. He discarded his first pencil and went to some trouble in selecting another. It occurred to me that doodles consisting entirely of open boxes, neatly drawn in fine outline and sharp perspective, must tell one something or other about the doodler. I promised myself to ask Otto Feld for a diagnosis.

'Anyway,' Pabjoy was saying, 'the Foreign Secretary wants me back in his office at four and I suppose you'd better come too. He says he wants to see personally whoever's going to look after the French end of the business.'

We trooped into the Foreign Secretary's room and sat ourselves in a rough semi-circle round the big desk. Curzon and Salisbury looked down at us without interest from their heavy gilt frames and there was scarcely more animation on the face of the chinless wonder in dark grey pinstripe who stood stiffly behind the Minister's chair, waiting deferentially for the great man. 'The Foreign Secretary,' he said fussily, 'has been delayed at the House. I am very sorry about it, gentlemen, but he's on his way over.'

'What did Claridge's switchboard throw up?' Pabjoy asked no one in particular. There was no reply. 'Well, Killigrew,' Pabjoy turned to the man on his left, 'you must have looked into that by now.'

The man called Killigrew turned his head slowly and looked at Pabjoy as if seeing him there for the first time. He was lean and intense and all of him seemed to bristle fiercely. 'Nothing,' he said, and swivelled his head back to its original compass reading.

'No goddamn calls *at all*?' Pabjoy was not intimidated.

This time Killigrew's head did not turn. 'Nothing of interest,' he said. The words were extruded reluctantly from his thin mouth. Whatever he enjoyed, it clearly wasn't talking shop.

'Do you have any leads?' Pabjoy worked on him like dripping water on stone. The results were comparable.

'None that I know of.'

'What about the French?'

Killigrew decided on a small investment of energy and turned his head. '*What* about the French?' he asked.

'How have they taken it – the Embassy people, security, the Quai d'Orsay, I don't know?'

The head turned back before emitting an answer. 'As you'd expect. Hysterics. Normal.'

'The Foreign Secretary,' pinstripe said, 'won't be long. He's on his way across from the House. The PM wanted him there for question time . . .' He clearly couldn't stand the cheery atmosphere. No one paid any attention to him.

'Was anything useful found in his hotel room?' Pabjoy asked, exactly as if he expected an answer.

Killigrew shook his head carefully, still conserving energy. 'No,' he said.

'And the suicide note. Anything in that?'

'No.'

'Where is it?'

'The French have it.'

'So you fellows at Special Branch aren't exactly over-burdened with stuff to go on.'

'We'll see,' Killigrew said. Then he added: 'It's early days yet.' From him it was a whole speech.

'Too true,' said the pink and ginger man seated beyond him. He was in mufti but he looked as if he was in uniform.

'Have you got anything, Alan?' Pabjoy asked.

'Afraid not, old boy. Matter of fact, I'm not all that clear why I'm here. I can't see it as a War Office matter. We wouldn't really know which end to get hold of. Told my Minister but he said the Foreign Secretary wanted us along. Comes from the PM, I shouldn't be surprised. Toothbrush mislaid at Number Ten? Call in Intelligence. Panic, wouldn't you say?'

'I would say,' Pabjoy nodded. 'Wouldn't you say so, Killigrew?'

Killigrew decided if his head was to turn it would prefer to turn towards the man from the War Office. 'I doubt that,' he said. Eyes front again.

'So do I.' The sound came from a wizened and diminutive figure who had not opened his mouth so far. No one had bothered to introduce him and I'd concluded he was either representing the KGB or was the deaf mute security man from the FO. His left arm hung loose at his side and he wore a white lisle glove.

We all looked in his direction. No one knew what to make of him. He clearly wasn't going to add further to the general gaiety. 'Christ!' Pabjoy said suddenly. 'We're a cheery lot.' He turned to pinstripe, still erect behind the Foreign Secretary's desk. 'What about a nice cup of tea all around?'

'I think we should wait for the Foreign Secretary, don't you?'

'Not really,' Pabjoy said, 'since you ask. But never mind.'

Then the door opened and the familiar stubby figure of Her Majesty's Principal Secretary of State for Foreign and Commonwealth Affairs shot across the room, grasped each hand in turn and propelled itself to the big chair behind the big desk. The Foreign Secretary brought with him a kind of Welsh huff and bustle. I felt we could do with it.

'Well now, gentlemen,' he said in a pleasing Merthyr sing-song, 'it is good of you to come to see me. Very good of you. Vivian, why haven't you got some of our appalling Foreign Office tea for these gentlemen?'

Pinstripe muttered something about waiting for you, sir, and disappeared through the door. 'Without tea,' the Foreign Secretary was saying amiably, 'we cannot reach any sound conclusions. That has been my experience. But never mind, we shall have some shortly. Now then, yes, what about this sorry business?' He repeated 'sorry business' twice. He seemed genuinely upset that his French counterpart had decided to kill himself.

'I should explain that the Prime Minister's main concern, as it is mine of course, is that Monsieur Marchand may have ended his life as a way out of an intolerable situation. We are not concerned with the inconvenience, though inconvenient it certainly is. No, we need to know why Monsieur Marchand killed himself, why he did it now, and why he did it here in London. You see, gentlemen, I cannot simply turn my back on the fact that a colleague attends by special invitation a meeting of the NATO Council on Monday to review a certain new matter of the highest confidentiality – which happens, by the way, to be of far more moment to us than it is to the French – I cannot turn my back, I say, on the fact that he proceeds on the Wednesday to take an overdose of barbiturates. I'm not saying it was the result of pressure, you understand, but I am saying it *could* be the result of pressure. The PM wants to assess the damage to security, if damage there be.'

The Foreign Secretary's breathless syntax was interrupted by the return of pinstripe, closely followed by a prim person bearing cups on a tray.

'Ah,' he said, 'Tea. Excellent. See that these gentlemen have biscuits too.'

When the tea ceremony had subsided, the Foreign Secretary resumed. 'At question time just now we had a question by arrangement with the Opposition which gave me an opportunity, you know, to say something appropriate about Monsieur Marchand. Deep regret, much-missed colleague, so on and so forth. The Ambassador had made it clear to me that Paris would appreciate as little fuss as possible, which I can well understand. So the Opposition have agreed to play it cool. But then that stupid burk Darby-Wills pops up on our side to ask the Foreign Secretary if he is aware that certain French newspapers this morning have expressed alarm at the implications of the Foreign Minister's suicide, and will I take whatever steps are necessary to satisfy myself . . . security considerations . . . and so on and so forth.

'Naturally, I pooh-poohed it all, but of course, the bloody fool was quite right. We *do* need to take whatever steps are necessary to satisfy ourselves . . . and so on and so forth.'

He paused for breath and a drink of tea. 'You should also

know the Ambassador said something else. It was wrapped in French diplomatic flannel but it was clear as God's daylight. He said, when you'd rendered it down, that his Government wouldn't take kindly to our seeking the *reason* for Monsieur Marchand's action. Short of telling me straight out to keep my nose out of French domestic affairs, he warned me off as clearly as you could wish for. From which I can only conclude that they have a case of the jitters. And if they have the jitters it must be because they fear the worst if they look too closely into this Marchand business. From which I further conclude that they won't look.'

He drank again, holding up his hand in the authoritative gesture of a policeman halting the traffic. He had more to say. 'I have talked it over with the PM. We conclude, gentlemen, that we cannot leave it to the French. They have a long and honourable tradition of shoving stuff under rugs, or not telling their allies what their allies need to know. We must therefore use our own resources to find out.' He turned to Pabjoy but pointed at me. 'Is this your man, Andrew?'

'Yes, Foreign Secretary. Charles Carey. Very experienced.'

The Foreign Secretary funnelled his Welsh charm in my direction. 'You have a bloody important assignment here,' he said. 'Bloody important. Bloody difficult. Bloody urgent. How you accomplish it in the face of the French is your problem, thank God, and not mine.' He beamed cheerfully. 'But what I urge upon you is discretion, man, discretion. I want no embarrassment, you understand? Nothing which will bring their Ambassador scuttling back across the park. Is that clear?'

'Yes, Foreign Secretary.'

'Good. Now, Commander Killigrew. What of the London end of things?'

'Enquiries are being made, Foreign Secretary.' Killigrew now bristled in the general direction of the Foreign Secretary. His hostility was dispensed without fear or favour. There was a kind of perverse integrity in the man.

'Anything to tell us, Commander?'

'No, Sir,' Killigrew said.

The Foreign Secretary retired defeated. 'What about you, Alan?'

'Nothing yet, Foreign Secretary, nothing yet, but we'll work with Andrew Pabjoy and his people. I think it will be up to them to call on us at the War Office if they feel the need.'

'Yes, well that is something you gentlemen will decide between you. All I require from you is a co-op-er-at-ive effort.' The Foreign Secretary sounded all five syllables of the word in Welsh cadence, looking straight at Killigrew as he did so. Killigrew looked straight back. 'My experience has been that a co-operative effort is difficult of accomplishment among our security services. There are no doubt good and sufficient reasons for this. Our Lord doubtless knows what they are but it has not been considered appropriate to explain them to me, with the result that I have suffered certain disappointments on this score in the past. However, hope springs eternal, as you well know, and on this occasion I hope – and the Prime Minister hopes – that a useful measure of co-operation will be achieved and, if I may so express it, no one will spit in the beer. So let us get to work on this matter.'

He trotted round the desk and grasped each of us by the hand. When it came to my turn he looked hard at me. 'Be careful, young man,' he said. 'I know nothing of your trade but I am a case-hardened politician, you know. I smell trouble. The French are charming people, good cooks, witty, very intellectual and all that, but bloody difficult sods. I have enough trouble with them as it is. Please don't create more for me.'

'We'll get no help from Special Branch,' Andrew Pabjoy said as we turned into Horseferry Road on our way back to Smith Square. 'Killigrew's on great form. Haven't seen him as friendly and communicative for years. Even said goodbye. A new departure, that. But he won't co-operate – to use the Minister's word – because there's nothing in it for his mob. Which means, Carey, that you'll be on your own.'

'How hostile are the natives?'

'Well, I can tell you I've already heard from Wavre. In translation, what he said in essence was "keep out". It's what I'd expect.'

Later in the office we fixed the details.

'What cover have you got?' Pabjoy asked.

'Panmure, George Richard. Chief European Correspondent of the Transtel Features Agency, Fleet Street.'

'Thin stuff,' Pabjoy said.

'It feels comfortable.'

CHAPTER 2

Avram Artunian

'Je prendrai un café et un sablé, s'il vous plait.'

'Noir?'

'Noir.'

Three tables in the *boulangerie* were occupied. At two of them, two men, and at a third a man pushing seventy with his black homburg still on his head. When the coffee and biscuit arrived I asked the *serveuse* if she knew a Mr Artunian.

'How should I know people by name? Hundreds come in here.' She was three yards away before I could pursue our friendly chat. The elderly man leaned towards me.

'Excuse me, I heard you asking for Artunian. He hasn't been in lately. A heart attack two months ago and he is still recovering at home.'

'How can I contact him?'

'You have business to do, perhaps? In emeralds?'

'Not, it's personal.'

The old boy's face fell. He had smelled a deal, snatched from the prostrate Artunian. All in a day's business.

'I have a telephone number.' He was looking in a small red address book. 'Yes. Avram Artunian: 983 8879.'

'Thank you,' I said. The old man nodded and shrugged and returned noisily to his coffee. At the next table something like a flaming Levantine row was under way in heavily accented French.

'I said thirty-two thousand.'

'And I said twenty-five thousand.'

The other laughed sardonically, packing into the guttural sound the accumulated guile of all the Greeks, Phoenicians, Levantines and whoever else had traded and bartered back and forth across the Mediterranean in the past two millenia.

'Five thousand a carat. Ridiculous!'

'They're selected. Look at the colour: perfect!'

'A joke.'

'I'm making nothing on them. Nothing.'

'Another joke.'

'So buy elsewhere.'

'Why should I buy elsewhere when I want to buy from you?'

'Thirty-two thousand. You'll never do better.'

'Twenty-five thousand. My last offer.'

'Ha!'

'Ha!'

An overweight, thickset man in a dark grey overcoat and weatherbeaten soft felt hat came into the shop, made a pretence of looking at the pastries displayed under the glass counter, glanced around as if to say, 'What on earth do I do next?' and dropped heavily onto a chair at a table nearly opposite me. He asked for a *café crème*, pulled a copy of *l'Aurore* from his pocket and settled down to pretend he was not a policeman. The effect on the assembled businessmen was curiously soporific. A solemn hush descended on the table where buyer and seller had been struggling for a meeting of minds. The silence seemed to be connected with a reluctance to be seen to be doing any business at all and thus to become liable to pay taxes. But that was *their* problem.

My problem was that I'd already caught sight of the big man at the corner of the boulevard Haussman when I'd paid off my taxi. I felt like announcing to the paralysed merchants: 'Gentlemen, you may resume your bargaining. This policeman is not interested in you. He is interested in me.'

I prepared the exact change to pay my bill, and in one neat move, rose from my chair, plumped my money down on Madame's desk, and was out into the street before the policeman had got his newspaper folded. I was into a taxi and away before he emerged onto the pavement.

At the Gare du Nord I paid off the taxi, plunged into the thick of the crowd pushing into the station, advanced maybe twenty yards, about-turned and came out again and was at the telephone in a *tabac* opposite in twenty seconds.

A woman's voice answered almost at once.

'I would like to speak to Mr Artunian.'

'Who is speaking? This is Madame Artunian.'

'*Bonjour, Madame.* I am a friend of your husband's from London – a business friend. I only just learned of his illness. How is he?'

'Better, thank you. But the doctor says he must still rest. He has been very bad.'

'I am sorry. Do you think he could come to the telephone?'

'I will see. Give me your name please.'

'Please tell him simply that I am a friend of Andrew in London.' There was a pause, footsteps on parquet, then the handset was picked up again.

'Avram says you may come this afternoon at three thirty. We are at sixteen quai Voltaire, on the first floor.'

'Thank you, I'll be there.'

As I came out of the *tabac* a young man with *flic* written all over him was examining the merchandise in the window of the shop next door. So they had some kind of team on the job. It called for evasive action. But after lunch.

At the Brasserie du Nord I had a half a dozen *belons*, a *choucroute garnie* and a half carafe of the house red. The young man hung around outside. A lousy job, surveillance. I felt sorry for him. I called for a newspaper and took my time catching up with the news. The Communists were accusing the President of pursuing a policy to impoverish the labouring masses, and the President was reported to be hunting wild pig with the King of Spain. There was a modest scandal brewing, to do with cost overruns on the Lille–Boulogne section of the Autoroute du Nord. Charles Aznavour was at the Olympia and the stagehands at the Opèra were on strike. A UP despatch from Washington reported the defection of one Leonid Serov, a Third Secretary at the Soviet Embassy. The Basques had killed some more policemen.

When I came out into the street after my coffee, the young man was leaning sadly against a hoarding, pretending to read a newspaper. I walked slowly to the top of the cab rank and took a taxi to the Galeries Lafayette. As we drove away, I saw the young man scramble for the next one. And a car which had been parked in the *zone interdit* all through my lunch without being troubled by anyone at all pulled away from the kerb. We were travelling in convoy. A very safe way to go.

I had no trouble shaking them off in the Galeries Lafayette. I went through a half-dozen departments, crossed over into the store's neighbouring block on the second-floor bridge, and emerged in the rue de Charras. Using the usual tradecraft I decided I was clear.

'I am at your service, Mr Panmure.'

Avram Artunian was a small, neat man with eyes of a deep brown liquidity, iron grey hair with a generous moustache to match, and small expressive hands. His manner was gentle but self-assured. He sat in a long purple dressing gown in an armchair which was as uncomfortable as the rest of the Louis Quinze furnishings of the drawing room. Through the high windows I could see the honey-coloured mass of the Louvre over on the right bank of the Seine. Madame Artunian had served China tea, very weak, in a fine Sèvres set, and had left us. I did not much care for the tea.

'Andrew Pabjoy sends his best wishes,' I said. 'He would welcome your advice.'

The slender fingers went up in a deprecating gesture. 'You know I am a figure of the past, Mr Panmure. I am not only seventy-one years of age. I am also an invalid, or so my doctors tell me. And I have few contacts these days. Also, my memory is not what it was.'

'But we think you will be able to help.'

'I am listening.'

So I presented the British view of the improbability of Marchand's suicide, the indifference of Wavre – the head of the DST – leading to the conclusion that HMG in London seemed more concerned at the death of the French Foreign Minister than the French authorities themselves. Artunian sat motionless, oriental and faintly sardonic.

'And . . . ?'

'And that is all. We want to know why the Minister killed himself within twenty-four hours of taking part in a highly classified NATO meeting and without even waiting to get back to Paris. My people do not believe he was undergoing a personal crisis.'

'But *I* do not know why he did it.' A trace of a smile lurked below his moustache. 'There are so many reasons that a man has for killing himself – women, money, the burden of responsibilities . . .' The delicate hands fluttered again. The din of the traffic beat against the tall, narrow window panes. The November light was fading but no lights had been switched on in the room.

'Can you tell me about the Minister? Anything you can recall. Any impressions. Any doubts.'

'Doubts, you know . . . there are times when one has doubts about all kinds of people . . . in the aftermath of the war, the Resistance, the honeymoon with Moscow.' He paused, looking straight at me.

'What do I know about André Marchand? A lot and yet very little. In any event, I advise you to look at his cuttings in the morgues at *l'Humanité* and *Le Monde*. They will mostly overlap, but a Communist with a pair of scissors and a paste pot produces a different cutting file from an anti-Communist armed with the same equipment.'

'I'll be going to *l'Humanité* from here,' I said.

'Then you should also talk to Georges Wavre at the DST.'

'I intend to, but I expect no co-operation. That has been made clear.'

'You will be so good as to pour me a little more tea.'

I was dying for a cigarette but somehow did not like to ask this strange, authoritative guru from the Near East for permission to smoke. So I said nothing and waited, and in a low voice with soft, guttural rolling of the consonants, Artunian talked about André Marchand.

'You know, in many ways he was a most remarkable man. Not quite of the very first calibre, but certainly a man who was bound to make a career in Cabinet or in the boardroom of a major enterprise. That he went into government isn't surprising, since he came from the highly political generation whose *formation* was in the Resistance.

'I knew him between '60 and '61, when he was at the Interior and the DST headed to him as Minister. He was the most *prepared* man I ever knew. A very good brain with a prodigious capacity for work. A grasp of the essentials of a problem. A man deeply impatient of other people's limitations. I met him maybe a couple of dozen times.'

Another pause. It was now quite dark in the room, and a discreet knock on the glass door brought Madame Artunian to switch on a solitary standard lamp and remove the tea tray.

'But I didn't *like* him.' He said this quietly, almost reluctantly, as if he had never before faced up to the fact of disliking his Minister.

'Why not?' My question sounded like an impertinent interruption and he ignored it.

'Remember that we were exclusively in the business of counter-espionage at the DST. Security dominated our lives, as you will understand very well. We developed feelings of almost feminine sensitivity about everyone. And as I say, I did not like André Marchand.'

'You felt he was a risk?'

'Not at all. He had had the highest, the very highest clearance for the Ministry of the Interior, of course. His record was impeccable. A member of the National Council of the Resistance in occupied territory from 1942 until it was destroyed by the Gestapo in 1943. Later, a fine record in the battle for Paris. All very good. Very good indeed. And in any case, why should I like him? I did not like de Gaulle either – who did?'

A slight raising of the shoulders at his own question. A faint smile at the lese-majesty of the reference to de Gaulle.

'Read the clippings carefully, look for any break in the consistency of his political outlook. Form a view of his personality and then ask yourself: is this or that act in character? Can it be logically explained or does it require an exotic explanation of some kind? I will tell you some people to see and no doubt they will lead you to others. In particular, I will recommend you to Alfred Baum at the DST. He knows more than anyone because he has been there longer than anyone. And that, in turn, is because he knows more than anyone and there is nobody to dare to clear him out.'

He stopped and I ventured a 'thank you'. But the wise brown eyes were closed and for a moment I thought he might actually have fallen asleep in the gloom of that very French drawing room.

'You will come here tomorrow evening at seven o'clock to tell me of your progress. At that time I will have more information for you. I will have seen someone who will talk only to me.'

'If I am to have suspicions, what should they be about?'

Artunian took a long time replying. He put the tips of his fingers together and examined them carefully. He threw his head back and looked out towards the Louvre. A *bateau-mouche* hooted briefly as it approached the Carrousel bridge.

'If I wanted to harbour ungenerous suspicions about André Marchand –' the words were spoken so softly that I had to strain to hear them above the traffic '– if I wanted to do that, I think I would finally ask myself the subversive question that none of us has any right to ask about colleagues of the Resistance. And that question is: *why did he survive the war?*'

I waited, but clearly there was to be nothing more.

'I will be happy to receive you at seven tomorrow evening,' Artunian said. 'And now, a very good day to you, my dear Mr Panmure, and please forgive me for not seeing you out.'

I took out a business card and scribbled the name of my hotel on it. 'In case you want to contact me,' I said.

And that was that.

A damp autumnal dusk had fallen on the river and the *quais*, and the booksellers were closing their stalls on the thick walls along the riverside. The rush hour had not started but the traffic was doing its best to make the city uninhabitable. It took me ten minutes to find a taxi and another fifteen to reach the offices of *l'Humanité* in the faubourg Poissonière. My press card got me into the morgue with its steel cabinets and box files full of cuttings. A plain girl in a grey smock found me two big boxes marked MARCHAND, André.

For the next three hours I read cuttings, while somewhere below in the bowels of the place the big rotaries roared into life, spewing out the early provincial editions of the Communist paper. Gradually I began to know André Marchand, graduate of St Cyr, junior officer of cavalry in the 43rd chasseurs, wartime Resistance leader, Deputy for the Aveyron constituency since 1946 and Mayor of Rodez, former member of the National Council of the Resistance, Under-Secretary for War in de Gaulle's first postwar Government and later Minister for Overseas Territories; twice Minister for Posts and Telegraphs, Minister of the Interior, Minister for War, Chevalier of the Legion of Honour, *Croix de Guerre* and *Croix de la Libération*.

My attention was caught by three items in the file, on which I proceeded to take notes in my crippled shorthand.

The first was a cutting from the 14 March 1953 edition of *Le Parisien Libéré*. It was a brief report of a speech by Marchand, in which he had talked about 'the flower of our leadership, our cadres, wiped out by the invader, leaving us to struggle as best we can to repair the ravages of war'. A harmless piece of postwar rhetoric, leading nowhere. But someone had marked the passage and against it had scribbled in the margin: 'Hypocrisy!'

The second thing which struck me was the vendetta which *Libération* seemed to be running against him from 1945 until 1950, when the campaign appeared to stop abruptly. Most of the pieces had been signed M. Ségur. I noted such phrases as 'this man who pursues a certain policy which does not correspond to his public reputation', 'formerly connected with certain dubious circles', 'so-called member of the cream of our Resistance fighters' – typical French newspaper double-talk hinting at untold secrets and dangerous connections without saying anything outright.

Who was M. Ségur? Why did he have it in for André Marchand? And why did he suddenly lose interest in 1950? I made a note of my three questions.

Thirdly, there was the fact that on two quite separate and dissimilar occasions, André Marchand had tried and failed to form a government and thus become Prime Minister of France. The first was in 1953, when the cuttings made it clear that Marchand was the obvious choice. But he had botched his negotiations with the Socialists and seemed to have gone out of his way to insult their leadership. He had done much the same thing to the Radicals in 1964. It was as if the man didn't *want* to become Prime Minister. And I agreed with Pabjoy's view that every politician wants to be Prime Minister.

Why? Perhaps M. Ségur had a theory.

I thanked the girl in the smock, who bestowed a brief '*de rien*' on me, and made my way back to my hotel in the rue de Castellane, behind the Madeleine church. The night porter was on duty and handed me the key to No. 32 without looking at me. I thought the indifference was a bit studied, even for a part-time Portuguese concierge, just as I had thought the van parked opposite the hotel entrance was somewhat superfluous: its side proclaimed *A. R. A. Quincaillerie*, but there wasn't a china shop in sight. No matter: the police had their job to do.

My room looked all right but wasn't, because the single hair

I'd left hanging out of the flyleaf of the latest Le Carré in the writing desk drawer was no longer there, and French chambermaids do not dust inside drawers. And someone had put my shaver back in its case the wrong way round.

I tore my notes out of the looseleaf book and stuffed them into my inside breast pocket, put another hair in the Le Carré for luck, placed the now empty notebook exactly its own length from the edge of the bedside table, and went down to find some food. The night porter glanced at me casually. The van was still there, no doubt with an eye glued to a hole somewhere in its side. I treated myself to the small pleasure of a friendly wave at the watching eye, and turned left into the rue Tronchet in search of an omelette and a good Pont l'Evêque.

CHAPTER 3

Marc Ségur

I got nowhere with Wavre. I followed the usher up the stairs and along the bleak, grey corridors on the first floor of the DST headquarters at 13 rue des Saussaies. The office of the Director, arguably one of the half dozen most powerful men in the Republic, was bare, dreary and faceless: a suitable background for the work of a super-policeman. There was still a photograph of de Gaulle on the wall behind Wavre's desk, though it had clearly been shifted to make room for President Mitterand alongside. The other walls were bare. The furnishings were standard French Government issue, designed to go into ornate eighteenth- or nineteenth-century rooms. They looked absurdly overdesigned and pretentious in this barn of a place.

Wavre wasted no time at all.

'I have received you because I wish to issue a warning to you, Mr Carey.'

I said nothing and looked at Mitterand.

'My warning is this. You are wasting your time and your Government's money. There is no mystery attaching to the death of the Minister. Our services are satisfied on that matter. I am personally satisfied. Furthermore, we do not need a political scandal at this point. The Government is not homogeneous and could not readily assimilate a scandal. So I advise you to return to London, Monsieur, and report to my friend Andrew Pabjoy that there is nothing behind this tragic event. Nothing at all.'

The Director was very relaxed, and a broad, disarming smile

spread across his pale and somewhat fleshy face. The eyes betrayed nothing.

'That's not so easy, *Monsieur le Directeur*. I have my instructions and I am not breaking any French laws.'

'It would pain me if you were because it would force me to act.'

'Don't worry, your people or maybe the men from the Préfecture de Police are watching me night and day.'

Wavre shrugged his shoulders. 'I can, of course, arrange for you to leave with or without legal cause.'

'I know,' I said, 'but I hope you won't, because London might retaliate against one of your men. Troyat, say.'

Wavre ignored the callow threat. He rose and held out his hand. His manner was affable but he looked dangerous.

'I have said what I have to say, Mr Carey, and now you will excuse me . . .'

I hadn't decided yet how to contact Alfred Baum. I couldn't ask for him openly at the rue des Saussaies. If his superiors knew, they would find ways of frightening him off. And the man had a job to hold down.

I left Baum until later, walked the 300 yards to the Chancellery of the British Embassy in the faubourg St Honoré and asked for Isabel.

When I reached her office she closed a file and looked up.

'Business or pleasure, my sweet?'

'Both, Isabel, both. Let's have a little music. This place has never been properly de-bugged.'

She turned on the transistor on her desk and we talked to a background of Haydn. Electronic surveillance is what they call bugging, and a love of the classics is a simple way of messing up the signal.

Breaking the rules, I told her why I was in Paris and what progress I had made. She listened with one long leg slung over the other, her cool green-flecked eyes unwavering, hands immobile. Repose was one of the things Isabel had acquired somewhere between Roedean, Lady Margaret Hall, and her parents' place at the better end of Shropshire. It is a very expensive commodity.

'Put this in the bag, love.' I handed her a note addressed to Andrew Pabjoy via the diplomatic bag and a circuitous London route of my own devising. Anyone reading it would think the writer mad.

'Can I help?' Isabel asked.

'Yes, have dinner with me. I'll pick you up at nine. Be patient if I'm late. My seven o'clock appointment may run on a bit.'

I spent the afternoon in the morgue at *Le Monde* and while I was there I looked up Baum in the telephone directory, but there were a dozen A. Baums and I did not know how to choose. The Marchand file contained two more pieces by M. Ségur which had not been in *l'Humanité*'s collection, and a profile from *Le Monde* itself which gave information on André Marchand's early life.

I asked if they could find me anything on M. Ségur, a writer on *Libération*. The librarian offered a file marked SÉGUR, Marc. It consisted almost entirely of cuttings dealing with the death on 3 June 1950 of Marc Ségur and the subsequent and abortive police enquiries.

LIBERATION: 4 June 1950

Marc Ségur, our esteemed and much-loved collaborator, was killed in the early hours of yesterday morning when his car went off the N 144 between Bourges and Levet. With him was his wife Ariane, who is in the Charité Hospital at Bourges with multiple injuries. The car appears to have been travelling at speed when it went out of control on a bend and smashed headlong into a tree by the roadside. Mme Ségur is still unconscious and unable to throw any light on the matter.

Marc Ségur was working on an assignment for this newspaper: a series of articles which he planned on certain aspects of the Resistance and its postwar ramifications – a subject which he had made his own in recent years. He was travelling south from Bourges but his exact destination was not known.

There followed more about Ségur's talent etc. which offered nothing of interest.

LIBERATION: 7 June 1950

For the first time yesterday Ariane Ségur was able to speak to Inspector Freyssinet of the Bourges police regarding the car accident in which her husband Marc, our distinguished collaborator, was killed last Thursday night. She could shed little light on either the event itself or the circumstances surrounding it. She had been dozing, she said, at the time of the accident, and could recall nothing. However, police examination of the car reveals that a pinion in the steering system had sheared, thus putting the vehicle out of control. The part appears to have been sawn partly through, and had finally broken, as it inevitably would.

Mr Alfred André has been appointed Instructing Magistrate in the affair and has opened an enquiry.

How like the French press to bury the whole point of the story halfway down! It became interesting.

LIBERATION: 28 July 1950

Mr A. André, Instructing Magistrate in the Ségur affair, stated yesterday that he would be filing the dossier for the time being as 'crime unsolved'. The recent judicial procedures and extensive police investigations have failed to produce any suspects. However, there is speculation that there could be those whose interest it was to eliminate Marc Ségur before he could put together the *reportage* on which he was working. But his collaborators on this newspaper were not in his confidence and have been unable to help forward the enquiries.

One final mystery has been insufficiently commented

upon: when visiting the Ségurs' apartment two days after the crash, the police failed (or claim they failed) to find any notebooks or working papers dealing with Marc Ségur's last assignment. Nor, according to the police, were any notes found in the car or upon the body. Do we find a certain complicity here? What interests are being served by the suppression of this material?

I could not believe that the very newspaper for which Ségur was preparing a series of articles knew nothing about what they would be dealing with. Off to the country to a secret destination to investigate a nameless story? And what about his notes? No notes? It was absurd. But since the whole thing had happened over twenty-five years ago, speculation would not serve. Unless of course, Ariane Ségur could somehow be found and could remember anything. But how on earth did you find the wife of a man who had died all those years ago, even supposing she was still alive? I could see I'd need help from someone like Baum.

Back at my hotel at six thirty I did the following things: checked the hair in the Le Carré and put another on the small pile of underwear and shirts in the cupboard. Locked my room, walked down to the desk, left my key and asked how far it was to the avenue de Villiers (which seemed as good a street to choose for the purpose as any other). Walked to the Madeleine Cinema, bought a ticket, got myself shown to a seat close to the door marked SORTIE and immediately darted through it, glancing back to see my young friend from the Gare du Nord being shown into a seat a couple of rows back. Then up the stairs to the side door of the cinema in the rue Vignon, and into a cruising taxi. The whole exercise from hotel to taxi had taken seven minutes and I had shaken myself clear.

I dismissed the taxi on the right bank of the river at the Carrousel bridge and walked across. It was dark, cold, and wet underfoot. The rush hour was still in full spate and the traffic was solid on the bridge and along the riverside.

Before the tall green-painted double doors of No. 16 stood a policeman. At the curb was a Citroën DS with a Préfecture number plate. I walked straight past, turned into the nearest café and dialled Artunian's number. A thick southern voice answered at once. I manage a fair imitation of an Italian waiter, even in French, and reckoned it could hold through a few sentences.

'Mr Artunian, please.' I kept the talk to a minimum.

'Who wants him?'

'Mr Franconi. A friend.'

'Mr Artunian cannot come to the phone.'

'What is the matter? Is he worse?'

'I can't tell you.'

'Who are you?'

'Police.'

'Can I speak to Madame Artunian?'

'Not possible.'

I rang off. Further down the road I went into another café, dialled Reuters news agency and asked for Arthur Wedderburn.

'Keep the hallo's till later, Arthur. Just tell me if any murders are coming over the AFP wire.'

'Where?' said Arthur, as if old friends phoned him with that question twice daily and once on Sundays.

'Paris. Quai Voltaire. Man named Artunian.'

'Hold on.' There was a short pause. 'Yes, here's a flash at eighteen forty-nine hours. Police report on Avram Artunian, dealer in precious stones, found shot through the head in his apartment at sixteen quai Voltaire. Theft suspected. Wife out at the time, called the police on her return, finding front door bolted from inside. That's all.'

'Thanks, Arthur. I'll be back to you for more later.'

'I say, what . . .' But I had rung off.

By eight I was in Isabel Reid-Porter's studio in a street off the rue de la Convention and she kept me quiet with scotch and ice while she bathed and did things to herself. I used the time to do some thinking, against a background of splashes through the open bathroom door and the Pink Floyd which she had put on the record player. Isabel came out of the bathroom draped in a bathrobe and chatted about the office as she prepared herself to go out. She did a neat demolition job on the Ambassador's wife.

'A little-does-she-know type,' she said as she held still for me to fasten her bra and slithered away as I sought to adjust the thing in front. 'A harbinger of small personal dooms. Probably a breaker-up of marriages too. Sir Roy is, beyond doubt, your original free-range twit, but I wouldn't wish that woman onto anyone, even him. As they say, if she were in India she'd be sacred.'

She picked up from the floor a crumpled grey rag which turned into a perfectly fitting Missoni creation as it slipped over her shoulders and hips. She added pale lipstick, two squirts of Cabochard at the ears and an expert flip of the head to get her hair into place.

'*Allons*,' she said. 'I need feeding.'

We dined at a familiar haunt in the rue de Vaugirard. I recounted my professional troubles and tried out my theories. Her fine eyes resting steadily on mine, Isabel listened without a word to my account of what I'd dug up at the two newspapers. I added what I knew about Artunian's death. She dabbed delicately at her rather wide mouth with a corner of her napkin and moved a blonde hair back from her forehead with a long, tapering finger.

'We have to assume your friend Artunian was killed because of you,' she said. 'A stray burglar blundering in the day after you were there is too much of a coincidence.'

'Let's assume it,' I said.

'I can think of four categories of people who might want to do it and that's before I've had my coffee.'

'Such as?'

'A foreign service, the DST, the police or some freelance outfit.'

'All possible.'

'And whoever killed poor old Artunian isn't going to feel squeamish about you.'

'Correct.'

'You have a rich choice of enemies. You'll need to keep moving, Carey my love.'

I grinned. 'What did the Chinese gentleman say: of all the thirty-six alternatives, running away is best? But it isn't in my contract.'

'Be careful. I'm fond of you,' Isabel said.

We had finished our coffee and I had called for the bill. 'Then show you mean it.'

Isabel gave one of her chuckles, deep in her throat. We used to tell each other that that was her mating call. 'I don't live that far away, so tell the man to hurry with your change.'

CHAPTER 4

Albert Chavan

The night porter handed me a message with my key. Mr Chavan had telephoned. Would Mr Panmure call him when he came in. It gave a number. My room appeared to be untouched. Perhaps they found me boring. I toyed with the idea of going out to a *tabac* to phone Mr Chavan but couldn't really see the point. That, and the fact that I was tired. So I dialled the number.

Now, the technical resources of the PTT in France are limited and on the whole obsolete, and if you know what to listen for in the way of clicks and unnatural intervals between the last ringing tone and the change of background echo as the handset is picked off its cradle, you can tell as near as dammit whether or not your phone is being tapped.

My phone was being tapped.

'Yes?' The voice contained a certain amount of gravel and a lot of natural authority.

'Panmure. But I am phoning from my hotel.' I thought the 'but' would be meaningful to anyone who was alert to meanings.

'Right. Be in thirty minutes outside the office you visited next after the quai Voltaire yesterday.' The receiver was replaced. This was clearly Artunian's contact.

I had no trouble losing the police tails. I arrived outside *l'Humanité* at 11.50, paid off my second taxi and waited on the pavement for someone to take an interest in me. After five minutes a man got out of a black Renault which was already parked across the street when I arrived, dodged a *l'Humanité* van which was picking up speed as it headed east, and walked slowly along the few yards of pavement to reach me.

'Monsieur Panmure?'

'Yes. Monsieur Chavan?'

The man did not answer my question. In the lights from the newspaper building his face was unnaturally white and blotchy, like a plateful of curdled milk. His black hair had been painted onto his skull in heavy impasto. His clothes had sharp edges. He was maybe twenty-two and looked very precocious indeed: an extraordinarily unpleasing young man.

'Follow me.' He said it as if it had been forced out of him.

I crossed over to the Renault, the young man held open the back door and I got in. I found myself sitting next to another rather similar young man who never once glanced in my direction. I wished I'd thought of calling Isabel to let her know Chavan's number and my present plans. Plans? If there were any plans, they were theirs and not mine. The car pulled away from the kerb.

'Where are we going?'

'To see Monsieur Albert.' This from pasty-face, who drove like a professional – heel-and-toe, finger touch on the steering, left elbow on the window ledge. The car moved eastwards through the late traffic. It was beautiful driving, utterly without regard for the inalienable rights of other road users. No one said anything. I settled back to get my bearings. At the République we turned northwards and at Barbès-Rochechouart we turned left towards Clichy. Now we were into the nightclub district of rip-off *boîtes*, cabaret theatres and small eating places. The whores stood in clumps like out-of-date shop manikins. They were still in minis, twenty years after other women had got tired of showing their thighs. Maybe the miniskirt had been designed for the trade in the first place. The whores came in a range of colours and sizes and waylaid anything that moved.

At the place Pigalle we turned left and left again in the rue Victor Massé and nosed fast into a parking space. We got out and made our way ten yards back to what had once been a shop. Now it had a curtained window and on the fascia a legend in blue neon: SEXY-BIZARRE. Next door was LA POULE and opposite, DANCING PIGALLE. Outside SEXY-BIZARRE a North African in a battered trenchcoat and a braidless peaked cap stood guard miserably. Without a flicker of recognition for the two young men he pushed open the door and we marched in – pasty-face, me, the silent one, in that order.

The place was packed and cigarette smoke hung in a dirty grey mist over the solid mass of humanity. Somewhere, invisible through the haze, someone was thumping out 'Basin Street Blues' on the piano. There was someone else on drums. At the end of the room a small platform was curtained off and would presumably be used later for the show. A placard propped in front of the curtain proclaimed ESTELLA – UNE EXPERIENCE BIZARRE. If these people were willing to cram themselves into this tiny room where oxygen was at a premium and the scotch probably of Turkish origin in order to see Estella, then Estella presumably had something to offer. I was wondering idly what that might be when my young friend grunted 'this way' and thrust his way through the mass of humanity and on through a small door by the side of the stage. We were in a short corridor with the stage on our right and a door opposite us at its end. Through the second door we entered a room with a mirror and shelf along one wall, and three chairs. On one of them sat a girl with cropped, blonded hair. She was fitting on a long black wig, and as she did so the grubby kimono round her shoulders slipped down to her waist. In the mirror I could see her face: the pinched, hard, Parisian and not unbeautiful face of a pro of the nightclub circuit. Her shoulders were smooth and white. Her breasts, which were bare, were firm. Her nipples had been pierced and through each of them a fine gold ring, maybe an inch in diameter, had been threaded. And on the rings hung lengths of gold chain. It was what the customers had paid to see.

We reached another door and pasty-face knocked. In response to a gruff '*entrez*' he beckoned me forward, held open the door and closed it behind me. I was glad to lose the terrible twins.

Albert Chavan was sitting at a small desk made up of two plastic-trimmed pedestals and a smoked-glass top. He was a very big man, balding and grey, with a face bearing the pitting and florid colour of a lifetime of serious wine drinking. The eyes were small, light brown, very alert beneath rather heavy lids. The hands were huge and capable. A cigarette hung in the left corner of his mouth in the French manner, and the smoke drifted up into his eyes without bothering him at all. There was a touch of humour about the mouth. Despite the brutish twins and the SEXY-BIZARRE and Estella, I began to relax. Chavan's handshake was firm, decisive and reassuring. I sat down and lit a cigarette.

'I owe you an apology, Mr Panmure,' Chavan said. 'I had to have you brought here by my rather unsavoury young men. It was a small additional precaution.'

'They didn't actually hit me,' I said.

'I won't say there is no harm in them. In fact, they are rather vicious and there is a great deal of harm in them. But they are young: they don't understand that a snake is not called upon to hiss all the time. In my business there is a role for such scum.'

He said it dispassionately. If he was ashamed of his associates, he did not appear all that ashamed.

There was a bottle of Armagnac on a shelf and he poured me a glass without asking if I wanted it.

'You heard about Avram?'

I said I had.

'I saw him at two o'clock and left him just before three. We talked about you.'

'He was an impressive man,' I said.

'A very remarkable man. If he had not been an Armenian by birth he would have been deputy-chief at the rue des Saussaies. And he was a good fellow to work with . . .'

He paused, moved. Then he went on: 'He explained your

little problem. I suppose you realise that you will attract cross-fire, and though I never received a formal military training, I learned in the service that no sane individual gets into a position where he is exposed to cross-fire.'

'I suppose I am not a sane individual,' I said. 'I have a job to do. It has nothing to do with sanity.'

Chavan allowed himself a brief smile. Through the closed door came the sound of a female voice, screeching, followed by the angry voice of a man. The racket subsided quickly.

'I am getting no official co-operation here,' I said. 'That isn't surprising, of course, but it does create a delicate situation. Our people don't want an inter-service squabble with the DST. But they want answers to their questions. And I can only provide these answers if people will talk to me despite the DST. I gather you are one of the people who will do that.'

'I will do what I can,' Chavan said, 'but you must know that I have no special knowledge of André Marchand and his past. If you want help from me, you must formulate the questions and I'll do what I can to answer them or put you on to people who may have the answers.'

'I am making a number of suppositions,' I said. 'Let us suppose, one, that Marchand was someone's asset; two, that he was recruited at almost any time from the war onwards; three, that the various French services, such as the DST, are unaware of the fact. Then let us assume that his personal dossier at the rue des Saussaies contains nothing that is suspicious *in itself*, but that there are things in it which become significant if you read them with an eye to treason. In other words, that the dossier, properly read, can point the direction my enquiries should take.'

'A reasonable approach,' Chavan said.

'From which you will have deduced that I need a sight of his dossier.'

Chavan scratched his head. 'If anyone can do it for you,' he said, 'it's Alfred Baum.'

'Artunian mentioned him.'

'I can find a way to put you in touch with him. But my own view is that you'll be wasting your time.'

'Why?'

'It is very simple.' He leaned back in his chair and gazed steadily at me through the curling smoke of his cigarette. 'Your people suspect that Marchand was the subject of blackmail, or maybe demands for information which he could no longer bear. You think he was betraying his country because at some time in his past someone got a hold on him. You may be right. But what if you are right? Do you think the intelligence services of this country will thank you for doing now what they should and probably could have done twenty years ago? Will the Government vote you a medal for exposing one of their most distinguished cabinet ministers as a spy just four months before the elections? And what view will be taken by Marchand's masters, if he had any? Will they shrug and say it doesn't matter because he's dead anyway? Or will they reckon that the truth about Marchand is likely to lead to other truths and other men who are still alive and still useful? My dear friend, why should anyone allow you to stir up a hornets' nest of such proportions?'

He leaned forward and brought his great fist down on the desk top, delicately, without a sound. 'The answer to my question is that they will not allow it.'

'Did Marc Ségur of *Libération* know Marchand's secret?' I asked.

Chavan leaned forward a little. 'Ségur has been dead a long time,' he said. 'What makes you think he knew?'

I explained my reading of the newspaper files. 'Could one find Ségur's wife?' I asked.

'It might be possible. I'll see.'

'Before we go any further,' I said, 'I have to ask you what a man like you is doing in a dump like this, surrounded by bully-boys and entertainment of doubtful legality. I would like to know who I'm involved with.'

Albert Chavan took the stub of the cigarette out of his mouth, lit another from it and put that where the first had been. Then he reached for the Armagnac bottle and it seemed even money to me that he'd bring it down on my head. But instead he poured us both another couple of fingers. Then he settled back in his chair.

'A reasonable question,' he said. 'The answer is not complicated. I am from Corsica and we Corsicans usually choose one of two careers when we emigrate to France, as most of us must: we choose crime or the police. I have three brothers over here and two are policemen in Toulon and one is in the *milieu* here in Paris. During the war I was active in one of the Resistance networks. When they transferred the DST from London to Paris after the liberation they were on the lookout for lads like me, and I joined, though I might just as easily have gone into the rackets. I had six good years in counter-espionage at the DST, but through my brother I kept in touch with the *milieu* – the underworld. And, of course, what I saw was my friends drinking champagne while I drank *ordinaire*, and vacationing in Chamonix while I took my wife and kids camping.

'So I decided to cross over. I took the decision soberly, as a family man with financial responsibilities, and I did it the right way. I went to my boss and told him what I intended to do, and on the day I finished we all had a drink in the department and the lads clubbed together and they gave me a clock. It's a fine clock.'

He paused and drank some Armagnac. 'So now I have money and my daughters both had decent dowries. We live in Auteuil and have a nice summer place near Hyères. I do well: this place and another like it, some girls on the game, other interests . . .' he waved a hand. 'And I keep in touch with my old friends in the department. I have contacts. Sometimes I can be useful. It is insurance.'

I must have looked a bit surprised because he added: 'There is nothing unnatural in all this, Mr Panmure. At least, not for a Corsican. We are flexible people who recognise that you can't have police without criminals, nor criminals without police.

They are mutually dependent and the dividing line is very fine, very fine.'

'Do you have friends in the police, at the Préfecture?' I asked.

'Do you think I could run my business if I hadn't?'

'What about getting them off my back?' I said. 'I have to waste a lot of time losing them.'

'I might manage it if it is the Préfecture,' Chavan said. 'But it may be the DST or some other outfit. I'll make some enquiries. Come here after eleven tomorrow night and I'll give you whatever else I can. After that, you'll be on your own.'

As I went out through the pall of smoke, Estella was on the stage dressed only in a see-through skirt made up out of a yard or two of cheap black net. She was going through a do-it-yourself dance routine to a sleepy version of 'Adios Muchachos' from the combo in the corner. But no one was looking at the steps. The gold chains loosely connected her breasts to the gold bracelets which encircled her wrists, and she was making the most of her arm movements. The customers in the tightly packed room were silent as they gazed at Estella's delicately mutilated nipples, pulled this way and that at the ends of their chains.

I caught a remark from a plump, well-tailored man as I pushed past his table. '*Evidemment*, for real S/M,' he said, 'you have to go to Hamburg. This is nothing. On the Reeperbahn they have girls who've had more interesting parts of their anatomy doctored.'

I didn't catch his companion's reply.

CHAPTER 5

Baum I

Next day I bought all the newspapers and a couple of books and spent most of the day in my room, reading and making notes. *Le Figaro* said the police view was that Avram Artunian had been killed by a common burglar who had been disturbed before he could rifle the apartment. *Le Parisien Libéré* said the police theory was that Artunian had underworld connections and it looked like a crime of revenge, but *Le Monde* in the afternoon said the police had no theory. My books produced a dozen pages of notes and cross-references.

At four I called Isabel. 'If I come round, will you give me tea?'

She said she would, so I did the ten-minute walk to the Embassy, and to a background of Liszt we took tea and I filled her in.

'Will you take me with you tonight?' she asked.

'Who do you want to see, Chavan or Estella?'

She said, 'Estella, of course. Ugh!'

I said I'd take her; but didn't she think the FO would be livid if she got mixed up in this and the French demanded her recall?

'Oh, yes, quite livid,' she said. 'I'd have to see Cousin Cyril. What's the point of having the Permanent Under-Sec. in the family if he can't stop them being livid?'

'This tea is filthy,' I said. 'It's Algerian.'

I met Arthur Wedderburn downstairs in the bar of the Scribe, which was his base away from the office. I'd called him again because I wanted more help. Arthur is a shaggy and laconic man, misleadingly slow of speech and movement and no one's fool. Half a lifetime in the rootless world of the foreign press corps had drained all the ideology out of him. He preferred a decent Communist to an ill-natured champion of democracy, though if pushed he would admit that among a lousy set of choices he would, if he must, choose the Western brand of mismanagement over and above the others. This dispassionate and pragmatic cast of mind had earned him a vast and ill-assorted crowd of useful contacts. He'd done one or two fringe jobs for the Section in his time but didn't like the work. Nor do I, but that's another story.

'I want to find the widow of one Marc Ségur,' I said. 'He was on the staff of *Libération* and was killed under odd circumstances in June 1950. It's urgent.'

Arthur grunted. 'All right, tell me what you know.'

I told him and he grunted again and said he'd call my hotel when he had something.

'Also,' I said, 'I need a good list of people who worked with André Marchand. As many as you can find. Ideally, I'd like the phone numbers of all his private secretaries and his heads of secretariat for as far back as you can go. And anyone else who knew him well.'

'And what do you plan to do with them?'

'I shall keep phoning until I hit on someone who wants to talk. I shall be a Reuters' correspondent in search of a story.'

'You know London office doesn't like that at all,' Arthur said.

'That's right,' I said. 'But then London office doesn't need to know.'

Arthur drank again and shook his head. 'Given time, you'll get us closed down,' he said. But he didn't refuse the assignment.

'Thanks, Arthur,' I said.

'I don't want your thanks, I want the story.'

But I didn't respond. I made my way upstairs and out into

the rue Scribe, leaving Arthur hunched at the end of the bar, a wary old spider, waiting patiently for flies.

As I got out of the taxi at the SEXY-BIZARRE it all happened in maybe fifteen seconds – not more. I'd handed the driver thirty francs and told him to keep the change, and Isabel was following me out of the cab when two coppers in mufti closed in on me, one on either side. They were businesslike and they knew their job.

'Monsieur Panmure?'

'Yes. What's all this?'

'We are from the Ministry of the Interior. You will please come with us.' This with a rapid flashing of identity cards.

'I have no business with the Ministry. Please leave me alone.'

By this time there was a hand grasping each of my sleeve cuffs and the grip was firm.

'Please remove your hands,' I said with less hope than bravado.

At that point one of them said '*Allons-y*', and with quite astonishing violence I was frog-marched towards a waiting DS and thrown headfirst onto the rear seat. I'd caught sight of the tell-tale Interior number plate as I was whisked inelegantly past the front of the vehicle. And as I careered through the rear door I caught my elbow and shin on the hard edge of the metal door frame and gasped from the pain. The gasp became a grunt of agony as one of the men followed me into the back of the car, sat hard on my extended leg, and calmly rammed a practised fist into my face. I felt and tasted blood spurting from my lower lip. The next blow landed below my rib cage and as I fought desperately for air something hit me somewhere on the back of the skull and that, as far as I was concerned, was that.

Some time later the world, fragmented and hazy, reimposed its ordered patterns on my mind. I first became aware of a heavy smell of Gauloises mixed with petrol fumes. Then I realised it was dark, with a faint electric glow coming from somewhere behind me. I heard talk close at hand. Then memory partially returned. I remembered the arrest outside the SEXY-BIZARRE. A thought of Isabel obtruded itself. What had happened to her? Surely she hadn't been in the police car with me. Why not? Why had they beaten me up? What were they after? I stopped asking myself stupid questions and addressed myself to my present predicament.

I appeared to be still in the back of the car with my two coppers, but the car wasn't moving and there were no traffic noises. I guessed it was a dimly lit garage. The two men were talking to each other. I tried to move my head and let out a heavy groan as a six-pound hammer started beating at my skull from the inside.

'He's come round,' said the man next to me. 'Come on,' and he gave me a vicious shake designed to annoy rather than reassure. I groaned again and meant it. Another shake, another groan. I was not in good company.

They dragged me out of the car and across a concrete floor between the dim shapes of other cars. I still felt winded and nauseated from the blow to my stomach and I had imperfect control of my legs. Inside a large lift I simply slumped to the floor and got kicked for my pains. But I was just alert enough to see that the lift indicator showed a seven when we stopped. I was hauled to my feet and hustled along a familiar-looking corridor. It was a shorter version of the corridor leading to Wavre's office at the DST. Similar paint of vague grey, similar panelled wooden doors. Similar cheap lino on the floor. I knew where we were.

They must have worked me over in one of the offices – not that I remember leaving that corridor. I recall spells of consciousness and a foreshortened view of heavy black footwear, dark blue trousers, a shirt-sleeved torso with a head atop of it. I must have been lying on the floor, but then presumably someone hit me again and all memory was cut off. I recall that my head hurt, my ribs hurt and my legs hurt. Maybe all of me hurt. I think I vomited over someone's boot. I struggled a good deal but I don't honestly think I managed to hit anyone. I wasn't a movie superman. I was a citizen who'd been jumped by two properly trained gorillas under instructions to teach him some kind of lesson. If a professional blow lands first you haven't really a chance. And if the beating is being done for its own sake and not to get answers to a lot of questions you simply have to put up with it until they get tired, or scared of killing you. If I hadn't lost consciousness so readily and so frequently they would have made a far worse hash of me. Being conscious in such circumstances is an invitation to be hit.

How long the treatment continued I have no means of knowing, but eventually I drifted back to consciousness again and was not slapped across the face or kicked in the ribs. It must have been some kind of tea break. I pulled myself into a slouching position against a wall. I was alone in a typical Ministry office, an underling's pale copy of Wavre's room – grey, anonymous and now pretty messy. I had made the mess – a nasty mixture of various excretions, much of it blood, which the body produces when you attack it. I still wanted to vomit, but retching produced nothing but streams of cold sweat on my face, neck and chest. To judge from the light and the occasional traffic sounds from the outside, it was earlyish in the morning.

I moved my legs and could not identify any breakages. I toyed with the idiotic idea of simply walking out of there – right into the street and over to the Embassy. No doubt I would wave cheerily to the door staff on the way out and say: 'Pay no attention to the blood, and if I'm on all fours it's because that's how I like to get around.' Or maybe I could get out through the underground car park, the way I'd come in. Better scheme, that. Provided no one joined me in the lift.

I pulled myself over to the door and tried it, knowing it would be locked. It was. The window was at waist height. I was on the mansard floor of the building, with a sloping outer wall as in any maid's bedroom in Paris. Outside was a wide gutter and beyond that a heavy parapet. The gutter provided a possible crawl to the neighbouring windows.

Getting out took as much effort as a 100-yard sprint. Once out, I crawled. It was easy. The first window along to the left was locked. I crawled on. The second one was unfastened and the office unoccupied. Someone had kindly left a chair within reach of the window. I found myself in a replica of the room in which I'd been beaten up: grey walls, battered desk, a couple of chairs, metal filing cabinet and a squat safe in the corner.

Now I had to move fast before the staff arrived, presumably some time between eight and nine. I opened the door. The corridor was empty and I could hear nothing. I glanced at the outside of the door I was holding and my heart thumped hard. I couldn't believe my luck. Metal numerals had been screwed to the centre panel. It was room 719. Beneath the number a typed card was fixed in a frame. It said: *Chef des Services de Documentation*, and beneath that: A. Baum.

I retreated into the room and closed the door after me. Should I wait for Baum and risk being found before he arrived, or should I try for the car park? And if Baum did arrive, what could he or would he do for me anyway? The matter was settled by noises in the building. I could hear the lift and soon I heard voices in the corridor. So I did the only thing I could think of. I sat down in Baum's swivel chair and waited while footsteps passed along the corridor. I'd been there maybe fifteen minutes when I heard the lift again. A brisk tread stopped outside 719. The handle turned and a man in a fawn raincoat came into the room. He was maybe sixty, with a sharp, sallow face and sparse hair. When he saw me, a dishevelled wreck slumped in his office chair, he did little more than raise an eyebrow in mild interest. He closed the door behind him, took a couple of steps into the room and put his briefcase on the desk.

'What's this?'

'Avram Artunian sent me,' I said.

'But at this time of the morning, unannounced, and in such a condition?' I couldn't blame him for the disbelief in his voice.

'No, no. Two of your friends along the corridor brought me here some time during the night.' I explained the rest.

Baum shrugged. 'I know who that would be. They're a pretty rough pair. You're lucky to be sitting up.'

'That's just the point,' I said. 'I've had enough of your department's rather simplistic way of communicating with people. I would like to get out of here before they resume the dialogue.'

'Wait here,' said Baum, as if I was likely to do anything else, and left the room, closing the door firmly behind him. I heard his footsteps retreating down the corridor. Then silence for maybe five minutes. Then a return of the footsteps and he was back in the room.

'Listen to me,' he said. 'They'll be back in about twenty minutes, not sooner. It gives you a chance to get out of the building if you do exactly as I say. But one thing must be clearly understood: you did this on your own. When you climbed in here and found the room empty you went out into the corridor and made a dash for the lift and reached the car park without being seen. How you got away from there will be anyone's guess. In fact, I will escort you downstairs and take you to my car. You will hide in the boot until I come down again in a couple of hours and drive out. Now let us get moving. Put this on.'

He offered me his raincoat and I managed to get into it and he buttoned it up to the neck. His hat, pulled well down, presumably obscured part of my bruised face.

'Can you walk on your own?'

'I'll manage a few yards.'

'Good. I'll get the lift up and come back for you.'

Two minutes later we started out. It was dreadfully slow, but we got into the lift just as a door opened ominously at the far end of the corridor. So far so good. Baum kept a finger on the button to prevent any interception of the lift on the way down. In the underground garage the coast was clear, and with a few grunts I heaved myself into the car boot and saw the lid descend on me.

I must have dozed towards the end of my wait. I was jolted awake by slaps on the outside of the boot lid. I took them to be friendly. The car started and we drove for maybe an hour. I ached a good deal but I'd known worse. When the car stopped and Baum opened the boot I saw we were parked in a courtyard of the kind most buildings have in Paris.

'Quick! Out before anyone sees you.'

I obeyed as fast as my legs permitted. Stiffness was beginning to set in.

Baum took me up in a lift to the third floor, opened a front door with a latchkey, beckoned me inside and showed me into one of those French living rooms without style, comfort or personality. I sat down on a hard chair and he sat opposite me.

'So – you've been in trouble,' he said. 'Would you like to clean up? Maybe some plaster on some of those cuts?'

'Never mind,' I said. 'I prefer to talk first.'

'I am listening,' Baum said.

So I told him the story – everything up to date. He sat impassively, expressionless. When I'd finished he went to a cabinet, poured a generous portion of Black Label into a tumbler and handed it to me.

As I drank, my bruised stomach knotted around the burning liquid and nearly rejected it. I gasped a bit. My head was throbbing like a metronome and I found it difficult to keep my attention properly focused on the matter in hand. I suddenly wanted desperately to sleep, and I told myself sleepiness after a blow on the head could mean concussion. It was something I couldn't afford.

'I don't think you should stay here,' Baum said. 'Furthermore I have to get back to my office. I will put you in a taxi so that you can go somewhere of your choice, and I will think about your problem. I will meet you tomorrow at six thirty at this place.' He scribbled a name and address on a scrap of paper and stuffed it into my jacket pocket. 'Under no circumstances whatever call me at the rue des Saussaies. Nor will I give you the number here: it would be unsafe to use it.'

Downstairs, we climbed into his car and drove out of the courtyard into the street. On the corner I watched for the street sign: rue Etienne Marcel. We were in the centre of town. Baum must have taken a fancy route to make the journey from the rue des Saussaies last so long. A cautious man.

Minutes later I transferred to a taxi and gave the driver the address of Reuters' office.

'Christ, you look foul,' Arthur said. He dabbed at me with some wet cotton wool provided by his secretary, who had also come up with codeine, adhesive plasters, a needle and thread to sew the rents in my jacket, and a mug of strong tea.

'I need a bit of legwork,' I told him. 'A change of gear from my hotel, and a message to Isabel to come here, shedding any followers.'

'I'll fix it,' Arthur said. 'Give me the details.'

An hour later I'd changed my clothes and Isabel was sitting on Arthur's battered sofa, sipping gin and looking at me with considerable distaste on her fashionable face.

'You look foul,' she said. 'Tell me all.'

I told her what I knew and asked for her end of the story.

'Well,' she said, 'after they whisked you off I climbed back into the taxi and once I knew I wasn't being tailed, I directed him back to my place. Then I started phoning. The Sûreté said they hadn't got you. I didn't care to call the rue des Saussaies. The DST never admits anything anyway. I called your hotel and left my number. That did no good. So I got a friend at the FO to let the abominable Pabjoy know what had happened. It was done discreetly.'

I fancied there was concern and affection in Isabel's eyes. The thought was fleeting but consoling – fleeting because Arthur's phone rang at that moment and he beckoned her.

'Your office.'

'Yes?' she said into the instrument. Then, after a pause, 'Thanks,' and she rang off.

'The FO on telex. It says: "Tell George to come for a chat." It must be from Pabjoy, so off you go.'

I fixed the practical things: a note to Arthur to get my things from the hotel and pay the bill; a phone call to Chavan to say I'd been unavoidably detained the previous evening – which was wonderfully true – and would call him shortly; details to Arthur of my appointment with Baum in order to make contact and fix something a week ahead. Then I got Arthur's secretary to book me on BE 025, and was in a window seat aboard the flight four hours later. I didn't even allow myself time to call in at a chemist's with the prescription Isabel had thoughtfully extracted from the Embassy's tame doctor. I'd never before been glad to get out of Paris.

CHAPTER 6

Hank

Andrew Pabjoy's pale eyes blinked unsympathetically at me. From time to time he stabbed at one of his yellow pads with one of his 2H pencils, or flicked imaginary dust from his sleeve. No boxes with lids this time. Just the blinking eyes and the occasional attack on the yellow pad. He didn't seem to like what he was hearing and whatever he felt in his reputedly passionless heart, it wasn't sympathy. When I'd finished he let out an ostentatious sigh, as if he'd been intolerably put upon, and straightened his already perfectly straight pad.

'You boobed, Carey,' he said. 'The whole trip's been a *non-starter*. How can I tell the Minister that my man went to Paris, got himself beaten up by Wavre's boys after provoking a murder and being put down by Wavre in person, and is now back in town covered in cuts and bruises? No way, Carey. It's what I'd call a *bad, bad scene*.'

At that point in time, to use a favourite Pabjoyism, I could have rammed the fellow's jargon down his throat. Fistwise. But Penny came in with tea and biscuits and it gave me time to collect my thoughts and swallow my irritation. Penny looked crisp in off-white over dark grey nylons. I asked her for a couple of aspirins.

We sat in absolute silence while she fetched the aspirin and a glass of water, then Pabjoy asked me what I proposed to do next.

'One, take a few days to improve my appearance. Two, get

back to Paris, which I should never have left. Three, contact Baum and Chavan. Four, find Ariane Ségur. Five, read some more history.'

'And how will you stop them pulling you in again and blacking the other eye?' Pabjoy's tone was nicely ironic. He had started on his boxes, too.

'I'll have to use fresh cover and be nippy on my feet,' I said.

Pabjoy looked at me reflectively and sipped his tea. Then he pressed the intercom and told Penny to get Wavre on the private line.

'*Mon cher ami*,' said Pabjoy, '*c'est un plaisir de vous parler*.' Then he told Wavre that he viewed with a certain amount of concern the fact that one of his men had been, er, interrogated at the DST. Perhaps a little more vigorously than was appropriate between friendly services? Was there, maybe, a misunderstanding? He paused, listened, even looked a bit nonplussed. Come now, he said, surely between colleagues one did not need to pretend? A certain, er, force had been used. It was regrettable, most regrettable. He paused and listened again. Then with expressions of cordial esteem he rang off.

'No dice,' he said. 'The man denies any knowledge of it. Says he spoke to you and that was the last time you set foot in the place. Insists we've got it wrong. And ends by telling us to stay away.'

'Everyone knows the French are the most consistent and barefaced diplomatic liars, so isn't it what you'd expect from Wavre?'

'No, it isn't what I'd expect from Wavre,' Pabjoy said, parrot fashion. 'If Wavre had you beaten up – a thing of which he is perfectly capable – I'd expect him to tell me that he'd do it again if we didn't leave him alone, only harder. Are you sure it was his lot?'

'Of course I'm sure,' I said irritably, 'and I bear the scars to prove it.'

'Well, I don't connect,' said Pabjoy. 'It isn't like Wavre. The game must be deeper than we thought. No doubt his Minister is leaning on him. But I'm *damned* if I'll have him treat me like this.'

'Treat *you*?' I thought I'd heard it wrong.

'Yes, how dare the man rough up one of my people. It's a personal affront to me as head of the Section, and he must know that perfectly well. I won't have it, I tell you. And I'll tell you just what I intend to do.'

Pabjoy's indignation seemed a bit spurious, but I obliged by picking up the cue.

'And what do you intend to do?'

'I intend to send you back to Paris,' he said, just as if I hadn't uttered a word about it myself. 'I'm sorry, Carey, and I quite understand your reluctance to go, but I have no choice. We cannot call off the exercise. And if I send Jock or Stephen Boddey in your place, it's one up to Wavre, and I won't have the man telling me who to send where.'

I said nothing. Pabjoy hadn't finished yet.

'In any case,' he said, 'there's a new dimension. An American dimension. I've heard from Langley.'

Whenever the Central Intelligence Agency came after him for anything, Pabjoy referred to it as hearing from Langley. It was his way of signalling that he had often been a guest at CIA headquarters, though the eager beavers at Langley, in Virginia, usually relayed what they had to say to Pabjoy through the Resident in London.

'They have an interest in the exercise,' Pabjoy said.

'Oh,' I said.

'And they want a piece of the action. Hank Munthe will be here tomorrow.'

'Oh, him,' I said.

'Yes, well, we could do worse,' Pabjoy said, with little conviction.

'We could,' I said, 'but it wouldn't be easy.'

'State wants to know what Marchand was up to.'

'Just like us only a bit slower,' I said.

'Don't underestimate the State Department,' Pabjoy said primly.

'I shan't,' I said.

'I want to see you tomorrow at ten,' Pabjoy said. 'In conference. With our American friend. We will play it straight down the middle, Carey. The Minister takes the view that what is good for State is good for us.'

'A view of the State Department which does him credit,' I said. It was wasted on Pabjoy.

Next morning I was in Pabjoy's office at ten sharp. Hank Munthe was already there, sprawled untidily in one of Pabjoy's leatherette armchairs. His big, square face with the baby-blue eyes had its usual deep tan, and his jaw showed its familiar shadow of stubble. The eternal pipe was clenched between his teeth and his tobacco smelled terrible. The thick head of hair had been chopped back to within a quarter inch of the scalp, ready for combat duty.

He heaved his big frame out of the chair to greet me, revealing the usual peculiarities of his dress. The trousers were baggy, uncreased and too deep in the crotch. His jacket, unconstructed and made of porridge-coloured alpaca, had the lapels curling forward to meet you. His shirt showed no cuffs, and creases had been ironed firmly into the front seams of the collar by the lady he always referred to as 'my lovely wife'. He was as untidy and improbable a figure as ever.

'Hi, there,' said Hank. 'Good to see you, Charlie. Been busting broncos and fell off?'

'Hello, Hank,' I said.

I'd had dealings with Hank Munthe on and off for a dozen years. He ran a small section which was not even listed in the complex organisation charts maintained by the CIA – charts so very comprehensive and up to date that two old trusties were engaged full time in amending, checking and constantly refurbishing them. Needless to say, their very perfection made of them some of the most sensitive documents in Langley's vast output of paper, so that most of the operating sections spent a good part of their time trying to get off the charts and stay off. But as far as I knew, Hank was the only one to have foxed the administration. The O & M people actually didn't know that he existed. This achievement dated from the time, very soon after his arrival, when he was given the task of doing to certain Governments those necessary things which the CIA's regular operatives were either too squeamish or too sensible to do. For a start, he had achieved the near-impossible: he was the only man to have crossed successfully from the hated FBI to the hated CIA – a task generally agreed to be harder than getting in from the Hungarian Security Services. He'd been reared on field work in the FBI during the McCarthy red scare of the fifties, and this had left him with a simple and rugged view of Communists, Socialists and Liberals of every kidney and their wicked ways.

But I was never inclined to dismiss Hank Munthe as a Southern anti-Communist nut. He looked and talked like a faintly dotty academic, but was in fact a very dangerous man, always willing to smash things up on behalf of his fierce and unforgiving ideology. That ideology consisted in the belief that men must be free at all times to make their own political choices. Like the Dulles brothers in their day, Hank would cheerfully commit mayhem to impose this ruthless liberty on us all.

Now I sat on the far side of Pabjoy's desk and fidgeted on my sore backside.

'We are truly happy,' Pabjoy was saying, 'to have our American friends take an interest in this matter. Hank here would like to brief himself, so perhaps you'd tell him where we are at this point in time.'

Pabjoy was doodling carefully. Hank pulled at his rough cut. I told him as much as I felt he was entitled to know. I don't know why, but I said nothing about Marc Ségur and his researches. When I'd finished, Hank shifted heavily in his chair and started the elaborate ritual of filling and relighting his pipe.

'I'd like to hear how you figure this thing out, Charlie.'

'Well, circumstantial, and nothing but circumstantial, evidence points to Marchand being an asset of the opposition. So let's assume he was controlled by the KGB, though any of the East European services would do. On this premise, one of three things has happened. He may have had an attack of conscience, refused to carry on, and was being threatened with exposure to bring him back into line. Or they may have stepped up their demands on him to the point where his elastic sense of what was permissible had snapped. Or a Western service, or even some private individual, may have found him out and threatened him with exposure. A simple case of your friendly neighbourhood blackmailer.'

'Good thinking,' Hank said. 'Which was it?'

'The first two don't make much sense,' I said. 'I don't think I believe in the moral conversion of a man who has done that sort of work for over two decades. You don't swallow Hungary and Prague and then choke on Afghanistan.'

'Right.'

'In the same way, you don't deliver the French military budget year after year but suddenly refuse to hand over what you know about the latest NATO exercise.'

'I am reading you,' said Hank.

'Which leaves blackmail,' I said.

'Improbable,' Pabjoy said. 'No one is going to tell me that a man like Marchand, with his experience and his friends, couldn't look after some blundering innocent who thinks all you have to do to nail a top-level agent is to get up and say "Look, he's a spy!" Why, people were saying that about Philby for years before anyone would listen. And then he got away.'

'So do you reject blackmail?' Hank asked.

'I don't reject blackmail or conscience or anything else. I regard the case as wide open,' Pabjoy said. 'I smell something a little more complex than blackmail, but I don't know what it is. I need more facts and less speculation. More input. I need you to be back in France, Carey.'

'I propose to go back in two or three days,' I said. 'I want to see one or two people here, including Otto Feld. And I want to heal a bit in the hope that I might slip back in without Wavre finding out for a while.'

'I guess I'll stick around in London until we learn more,' Hank said. 'I'll leave this one to you, gentlemen, but I would like you to know that our people want to get to the bottom of it. So please let me have what you can. And if there's anything we can do, why, it will be my pleasure.'

We took our farewells.

'For God's sake,' I said to Pabjoy after he'd gone, 'keep that scourge of the Almighty off my back.'

Later that morning I called Otto and we met for lunch at an Italian place off the Strand. I wanted to ask him about Andrew Pabjoy's boxes and about suicide. He was communicative in his *gemütlich* Viennese way.

'Andrew Pabjoy is your classical anal character as described by Sigmund Freud,' he said. 'I base my remarks on Freud's paper "Character and Anal Erotism" of 1908 – a seminal contribution to the theory and practice of psychoanalysis, using inductive investigation. Freud teaches that if there remains in the individual a preponderance of anal and sadistic components dating from early childhood – from the pre-genital phase, you understand – these give rise in the adult to what we call the anal erotic character. I refer you to Sadger, Karl Abraham, and particularly Ernest Jones for admirable work on the subject. You understand?'

So far I understood Otto but I expected to lose him shortly.

'Now, Freud and Abraham defined three character traits of the anal type: orderliness, leading to pedantry; parsimony, leading to miserliness; and obstinacy, leading to defiance. Sadger said your anal character is convinced he can do everything better than anyone else, leading to a certain contempt for colleagues and employees. Jones drew attention to his obsession with order, systems, tidiness, precise recording *und so weiter*. Commenting on this, Abraham drew attention to his carping criticisms of all who work with him.'

'That's our man,' I said.

'Wait,' Otto said, 'more and better will come. Jones made an acute observation which was borne out by other workers. He found that the anal character is obsessed always with the reverse side of things. If he lives on this side of the hill he is tormented by the possibility that life would somehow be better on the other side. As he reads page one of his newspaper he becomes increasingly concerned to see what is on the back of the sheet, on page two. And of course, my friend, if he is working in intelligence he has found the ideal occupation. For are we not obsessed, all of us, all the time, with what is being thought, planned, perpetrated on the other side? No?'

'We are,' I said. 'It explains what Andrew Pabjoy is doing in the Service. But does it explain his damned boxes?'

Otto's moon face beamed appreciatively at me as he disposed of the last of the *fettucine*.

'It does, it does,' he said. 'They are entirely the boxes of an anal character – precise, tidy, clean, symmetrical, and above all, always open. Into them – symbolically, you understand – he dreams of putting *money*, and he will then close them up neatly, securely, so. Only he prefers, as your true anal type, to leave that option always available. He will close them at the moment of *his* choosing, when he has filled them with whatever he is collecting and hoarding – as his unconscious reminds him that he hoarded his excreta as a baby until the wicked mother came and cleaned him up.'

'Your analysis conjures up a picture of the infant Pabjoy that one does not care to dwell on,' I said.

Otto beamed. 'You asked. I told you. It is simple.' We moved on to the cheese.

'Tell me about suicides,' I said. 'Who commits suicide?'

'It was my appreciation of the Marchand case which Pabjoy took to the Minister,' Otto said. 'It is again very simple. Suicide is predominantly a depressive manifestation. It says: the world is not good enough for me. Alternatively it says: I am not good enough for the world. Because this is a morbid condition – an *illness* of the mind, you understand – it will not respond to reason, to argument. Prove to your suicidal individual that he is good enough for the world; line up his wife, his children, his mother, his partner even, to tell him he's a splendid chap – and what happens? He knows better and he kills himself. His despair is finally total. His depression has turned to anger against himself and against others, whom he punishes by making them feel guilty on his account. Suicides always show their illness in many ways. They are *sad people*, withdrawn, anguished.'

'Are you sure André Marchand showed no such signs?'

'I know it. It is my business to know it. So he has to be the only other type of suicide known to us: the sane man driven to despair by some external event which creates internal conflicts he can no longer bear. For instance, he may be the brave man who knows there is no tolerable way out, such as the agent who will be forced to speak and prefers to die with his secret. Or the man who will bring disgrace on his family if he lives.'

'And in the case of Marchand?'

'In the case of Marchand –' and here Otto brought his round, pink face as close to mine as the intervening cutlery permitted, and tapped out the words with a pudgy forefinger on the white table cloth '– in the case of Marchand it is most likely that he was an agent who had reached the end of the road. I would wager my life on it.'

'I'm having to wager mine,' I said.

CHAPTER 7

Les obsèques Artunian

Three days later, partly healed, I picked up from Movement and Services a passport and accessories in the name of George Parrot, journalist, employed by Reuters News Agency, and caught AF 1885 for Lille at 17.50 hours. I reckoned Lille would be marginally safer than immigration at Charles de Gaulle airport. From Lille I took the train into the Gare du Nord, and booked into the Hotel Royal du Nord, across the way. I went straight to bed and slept soundly until morning. At ten I was sitting with Arthur over a *café crème* at a bistro nearby.

'I've found Ariane Ségur for you,' Arthur said. He pulled a sheet of paper out of a pocket and read from it. 'Born eighth August 1923. Married Marc Ségur March 1946. Remarried sixteenth June 1953, to Daniel Bontemps, artist. Now living at Chemin de la Fosse, Ver-lès-Chartres, which is about five kilometres south of Chartres itself. No number or house name, so it must be rural. Both Ariane and her husband were members of the Communist Party but resigned in 1956. There are no children. He paints and exhibits in a local gallery and has had shows in Paris, Zurich and Milan. A small but solid reputation. She's the features editor of the local rag.'

He handed me the paper, covered in his neat handwriting.

'I made contact with your Mr Baum,' Arthur said. 'He seemed a bit miffed by your failure to turn up. Seemed to think you'd come to a sticky end. Anyway, it's to be the same place at one today.'

'Anything on the Artunian story?'

'Not much. Police said to be mystified. Newspapers doing the usual. General consensus: some obscure Armenian feud. Funeral's at the Russian Orthodox Cemetery at Sainte-Geneviève-des-Bois at ten tomorrow.'

'And what about my list of Marchand's associates?'

'Here,' Arthur said, and handed me a typed sheet. There were sixteen names on it, all with brief descriptions and telephone numbers.

'Thanks,' I said. 'And finally I want you to contact Isabel for me and tell her to be at my hotel at six tonight.'

'When do you tell me what the hell is going on?'

'I don't,' I said. 'You don't need to know.'

'I never knew André Marchand personally,' Baum said, 'but I understand he was an exceptional man.'

We had worked our way through most of an indifferent meal, designed for foreign tourists.

'Do you have an opinion on Marchand's reasons for taking his life? Could it have been a question of blackmail?' I asked.

'I think blackmail unlikely because I think it unlikely that André Marchand was anyone's agent. It is difficult to believe a man like Marchand, constantly in the limelight, constantly undergoing screening for security-sensitive posts, constantly under attack from enemies such as any politician will accumulate over the course of a career, could survive for thirty years as the agent of a foreign power.'

'But why do you have to attribute such long service to him and then conclude that he couldn't have been an agent because the period was too long – a period which you've just invented yourself?'

Baum smiled thinly. 'I have invented nothing. I have made a simple deduction. Such a man could only have been recruited without our knowledge in the general turmoil of the war and the occupation. In normal times our services would have known he had Communist connections or would have uncovered something about him.'

'So you think I am wasting your time?'

'I do.' Baum's pale, thin face was expressionless.

'Can you give me a sight of André Marchand's dossier at the DST?'

Baum smiled slowly. 'You know what you are asking?'

'Of course I know. I am in the service too.'

'Why should I take such a risk?'

'I haven't the least idea. But Avram Artunian said you would help, and that's the help I need. In any case, I would have thought that as Head of Documentation you'd have ready access to stuff like that.'

'I haven't. Ministerial files are with the Director himself.'

'Are you saying you can't do it?' I had the impression he could do it and didn't want to. He was beginning to irritate me and I knew it wasn't reasonable. No doubt the man was scared.

'I'm not saying that. I am saying I will have to find a plausible excuse to go to the Ministerial file. It is a delicate matter and may take time.'

'But are you prepared to do it?' I was losing patience with this taciturn bureaucrat who may have saved my life but for whom I felt no warmth.

'I will try,' he said, 'but I have small hopes of the dossier being of the slightest interest. It is my view that you will do better on your own – among Marchand's colleagues and friends, his wartime associates if you can find them, and wherever else you think it useful to take a look.'

'I shall do that anyway,' I said. 'I plan to go down to the area where he was active in one of the Resistance networks during the war.

'How will you get down there?'

'Hertz or Avis,' I said.

'I wouldn't,' Baum said. 'Once it's realised what you are up to – and you certainly won't keep it dark for more than a few days at most – they'll trace you through the car. And if they fail to pick you up through the car-hire firm, they'll get the local police to keep an eye open for cars with Paris registrations. Sooner or later they'll locate you.'

'So what do you suggest?'

'I can get you a car in Paris with a spare number plate. It will be specially fitted with detachable plates. It will come from a hire firm we use on special jobs and no one will think of enquiring there. They will keep their mouths shut.'

'That,' I said, 'is useful.'

'The firm is Auto Ecole Marceau, and it's at thirty-four rue de Bassano. I'll talk to them myself this afternoon and they'll expect a call from Mr Panmure. You will find the spare plates in the boot.'

'Not Panmure, Parrot,' I said. 'George Parrot, journalist. I'll call the car people this evening.'

'I will let you know tomorrow whether I can give you anything from our files on Marchand,' Baum said.

Then I paid the bill and he left the restaurant ahead of me.

'I'd like to come with you, my dear.'

Isabel lay back luxuriously on the bed, her shoes kicked off, doing a mysterious toe exercise she said she'd picked up at yoga classes off the Fulham Road. She watched her toes as they moved down and back. I watched them too.

'You can't,' I said. 'Rules of the Section *and* the FO. You know it perfectly well.'

'Just dreaming,' she said. 'Where are you going?'

'First to Ariane Ségur. Then to the Aveyron area. That's where my reading tells me Marchand was active during the war. Maybe *la* Ségur can give me a lead.'

'Someone ought to keep track of you.'

'That's just what the DST would want,' I said. 'They'll have a tap on your phone as well as their usual on the Embassy.'

Isabel pulled a face and gently banged her big toes together. 'Then I'll be in the lobby of the Bristol every weekday from one till two until you get back. You can have me paged there as Miss Brown.'

'Good thinking,' I said. 'What do you hope to gain by doing that with your toes?'

'It helps the twenty-six bones and nineteen muscles in each of my feet to live happily together,' Isabel said. Then she rose from the bed, put on her shoes, kissed me and left behind her an aroma of Cabochard.

I turned to Arthur's list of sixteen names. Four were listed as *chefs de cabinet*, four as personal secretaries, two as deputy mayors of Rodez, in the Aveyron department, and three as vice-ministers serving at different times under Marchand. It wasn't bad. I settled down on the bed and started dialling. I had worked out a simple routine:

'This is Reuters news agency in Paris. We are doing a profile of the late André Marchand and understand you once worked with him. Are you willing to help us to be accurate by answering a few simple questions?'

The score after nearly an hour was depressing: eight refusals to talk to the press, three no-replies, and five replies but the person was said to be out, away or unavailable. Eight refusals, so firmly expressed, meant that someone – probably the DST – had taken the precaution of warning Marchand's former associates not to answer questions. It left me with eight possibles who had doubtless been similarly warned.

Next morning I started again and collected two more refusals. Score: ten blanks, six to go. My third call was to an Alain de Montand, *chef de cabinet* to André Marchand at the Ministry of Overseas Territories and later at the Ministry of the Interior. The previous evening Mr de Montand had been out. Now he answered the phone himself and I gave him my little speech. It sounded a bit hollow from over-use. When I'd finished there was a pause.

'You said Reuters?'

'Yes.'

'Who gave you my name, Mr Parrot? I haven't worked with André Marchand for fifteen years.'

'We have a good filing system, Mr de Montand.'

Another pause. 'Very well, if you will accept that the interview is off the record and no direct attributions can be made you may come to my apartment this afternoon if you wish. Say at two.'

'That will be fine,' I said, 'and thank you.'

'I am at seventy-eight boulevard Malesherbes.' And he rang off.

This left me three shots. The first two proved to be blanks: no reply. The third and last was decidedly better. A Mademoiselle Anny Dupuy, principal private secretary to André Marchand from 1953 to 1962. She must have followed him through several ministries. For her, at least, he could not have been such an ogre.

The voice was edgy. I told her my business, and as I spoke she interrupted with an occasional 'yes, yes'.

'Will you give me half an hour of your time, *Mademoiselle*?' I concluded.

'A quoi bon?'

The question was dismissive – not a question at all.

'In the interests of truth,' I said. And then I took a chance with this prickly woman. 'I am really looking for someone who can counter-balance the unpleasant innuendo I pick up almost everywhere when I ask about André Marchand.'

No impatient reply crowding on the end of my sentence this time. Perhaps I had reached her in some region where feelings and not bristling defences held sway.

'Very well. Where shall we meet?'

I suggested the upper floor at the Colisée at 3.30.

'I shall wear a red coat and my umbrella is red,' she said.

'I shall have a large bruise on my face,' I replied.

It was progress but it didn't look like being a cosy tea for two.

My taxi had some difficulty in finding the Russian Orthodox cemetery out at Sainte-Geneviève-des-Bois, so that it was nearly 10.30 when we arrived at the gates. A harsh, damp wind was blowing out of a sky of dirty, uneven grey with a lot of brown in it. I'd made a deal with the taxi driver to wait for however long it took me to decide that the whole expedition was wasted anyhow.

The gatekeeper was a giant blond with a Ukrainian head and an accent to suit. '*Les obsèques Artunian, oui,*' he said. '*Dans l'église. Vous êtes en retard.*' The r's rolled and disapproval was conveyed.

I walked over to the church, which proved to be a miniature Byzantine cathedral, heavily decorated in gaudy mosaics with liberal areas of gold leaf. The place had clearly been over-endowed by wealthy émigrés and the money had to show somewhere. Incense hung sickeningly in the cold, damp air. A stained-glass window over the altar filtered the grey autumn light through blues and reds, and a single chandelier added a touch of yellow from midway down the nave. There were perhaps twenty or thirty people in the pews, all muffled against the cold and each holding a candle. The points of candlelight did little to illuminate the place, but they made good religious theatre. The principal player was the priest, magnificently robed and coiffed, immobile before the altar. The voices of most of the congregation were raised in a solemn Gregorian chant, led by a wizened, fierce little man in black, who sang vigorously and beat time with his left hand. He would dart about the place, relighting a candle here and adjusting a prayerbook or tending the needs of the priest there, singing constantly and turning whenever he could to the congregation to keep them going in obedience and, hopefully, in tune. No one seemed to find the proceedings unusual.

I held the lighted candle I'd been given on the way into the church and winced when the hot wax fell on my fingers. To my untutored ear, the service dragged, but after twenty minutes the chanting stopped, and activity around the coffin, sombrely draped before the altar, signalled the end. I disposed of my candle, slipped out and stationed myself where I could see the mourners as they emerged into the biting wind, led by the attendants carrying the coffin.

The procession was short. Madame Artunian, in heavy black

and supported on either side by a young man and woman, presumably relatives. Then maybe a dozen others in what was clearly the family group. Then ten more people walking separately or in pairs. I recognised the old man from the *boulangerie* in the rue La Fayette, walking alone, a polite, self-effacing figure in black – certainly an old habitué of funerals. Two of the mourners bore the unmistakable stamp of police inspectors: perhaps former colleagues from the DST. A short, plumpish man in a dark grey overcoat walked alone. He carried a soft grey hat which he placed on his large head as a few spots of rain began to fall. He lacked the polite mourner's typical funeral stance. Unlike the others, his eyes were fixed neither on the ground nor on those just ahead of him. He looked constantly and carefully around him in the alert but relaxed manner of someone who spends much of his time making himself aware of what is going on. The others failed to impress themselves on my mind, save for the massive figure who brought up the rear. It was Albert Chavan, whom I had last seen seated at his fashionable little plastic desk at the SEXY-BIZARRE. He had come to pay his last respects to the old man, and there was grief on his heavy face, reddened still further by the November wind. As he passed me, he looked in my direction but gave no sign of recognition beyond the faintest inclination of the head. There was no sign of Alfred Baum.

Fifty yards along the broad gravel path, two young men stood together and watched as the procession approached them and turned up a side path towards the prepared grave. They then walked quickly away and out of the cemetery. As I emerged, their black Renault was pulling out of the car park. Neither of them looked at me.

I found my taxi and directed him back to Paris. Half a mile down the road, the black Renault pulled out from the position in front of a parked van where it had been waiting for us, and fell in behind. It took me an hour of simple manoeuvres involving two taxis and a Métro ride to shake them off. Perhaps it hadn't been one of my better hunches after all. For the DST and other interested parties would now know that I was back in France, even if they lost me again. And staying lost, even in a large city, is a good deal harder than you might suppose.

CHAPTER 8

Anny Dupuy

At two I presented myself at 78 boulevard Malesherbes. Mr Alain de Montand proved to be a white-haired gentleman, tall and spare and of considerable distinction of manner, like the better sort of ambassador.

'I am at your service, Mr Parrot,' he said, 'and I remind you that what I may have to say is unattributable.' He indicated a chair in the small study. He sat on the far side of an ormolu and walnut desk, bolt upright, his hands resting on a blotter, his eyes fixed on mine. A considerable presence.

'You worked with André Marchand for four years, at Overseas Territories and the Interior?'

'Yes, but I knew him in political circles for far longer. Since 1945, in fact.'

'I believe he was an able man?'

'Very able. A quick intellect. A prodigious capacity for work, and able to carry complete problems in his head.'

'Was he a difficult man to work for?'

'Very.'

I waited, but nothing more was volunteered. There was no trace of feeling in de Montand's features or in his voice.

'In what way difficult, Monsieur?'

'Excessively demanding of one's time and effort and one's personal loyalty. Impatient of one's intellectual difficulties. He expected his associates to master briefs as rapidly as he did himself. He expected full comprehension when often he did not bother to provide a full statement of the facts.'

'And yet you preserved a cordial relationship over many years?'

'Our relations were always correct.' This coldly. The eyes looked steadily into mine. He must have hated the man.

'Mr Marchand was a great French public servant,' I ventured. 'His tragic death must have been a shock to you and to many colleagues.'

De Montand dodged the question while purporting to answer it. 'He had a long political career. There will be those who miss him. And his death presents the coalition with certain problems.'

'What is your view of his political record?'

De Montand allowed a thin smile to touch the corners of his mouth. He raised his shoulders in the hint of a shrug. 'André Marchand's political career contains an element of mystery. Everyone knew that he could have twice become Prime Minister of France. These opportunities he refused to grasp. He was at certain moments a disruptive – in my view, wilfully disruptive – element in our coalitions.'

'Why?'

'I do not know why. I have thought about it often, and any solutions that presented themselves were unacceptable to me.'

'Can you explain that?'

'I think not.'

I tried a different tack.

'Did you like André Marchand?'

A brief hesitation. 'No. I have never *liked* men whose personality is largely turned inwards. I can respect them and, perforce, work with them. But I cannot like a man whose soul is protected by barbed wire – no, by a stone wall. One can at least see through barbed wire.'

'Can you tell me something of his work habits?'

'They were the habits of a work-machine. When he was in office he worked seven days a week, usually for twelve or fourteen hours in the day, and expected his associates to do the same. Much of his time was spent briefing himself with obsessive thoroughness. He made few notes, often none at all, but he forgot nothing. Even in periods of acute political crisis he would often drop everything at weekends and travel to his constituency in the Aveyron, where he showed as much impatience and energy over the local drains as he did in Paris over the armament of our motorised divisions.'

'Was it exceptional for a cabinet minister to devote such care to nursing the voters in his constituency?'

'Well, you must understand that in France our leading political figures often retain the mayoralty of a local town, though the detailed work is done by deputies. Nevertheless, it was very unusual for a leading minister to act as André Marchand acted, especially in periods of political tension. Furthermore, he enjoyed a massive majority and really didn't have to worry about wooing votes between elections.'

'How do you explain it?'

'I do not. Unless it was a kind of neurotic perfectionism.'

'Did you travel to the Aveyron with him?'

'Quite often.'

'What did he do down there that may be worthy of comment?'

'He would, as I say, fling himself into municipal affairs in Rodez, see constituents, undertake the usual grassroots political work.'

'When you went down, did you stay with him all the time?'

'Not when he went into the countryside to local meetings and to see political associates in other parts of the area. He liked to drive on his own. Very fast.'

'No bodyguards?'

'He was as impatient with them as he was with everyone else.'

'Why do you think André Marchand committed suicide?'

Again the faint, mirthless smile. An eyebrow gently raised, questioning: 'An emotional crisis?' He had turned my question to him into a question to me. It was a way of not replying.

'Come, Mr de Montand,' I said, putting on a little pressure.

'You worked closely with him for four years. You must have an opinion.'

'I cannot always share my opinions, even with an organisation as distinguished as Reuters.'

'That isn't generous,' I said.

'I fear not,' he said, 'but I do not believe one should speculate in public when one's data is inadequate. If André Marchand killed himself, you may be sure he had sufficient reason. I never saw him do anything without good reason and there seems to me no case for concluding that in this instance he acted blindly and with impetuosity. That was not his way.'

'Certainly,' I said. 'But why?'

His answer was to get to his feet. The interview was at an end.

'Mr de Montand, I imagine you have been asked not to talk to us,' I said. 'I am therefore doubly grateful for your time.'

'I talk to whom I please,' de Montand said, neither confirming nor denying my suggestion. As we walked to the front door, he stopped suddenly in the centre of the hall. 'I do not know what motivated André Marchand either in life or in his death,' he said. 'Perhaps that is why I ultimately feel alien to him. I am old enough, you know, to have come to terms with the motives of men. I understand ambition, greed, altruism, patriotism, even motives born of neurotic disturbance. No one of these motivations can account for Marchand the politician. Something else, at certain moments, is required.' He paused, silent, his head shaking slightly. 'I do not know what that thing was.'

And he showed me courteously to the door.

On my way from de Montand's apartment to the Café du Colisée in the Champs Elysées I stopped the taxi and bought *Michelin 80*, covering the Aveyron department, and buried myself in it for the rest of the journey.

She had arrived quite a bit before me so she must have been early. She was sitting bolt upright at a corner table facing the stairs, her coat duly red, her sharp, chiselled face with black hair pulled back into a knot matching perfectly the telephone voice. As I walked towards her she looked at me appraisingly and with no sign of approval. A woman in her late fifties for whom other people were a problem – *the* problem.

'I am George Parrot. Thank you for coming. I am sorry you had to wait. Not for long, I hope?'

'It's nothing.' Her handshake was curiously dismissive. Her glance met mine for a bare second and then slid down to the table before her. She had ordered a *pastis* and had drunk most of it already. I sat, called for a pot of tea and another drink, and bestowed a smile on Anny Dupuy. It was not returned. Instead, she took a cigarette from the pack before her and lit it, with the practised desperation of your three-pack smoker. It was like having a tête-à-tête with a very nervous cat which had not been kindly treated.

'No doubt you've been warned against speaking to me,' I said.

'What do you expect?'

'Why do you think the authorities don't want André Marchand to be discussed?'

Somewhere inside Anny Dupuy a head of steam must have built up over the years. You could feel it. The words came out clipped, charged with a kind of rage, as if they had half a dozen atmospheres of pressure behind them.

'They don't want the truth. They are afraid of what may be said.' The 'they' was spat out. The hysteria within found words upon which it could fasten.

'What truth?'

'That the Minister was the finest servant France has had since the war. He should have been Prime Minister, President of the Republic. But they couldn't stand an honest man, someone incorruptible, someone who would never compromise with the Left.'

She stubbed out her scarcely smoked cigarette and lit another.

'Who is "they"?'

'The old gang, of course. The Gaullists. And the Communists. The Minister used to tell me: "Thorez and his mafia are after me, and no doubt they'll get me in the end." And so they did.'

She referred to Marchand as the Minister. Her feelings and responses seemed to have frozen in the posture of more than twenty years before, when she had been his girl Friday and who knew what besides?

'But he killed himself, Mademoiselle, did he not?'

'Ha! There is suicide and suicide. Even supposing he did, have you asked yourself *why* such a brilliant and successful man should do such a thing? Have you asked yourself that?'

The second *pastis* had gone. I offered her an olive from the meagre ration that the waiter had banged onto the table. She shook her head.

'A problem of the heart?' It was an opening gambit.

'No!' The word was almost shouted.

'How can you be sure?'

'I am sure.'

'May I ask when you last saw him?'

She looked at me and simply ignored the question. I tried again. 'Have you been in touch with the Minister since you stopped working for him in 1962?'

'Certainly,' but with the slightest hesitation.

'May I ask why you gave up your work for him after nine years?'

'Our relationship was – different.'

'So that you are in a good position to form a view on why he committed suicide, assuming he did so.'

'No one is better placed. *No one.*'

I tried again, making my voice as gentle as I could. If this was a dangerous cat, she could not be tamed with kindness or tasty morsels. Her war with the rest of the world was hers alone, and woe betide anyone, friend or foe, who came within range of her claws.

'Tell me, Mademoiselle, why do you think André Marchand died?' Another stub. Another cigarette. Now her hands shook so violently that the flame burned a half inch of the cigarette away.

'May I have another drink, please?' I caught the whine of the alcoholic. I ordered the drink and waited, uncertain whether to repeat my question.

'How am I to know you aren't writing another disgusting article about him, trying to smear him with filth?'

'You have to take me on trust,' I said. 'I've been very surprised by the hostility towards the Minister that I encounter almost everywhere. I am looking for a truly honest opinion on this remarkable man from someone who knew him intimately. I want to tell the truth.'

The crazy suspicion did not drain out of her gaze. Probably, there was no one she trusted any more. She slipped her coat off her shoulders and onto the back of the chair. Her body was still neat, though no doubt it had thickened since the days when the racy, astringent personality and the wonderfully dark blue eyes had caught the Minister's fancy. You could still recognise what he had seen in her.

'They drove him to it,' she said with a kind of triumphant finality, as if she had spent infinite time and thought on the problem and had reached her conclusions, as no doubt she had.

'Who?'

'The Communists. Their friends. They have friends everywhere. Even at the Interior. The Minister told me.' She nodded knowingly.

'Why would they do that?'

'Because they cannot stand truth and decency. Because he was their implacable enemy.'

'And *how* did they drive him to it? What did they do that made him . . .' I trailed off, afraid of provoking some kind of outburst.

She finished her *pastis* in a gulp. 'They spread vile rumours about him. Vile, filthy rumours.' Great tears welled up in her eyes and trickled down her cheeks. She paid no attention to them. I waited, but she went no further.

'What were those rumours?'

'That he was a secret *collabo*, an agent of the Gestapo, in the war. You must have heard it.' It cost her a dreadful effort to get the words out.

'I heard it and I didn't believe it,' I said encouragingly. 'What I don't understand is where the stories came from. And why.'

'They came from the Communists, and the cryptos.'

'But when *Libération* was running a campaign against him in 1950, *l'Humanité* never picked it up. Wouldn't they have done so if they were after him?'

She snorted, not to be deterred from her obsession by anything as trivial as a fact. 'They aren't fools, the Communists. They let the cryptos at *Libération* do the dirty work while they kept their hands clean.'

'Do you know anything about Marc Ségur?'

'Only that someone must have had an old score to settle. Everyone knew he was killed. It was good riddance anyway. *Canaille!*'

She asked for another drink in a voice which brooked no argument and I got it for her. And gradually, painfully, I extracted from this tormented creature what she knew or thought she knew about André Marchand, the Minister, the dazzling man who had entered her trivial life of *petite bonne femme* and left it radiant and utterly shattered.

She first met him, she said, when she was working at the Ministry of Transport, and by 1953 he'd noticed her and had her promoted to his personal private secretary. Then, she implied, there started the days of her glory, serving this charismatic, masterful man, tending to his whims, protecting him from intrusions, gradually becoming a confidante, a necessity, a lover. For him, no doubt, the arrangement was convenient. For her it was life itself. How long he took to tire of her there was no means of knowing. Maybe her intense demands drove him away. Maybe the instability and hysteria began to show while they were still together. I could imagine how such a woman would have responded to the first signs of indifference. There must have been dreadful scenes in whatever discreet apartments or cafés they frequented. And eventually Marchand got rid of her, as he inevitably would. Brutally, no doubt. But not brutally enough to shake her obsessive adoration and her loyalty. And it was clear that she was lying about her continuing contact with the Minister. She could not have seen him at all since 1962. Perhaps the rest of her story was doubtful too.

As she talked she drank. The liquor slowed her speech but seemed to do little more.

There had always been rumours, she said. No, she didn't know what had started them in the first place, but they came from the Communists. No, she'd never seen specific accusations, except that it was said that the Minister had had close connections during the occupation with a proven traitor. No, she did not know who that would be, nor where. And she didn't believe it because the Minister had sworn to her that it was all lies. No, it was quite impossible that he himself should have been lying to her. This angrily, and I retreated carefully through the minefield. What she remembered mostly of him was work, work, work. And then brief moments of gaiety, happiness shared, opportunities to comfort him in times of political stress. Yes, she sometimes went with him to the Aveyron and those were the best times. They must have found each other at night, in his hotel room, away from the strain and the risks of Paris. For there was a wife in the background. Dead now, said Anny Dupuy. Died three years ago. But a matter of indifference to the Minister for many years before that.

'There was only one woman in his life. Only one.' And for the first and only time a serene and beautiful smile creased the corners of her eyes and with a gesture which had its touch of sexual pride she fluffed out the chiffon scarf which was tied high around her neck.

She did not travel about with him in his constituency, she said. There was an office reserved for her at the Mairie in Rodez, and she worked there on mail, his appointments, dealing with callers, while the Minister held meetings, travelled in the region and made his speeches. Where did he go when he left her in her room at the town hall? Oh, all over the constituency. He was the most conscientious, the most devoted of men. Even to such small places as Villefranches and Milau? I had remembered my geography from the taxi ride. Yes, he loved the countryside and the old churches. He knew a great deal about architecture. A cultured man. Any particular places that he loved to visit? I thought for a moment that I was pressing too hard but she was wrapped in her dream of the past now and her defences were lowered. All kinds of places, she said, Cordes and Sévérac and Conques. Particularly Conques.

'Why there?'

'It has a splendid Romanesque abbey,' she said. 'We would often visit it to look at the restoration work.'

'With you?'

'No, alone. I had my work to do.'

The reminiscences came at me across the table, staccato, in desperate bursts, like some confession to her priest. But all it amounted to was a hagiography of the Minister and a desperate cry of nostalgia for a past which must have borne little resemblance to her recollection of it.

'Mademoiselle, you have been very kind and helpful. If I need to consult you again, may I telephone?'

'You may.'

I paid for my bulk order of *pastis* and she left me to take the Métro. And through it all I felt I had got to know André Marchand a little better and to like him a little less.

CHAPTER 9

Ariane Ségur

I found Ver-lès-Chartres and the chemin de la Fosse with some difficulty. It turned out to be little more than a country lane bordered on one side by one of those immense cultivated fields such as you find on the plain of the Beauce, and on the other by a dense wood of chestnut and silver birch. Here and there the trees had been cleared and modest red-tiled houses had been plumped down. The Bontemps lived in the first of these as you arrived from the north, separated from their nearest neighbours by a hundred yards or so of undergrowth and trees, and lying some twenty yards back from the road. I had reached the place at eight that evening. Being a cautious soul, I'd left Paris by the porte de Charenton and worked my way westwards through the suburban streets of Ivry and Villejuif. I joined the motorway at Orly, certain that no one was on my tail but cursing the car rental people: the Peugeot 405 had a full ashtray, faulty heater fan and a jammed inertial reel on the driver's seat belt which rendered it useless. The lack of heat was going to be a nuisance.

As I nosed south on the Orléans *autoroute* I contemplated the state of play:

Item: Baum had so far come up with precisely nothing. Just a note at my hotel to say he'd try to get a sight of the document that interested me but it would take a little time.

Item: What would I say to Ariane Ségur/Bontemps? She might be glad to help unravel the mystery of her first husband's death. But as the wife of Bontemps she might prefer to leave the past buried and out of mind. As an ex-Communist – if she was truly out of the Party now – she might be interested to help an enquiry which would give the KGB a pain. But there are a lot of ex-Communists who retain a sentimental regard for the Party and their days within its cosy embrace. Was she one of those?

Item: Who had killed Artunian – the KGB, the DST, some other French secret department? And when would they take a pot-shot at me? Would I know the enemy when I saw him? And what kind of scandal would I create if I winged him first? Using a .38 with intent is one thing in the Maghreb or along the Syrian border. It is quite another in metropolitan France. And how long would I have before my friends at the DST caught up with me again?

'And so, *Madame*, my news agency believes there is an important story here with interesting political implications. We do not think André Marchand committed suicide because he was depressed. We think he was driven to it, and as I say, the only person I have been able to trace who appears to agree with our view that there was something unsatisfactory about the man was your first husband.'

Ariane Bontemps examined me shrewdly as I built up my cover story: muck-raking journalist working on a major international story. I didn't think all that much of it myself, but it was the best I could do.

She had served a delicious casserole of veal followed by a *crème au chocolat*, and now we were sitting in the book-lined living room of the house, tatty but comfortable. Bontemps turned out to be almost totally silent: a mute and bearded giant. He clearly left the management of the *ménage* to his wife.

'You read the cuttings,' she said. 'You will know that the police investigation of my first husband's death led nowhere. You will have concluded that that was not surprising. So what can I tell you that you do not know already?'

'Did Marc Ségur leave absolutely no notes at all?'

'If he did, they were stolen while I was in the hospital.'

'Did he tell you where you were both going on that last journey?'

For a moment she hesitated. 'No. He just said he had nailed André Marchand at last.'

'And he told you no more?'

'You know what the Talmud says: "Thy friend has a friend, and thy friend's friend has a friend." We followed the need-to-know rules. We learned them in the war.'

'Was your first husband a member of the Communist Party?'

'No. He had philosophical reservations. Let's say he couldn't accommodate himself to the *Realpolitik* of a practical revolutionary party, despite the fact that he regarded himself as a firm revolutionary. He was more interested in the moral absolutes – good and bad, justice and injustice, right and wrong. And he was not a man consumed with hot certainties.'

'And you were?'

'Yes.'

She helped me to more of her excellent coffee.

'You will stay the night,' Bontemps said. 'We have a spare room.'

'Thank you,' I said. 'I don't fancy driving all night.'

I explained that I intended to search out whatever I could in Marchand's wartime area of operations in the Aveyron. Then I turned to Ariane. 'There's something that bothers me about the whole business of Marc Ségur's death,' I said. 'I cannot understand why the Left – the Communist press in particular – never made a meal of the story. After all, on the face of it, the thing was a political godsend – dark forces of reaction conspiring with unknown assassins and corrupt police to silence crusading journalist who is about to expose leading Minister as a wartime traitor – a man who betrayed the Resistance. What could make better Party ammunition than that in the summer of 1950? But I've read the cuttings and they leave an odd impression. It seems to me the story was dropped too soon.'

Ariane's brown eyes rested steadily on mine. Her hands plucked at the edge of the black shawl which encircled her shoulders. She said nothing for a long while. Finally, she sighed as if a great weariness had built up within her through all those years.

'The Party decided it was not in the immediate interests of the struggle to pursue the matter,' she said. 'They let me know that they did not wish to press their quarrel with the bourgeois parties that far. They also believed that the Government would never allow the case to reach the courts. So they dropped it.'

'What did you do about it?'

'I had an interview with Mareschal after I came out of hospital. He was in charge of agitprop at the Party centre and also had a rather mysterious security role. But I got nowhere. We were in the grip of the Stalinists then. Maurice Thorez was still General Secretary of the Party. They would have had me out of the Party in ten minutes if I had argued. The fact that my husband had been murdered didn't really interest them, and why should it? They had larger matters on their minds, and he wasn't even a Party member. "It is not opportune," was how Mareschal put it.'

'Do you think they had other reasons?'

Ariane smiled faintly. 'Perhaps they didn't want to find out too much about André Marchand. Or perhaps they knew already what my husband was about to uncover.'

'What did you feel about the Party's attitude?'

'You must understand – I was a disciplined Party member. I had been in the Party-led *maquis* in the war. I'd seen the heroism, the sacrifices, the unflinching obedience. How could I applaud discipline in others and indulge the luxury of harbouring doubts myself?'

'But it was your husband's life,' I said.

'To me, it was only a part of the struggle for the lives of millions.' She laughed without mirth. 'The fact that I know better now does not make me either stupid or unprincipled then. I was a product of the Europe the Nazis created. Do you expect her children to be wise little Liberals? Look!'

She extended her hands towards me, palms down. I leant

forward. She had no fingernails. The fingers ended in unsightly stumps, as if nature had botched her work.

'A French Police Inspector did that, and far more than that, in his office in Rouen, with the radio turned up to mask the noise I made.' She drew her hands back and folded them, palms upwards, on her lap. 'The Communist Party won the right to obedience. If I never said a word in Rouen it was because I felt as a Communist – not as a French patriot, but as a Communist – that I owed it to my comrades and to myself to remain silent. And when, seven years later, the Party said that nothing should be done about Marc's death, it was the same Party, the same leadership, and I had no more reason to doubt them then than I had in the war.'

'And now?'

'Oh, now,' she said, and she smiled slowly. 'Now? I'm a big girl now.'

Bontemps had shuffled off somewhere and we were sitting on either side of the fireplace. The log fire threw an unsteady light into the corners. A single table lamp cast a yellow glow on her face.

'Why are you doing now what the Communist Party was doing then?' I asked.

She pretended not to understand though she understood me perfectly well. 'You must explain that,' she said.

'The Party would not help to solve the murder. You will not help to solve the murder.'

'You are seeking the reason for Marchand's suicide. You aren't looking for Marc's murderers.'

'They're part of the same story,' I said. 'Aren't they?'

Ariane did not answer. She looked into the fire, slowly shaking her head. Then she looked at me with her frank and rather overwhelming gaze. She got up slowly from her chair and went out to the kitchen without a word. When she returned she was holding a square packet wrapped in plastic film. The outside had traces of white on it. She handed it to me.

'Be careful of your clothes,' she said. 'That is flour. It

contains what you wanted – those of Marc's notes that they never found. Read them tonight and return them to me in the morning.'

I read and made notes by the inadequate light of a bedside lamp until two am. Some of what I read I understood. Some was incomprehensible – the jottings in private abbreviation that make up the raw material of any journalist's story. I found three categories of document: Marc Ségur's own notes; newspaper cuttings, some of them marked and annotated; and documents from the underground Resistance itself. The latter were on low-quality wartime flimsy, dimly typed or scrawled in pencil or faded blue ink. The spelling was uneven. There were brown stains from rusted paperclips, and marks where liquids had spilled onto some of the sheets. The authentic trivia of a step in the European historic process.

There was a quarto typed sheet headed ASTURIE COMMUNIQUE, followed by the note:

> Below is a warning list of dangerous individuals supplied by network N4 in the period June–July 1943.

There followed some twenty names with sketchy biographical details. Most of the entries referred to the Lyon and Aveyron areas. Against one of them a heavy mark had been made in the margin:

> BRACONY, Raoul Fernand: Born 1915 in Bollène, Vaucluse. Domiciled rue Alembard, Lyon. Carpenter and tiler. Active in various networks, including *Combat* since 1942, but now believed to be exceptionally dangerous double agent working for the SD*, Lyon. Known to use other names: Beranger, Bracante, Bellise. Married, but with a mistress, Suzanne Venant, at Chatelguyant. Venant's husband is a prisoner of war in Germany and the occupying forces may have a hold

* Sicherheitsdienst: German counter-espionage and security service.

on her through him. Bracony was briefly in the hands of the SD Lyon in 1943 and claimed not to have been identified. He is to be excluded from all clandestine work.

Ségur had stapled a sheet of paper to the Asturie communiqué. On it he had written: 'Bracony moved away after the war. Find address.'

Raoul Bracony's name cropped up again in Marc Ségur's handwriting on a sheet torn from a reporter's notebook:

RAOUL BRACONY: Member of Marchand's group 1942/3. Is Asturie report on Bracony correct? If so, was he ever caught? Who knew of his contact with SD?

At the bottom of the sheet, in ink of a different colour, Ségur had scrawled (presumably at a later date):

Bracony was never arrested. Marchand must have known about him. *Must find Bracony*. Find his files in SD archives, but where?

Another sheet from Ségur's notebook bore the following:

FLEDERMAUS* This cryptonym figures in SD archives. Seems to belong to an informer in *Combat* network.

Below this he had stapled a cutting from a German newspaper, the *Baden Tageblatt* of 14 March 1947:

FORMER SD MAN GETS 20 YEARS

Johannes Muller, 42, a native of Cologne, was found guilty in Baden-Baden today of crimes against humanity committed in France between 1942–4. He was sentenced by a French

* Literally flittermouse. German for bat, title of the Johann Strauss operetta, *Die Fledermaus*.

war crimes tribunal to 20 years' imprisonment with hard labour.

Muller was employed in the interrogation section of the SD (Abwehr) in France, first at the Hotel Lutetia in Paris and later at Abwehr headquarters in Lyon under Klaus Barbie, who has never been apprehended. On the evidence of returned deportees and former prisoners of the German occupying forces, Muller was found guilty of excessive brutality in the interrogation of prisoners, including the systematic use of the *baignoire* torture and severe beatings. Many of his victims had subsequently died.

He pleaded not guilty and claimed to have resisted Klaus Barbie's demands for more rigorous interrogations. His duties, he claimed, were administrative. He agreed that he was in Barbie's confidence and maintained the department's secret archives. But he denied using force on suspects.

There was a dramatic scene in the courtroom when evidence was being given by Jeanne Vallon, who claimed to have been beaten by both Muller and Barbie over a three-day period and had lost an eye and suffered other permanent disabilities. When Muller claimed never to have seen her before and was heard to laugh during her evidence, she rushed from the witness stand and scratched his face severely before she could be restrained. Muller's counsel gave notice of appeal after judgment had been passed.

On a fourth sheet, Ségur had asked himself a number of further questions:

Why is the editor lukewarm about the story?
Is it true the party wants it killed? Surely not!
Why have the SD archives disappeared from Lyon? Where to?
Can Johannes Muller be found? Which prison?
Who was Fledermaus?
Bracony. *FE says he lives at Conques, Aveyron.* Must check.

The next sheet was headed:

A THEORY FOR THE CASE OF
ANDRE MARCHAND

There followed a list of propositions:

* M. was a genuine *résistant*.
* M. was taken and turned by Barbie at Lyon SD. Barbie a specialist in such exercises.
* At end of war someone knew M. had been double agent. Who?
* Who runs him now? How was he sold? By Germans to Russians in return for favours? Political morality!

The clip of newspaper cuttings included several which were familiar to me from my earlier researches, plus a couple which filled out details of Marchand's career. I made some more notes, and shortly after two o'clock I turned off the light.

CHAPTER 10

Daniel Bontemps

A wind had sprung up, rustling the trees which surrounded the house and sighing and whistling under the eaves. It was a noisy night and I only just detected the sound of an approaching car. It came from the same direction as I'd come myself. The sound stopped abruptly before the car came abreast of the house. It surprised me because I was sure I'd seen no other houses before reaching the Bontemps' place in the chemin de la Fosse, so that there was no logical spot on that side for a car to stop. I lay alert in bed for thirty seconds, telling myself that no one could have followed me here. Then I got up and took my gun from the holdall.

Against the moan and swish of the wind in the trees there came the sharp crack of a dry stick breaking, presumably underfoot. Then I caught the distinctive crunch of gravel at the side of the house, like the milk hitting the breakfast cereal. The pattern of sounds told me there was more than one intruder. A stranded motorist would have rung the bell by now. I groped for my shoes and slipped them on, found my dressing gown and put that on too. I checked the .38, released the clip and slipped it into my pocket. Then I felt my way to the door and out onto the landing just as Bontemps in a livid red wrap-around switched on the landing light.

'Lucky I don't sleep well,' he said. 'You heard too?'

'Yes.'

'Do you have a gun?'

I patted my pocket. He was carrying what looked like an old Mauser pistol.

'Ariane thinks someone followed you to the house. These are not the kind of houses that usually interest burglars.'

'Impossible,' I said, 'I took precautions.'

Bontemps looked at me and smiled. 'Even in France they don't usually follow journalists about the country and raid them in the middle of the night.' He put his emphasis on 'journalists' and I pretended not to get the point.

'What about the jokers outside?' I said. We were halfway down the stairs by then.

'They can see the light,' said Bontemps. 'If that hasn't scared them off it's because they mean business, whatever their business might be. Let's try a couple of warning shots into the night.'

There was a side door with glass panels leading onto the gravelled path on which I had heard the footsteps. Bontemps signalled me to hug the wall and flattened himself against it as he put out a hand and unlocked the door. He was reaching for the top bolt when one of the panels shattered, almost drowning the *pphht* from outside. The bullet from the silenced gun lodged with a thud somewhere in the wall on my right.

Bontemps grunted, aimed through the broken pane and fired a single shot, deafening in the narrow passage. Nothing could be heard from outside above the racket of the windy night.

'I only heard one car,' he said, 'so we can reckon with four, maybe five of them.'

'I heard at least two on the gravel,' I said.

'So that's the minimum. Between two and five men.'

On the landing above us the light went out. Ariane's footsteps descended the uncarpeted stairs. 'We can do without a light behind us,' she said. Her voice was calm, matter of fact.

'Have you got your revolver?' Bontemps asked.

'Yes,' she said.

At that moment another pane shattered and I caught the whistle of the passing bullet on its way to the wall. This time there was the light, dry clatter of plaster falling on the floor.

'I reckon they're in the bushes across the pathway. Say four metres away.' Bontemps had clearly tasted small-arms fire before. He let off another round through the door. There was no reply.

'We need a diversion,' said Bontemps. 'Otherwise they'll be at us from the other side of the house. You two stay here. I'm getting out through the *salon* window and then I'll let fly a bit from the end of the garden. Maybe they'll find that too complicated for them.'

It was about two minutes later that three revolver shots cracked sharply from the garden. An answering salvo of *pphhts* came from the bushes. They were firing at the flashes from Bontemps' gun.

'He can look after himself,' Ariane said.

'I think I'd better show a little action at the other side of the house,' I said. 'You pin them down here with a shot from time to time.'

'Good,' she said.

As I passed through the open door of the dining room on the far side of the house I sensed someone in the room. The window was open and the racket of the wind outside filled the room. It was pitch black. I could hear nothing above the wind and see even less.

'There's one in here,' I shouted to Ariane, and dropped to the floor as I spoke. The flash from the answering gun came from my left, inside the room, maybe ten feet away. I fired straight at it and was rewarded with a mixed howl and groan as something heavy hit the tiled floor amid a crash of splintering wood.

'I got him,' I shouted to Ariane. 'Stay where you are. He may still have some fight in him.'

'And you?' she called.

'OK.'

I listened hard. Nothing from inside the room. The man was dead, unconscious or playing possum. I felt around, encountered a table leg, followed it up and found an ashtray on the table. I flipped it to the far side of the room and it hit the wall with a metallic sound. Anyone lying doggo with a gun would never have resisted the temptation to fire. But he didn't fire. I got off the floor, found a wall switch and turned on the light.

He was lying flat on his back, feet towards me, head propped against the far wall. My shot had flung him back and from the position of his head the impact may have broken his neck. There was a neat, blackish hole drilled in his forehead just above his left eye. A thin rivulet of blood led downwards from the hole into the eye socket and thence, in two tributaries, down the left side of his face onto his black leather jacket. His eyes stared, his mouth gaped. There wasn't much blood. I didn't need to check for signs of life. He was a young man of maybe twenty-two or so, dark and sallow, probably North African. There was garden mud caked heavily onto the soles of his neat town shoes. Whatever he was, he was no policeman.

I let off a couple of shots through the window to indicate a continued interest in violence, and gripping the corpse firmly by the ankles, pulled it out of the room and into the corridor. The head bumped unpleasantly against the doorpost.

I went through the pockets. The identity card gave me Mahmoud Ben Ballem. Algerian. A Paris address in Ménilmontant. Possibly a genuine document, possibly not. There wasn't much else: about one hundred francs, two house keys on a ring, some bits of paper with illegible scribbles, a pencil stub, two photos of plain blondes smiling nervously.

There was more shooting from the end of the garden, followed by the answering *pphhts* from the shrubbery on Ariane's side of the house. Only this time I thought I caught the sound of a shot from outside the dining room. They had had the sense to spread themselves about the place.

'You OK?' I called to Ariane.

'OK.' Her answering shout provoked more shooting. Bontemps fired in turn from his hideaway. I hoped our visitors were as confused by all the loose banging away as I was. I let off a couple of rounds through the dining-room window, to add to the gaiety of nations. I raced upstairs and let off two more from my bedroom window. I thought it would create the illusion of numbers, like the old movies where the three men left alive in the fort keep dashing round the perimeter loosing off dead men's rifles. Bontemps entered into the spirit of the thing, firing now from another position in the garden.

I rejoined Ariane, flat against the wall next to the shattered glass panes of the side door. 'They couldn't have come here expecting a shooting match,' I said. 'Maybe now they've seen how much firepower we have, they'll go away.'

At that moment a heavy tread in the dining room was followed by a thud and a noisy curse. It was Bontemps, back from the shrubbery. I went into the hall and showed him my corpse. 'We'll have to be sure they take it with them,' was all he said. He prodded the body with his foot. 'It's no use to us.'

Without any apparent effort he pulled the dead man off the floor and draped him over his shoulder. 'I'll dump him at their car,' he said. He picked up a torch from the hall table and strode out into the night as if he were delivering coals. 'Keep firing,' he said over his shoulder.

Ariane and I let off the odd shot from either side of the house. It was difficult, now, to provoke a response. I began to worry lest they'd given up the fight and might run into Bontemps back at the car. Soon we were failing to stimulate any answering fire. Then the sound of a car engine reached us above the howl of the wind, followed by the crunching of footsteps on the gravel. Bontemps strode through the front door. He was grinning.

'Car number is 4819 PP 75. That's a Paris registration. I'd just got it when they came up the road and I had to get moving.'

I made a note of the number. 'Did you hear them say anything?'

'Plenty. In Arabic. A row, I'd say.'

'What did you do with Mahmoud?' I asked.

'Put him in the driver's seat. But he wouldn't sit up.'

We did our best with the mess of mud, glass and plaster.

Then Ariane made Russian tea and served it in tall glasses set in heavy silver holders.

'Why?' she asked, looking straight into my eyes.

'I've no idea. Could they have been after you?'

'I think not.'

Bontemps grunted. 'No one is that interested in us any more.'

'Well, no one as far as I know is that interested in me either,' I lied. 'And in any case, no one knew I was coming here.'

'So you were followed. Maybe a homing device on the car.'

'I checked before I set out. I suppose I could have missed it, but it's unlikely. Anyway, if it was me they were after, I'm truly sorry about the mess. And truly grateful for your help.'

Bontemps shrugged. 'They didn't press home the attack. Odd, that. Means they were doing it for money. Not much cash so not much risk. A mistake by whoever hired them.'

'Well, let's get what sleep we can,' Ariane said.

Next morning Bontemps and I went over the car inch by inch. It was he who found the device – a square metal box with six-inch sides, welded onto the left underside of the rear of the chassis in such a way that it looked structural. They'd taken the trouble to weld an identical but dummy box onto the right side, on the principle that *two* welded protruberances would not be noticed by someone looking for a single object. The transmitter had its own cadmium cell battery, giving it at my rough reckoning about one hundred hours of life. It was enough to see me to my destination, where I would no doubt be picked up and kept in view by other means.

So who was it? The DST? The Auto Ecole Marceau, whoever they really were? Some interloper from outside? It couldn't be Baum, or rather, it was highly unlikely to be Baum because if it were, that would have to make a fool or a knave of Artunian, who had put me on to him. With Artunian a fool or knave, Andrew Pabjoy became a fool in turn. That I did not believe. And in any case, the old man had been killed for his pains – the pains of helping me.

'A pro job,' said Bontemps. 'Never seen better. Do we silence it?'

'No,' I said, 'I want it off undamaged.'

'Not difficult,' Bontemps said. 'Leave it to me.' He worked for nearly an hour, delicately, with a welding torch and a couple of tools.

'What now?' he asked, holding the transmitter intact in his hand.

'Thanks, I'll take it with me,' I said. I put it on the front passenger seat. Then I went into the house and got my things together. Ariane was writing at a desk in the living room.

'Here are Marc Ségur's papers,' I said. 'They were very helpful. It was good of you to let me see them.'

'Please forget that I have them,' she said. 'I lead a quieter life nowadays. Last night took me back to things I prefer to forget. I don't want that to happen again.'

'You have both been very kind. In return, I hope to shed some light on the death of Marc Ségur.'

She smiled her slow, disarming smile. 'I don't know who you really are or what your true purpose is, but I wish you luck. And be careful. Whoever is after you is not going to leave things as they are.'

She got up from her chair and kissed me on both cheeks, left, right, left, French-style.

CHAPTER 11

Raoul Bracony

I rejoined the *autoroute* at the access point south of Chartres and kept a lookout for a lay-by or service area with plenty of parked vehicles. A half hour later I found one – pumps, toilet and a cafeteria. I parked at the edge of the car park, picked the homing device from the seat and wandered along the line of vehicles. Soon I found what I wanted: a saloon with a laden roof-rack covered with a groundsheet. I lifted a corner of the sheet, wedged the device between two suitcases and covered them up again. I left the *autoroute* at the next exit and settled down to the journey south on RN154.

At Orléans I threaded my way cautiously through the mess of trunk and ring roads, found N152 and headed south-east through Gien, nestling on its isthmus in the river. At Nevers I had a plate of soup and some cheese at a *brasserie* opposite the Duke's palace. It was just after one when I'd finished. I called the Bristol in Paris from the call box in the basement and asked them to page Miss Brown. Isabel's languid voice greeted me.

'Yes, I'm fine,' I said, 'but never mind. Take this down.'

I gave her the details from the dead man's identity card and the car's registration number. 'Get Arthur to find out everything he can on the man and the car. I don't know when I'll call back but I hope you'll have something by the day after tomorrow. If I fall under a bus, what you've got may lead to whoever paid the man who pushed me.'

'Right,' Isabel said. 'Mind how you cross.'

'And note this down for the record. I hope I'm going to find a man named Bracony at Conques in the Aveyron department. I think he may have some of the answers if he's still there. You're the only one to know that, and you're to tell Pabjoy and no one else, but only if I get clobbered.'

Leaving Nevers, I picked up the N 7 and headed for Moulins. From there, southwards into the foothills of the Massif Central on N493. By now it was raining steadily, the roads were treacherous and I cursed the fact that the seat belt was jammed.

Why was the seat belt jammed? Why, in France, where it is compulsory to wear seat belts at certain times, was the seat belt jammed? Why was the seat belt of a perfectly good car, one year old, from a substantial central Paris car-hire company, jammed? A perfectly good car? Who said it was a perfectly good car? And if it was not perfectly good – if it was deliberately and with malice aforethought not a sound car – then what was more natural, more necessary, than that the seat belt should be jammed? I groaned at my slow-wittedness. What were the odds on some essential part, say some bit of the front axle, the steering assembly, the brakes perhaps, being so expertly tampered with that, given time and a few hundred miles, that part was bound to give way, and what happened to the Ségurs all those years before, would happen to me? The odds, it seemed to me, were favourable and short. The thing was obvious, and yet Bontemps and I had found nothing – no tell-tale saw marks, no severed metal – because we had been looking for something else.

I took from Vercors to Cusset, a distance of some fifteen miles, with the road climbing steadily and the rain slackening off, to decide what to do.

I pulled into the roadside and spent ten minutes with the road map. South of Cusset, the Allier flows parallel to the road after winding round the edge of the town of Vichy. The map showed two crossings, near Abrest and St Yorre. I chose the Abrest route because it was nearer and I was developing a growing distaste for driving my car. I found that the river at that point flowed swiftly along a bed which must have taken the odd million years to dig out of the rock. The approach to the road bridge had a useful curve to it. If the brakes, say, were to fail somehow, the car would have no difficulty in leaving the roadway and plunging over the low parapet into the river a hundred feet or so below. All I would need was a little luck – for the car to go, for it to happen unseen, and for the wreck to lie not too conspicuously in the ravine, say for a couple of days. And ideally, I could use another couple of days before anyone decided in the absence of a body that there had been no one in the car when the accident happened. I reckoned I might have as little as two and as many as four days before the thing was pieced together and they came after me again.

There was a one-in-ten gradient as the road curved round and down towards the bridge. It gave me the chance to arrange matters with the engine off. No explosion and fire to alert the locals. I stopped fifty yards from the bridge, walked down and inspected the parapet, which was scarcely more than a narrow ledge. The car would mount it and go over, I reckoned, at about fifteen miles an hour. On the way back up the hill I collected two firm branches of ash and stripped them down. Then I climbed back into the car and backed another fifty yards up the incline.

At 100 yards from the bridge I climbed out again and stowed my holdall behind a tree. Then I changed the number plates, reckoning that the Puy-de-Dôme registration could further delay matters for the odd hour or two. The Paris plates went into the bushes. I climbed back into the car and did some careful experimenting with the two strong but resilient sticks of ash. Soon I'd got them to the right length. I threaded the longer stick through the steering wheel, over the rim, under one of the radials and up over the far side of the rim. One end of the stick was wedged into the left-hand corner of the fascia. The other, with the stick descending diagonally, stuck firmly into the crack between the base and back of the passenger seat. It left the wheel limited play – enough, I reckoned, to control the car on the run down to the bridge. The other stick was to be pushed upright through the steering wheel to jam into the top edge of the windscreen. The lower end would, with luck, stick firmly into the driver's seat.

I tried it. With the two sticks in place there was no play at all on the steering and the car would keep a steady course, unaffected by the steep camber of the road. I removed the vertical stick. Then I jammed open the driver's door with a lump of wood above the lower hinge.

I started the engine, put the car into second, and with the door open commenced the descent towards the bridge. As the car gathered speed I started on the tricky bit: out of the seat far enough to wedge the vertical stick in place: engine off and into neutral; then the plunge out of the car into the long grass and nettles covering the roadside bank.

I managed a soft landing as the engine cut out and the car gathered speed. At about ten yards from the ravine I saw it start to leave the road, unable to follow the curve as the interlocked sticks jammed the steering. It hit the parapet at something close to twenty miles an hour, lurched violently as the nearside front wheel tried to climb the hard edge and the tyre burst with a sharp crack. The speed maintained the inertia of the vehicle and prevented it bouncing back into the road and capsizing. Then the offside front wheel was over the parapet and the car's speed did the rest. It disappeared over the edge and I heard it crashing down the precipice in a shower of tearing vegetation and buckling metal.

It came to rest among flattened bushes and smashed-up saplings on a ledge a little above the waterline of the river. You had to lean over the edge to see it. So far so good. I only had to hope that my sticks had been dislodged in the fall, which seemed to me a near certainty, and that whatever part of the vehicle had been tampered with had given way under the stresses set up as the car bounced down the mountainside.

I recovered my holdall and set out through the damp and

lowering winter evening for the main road. By nine I'd been dropped by a friendly haulier, wet and famished, near the railway station at Vichy. As far as I could tell, no one in the whole wide world knew where I was.

The village of Conques clings to the mountainside above the Ouche river like the detritus of a holier and more peaceful age. The village is in visibly straitened circumstances nowadays, but for nearly three hundred years between the eleventh and thirteenth centuries, Conques had its importance. For then it was a staging point on the long pilgrims' trail which stretched from the north of France south-westwards towards the holy shrine of St Jacques of Compostella on the Galician coast of Spain. Into the great nave of the church of Sainte Foy at Conques crowds of footsore pilgrims pressed almost daily – some on their way southwards with hope, others on their way back with absolution and a collection of those seashells which have since lent the name of St Jacques to one of France's seafood delicacies. Nowadays Conques lives from the few tourists who find their way up the endlessly winding road from Rodez and Entraygues, or by arduous forestry and hill farming. The Romanesque glories of Sainte Foy have been decently restored. The village itself has been left to its own devices.

I'd stayed overnight in Vichy, taken an early train and changed twice to reach Périgueux, and there hired a Fiat 127 from what I hoped was the smallest and most obscure hire firm in the place. Now I parked the Fiat at the edge of the village and made for the cemetery. Twenty minutes among the carved marble and the artificial carnations in their metal holders and I'd found what I had hoped for. A recent grave hid the last mortal remains of Marie-Louise, beloved wife of Raoul Bracante, departed this life 14 December 1972 and now in Paradise. Next to the inscription there was a space left blank, presumably for Raoul, spouse of Marie-Louise.

Bracony, alias Bracante, was either alive or, improbably,

buried elsewhere. And he was rather carelessly using one of his wartime pseudonyms. Carelessly, or with the confidence of a man who reckoned he had nothing to fear. Probably he'd had forged papers in that name when the war ended and had no means of knowing that Asturie had come to hear of it. My guess that he'd stuck to something beginning with B bore out the ancient truth that men do not like to abandon their identities totally and for ever. Even the continuity of a capital letter is better than a total break with the past. And in the dangerous conditions of wartime, Bracony had shown this familiar weakness with his three known aliases, all beginning with the letter B.

I walked back up the hill into the village and stopped at a shop which was hoping to sell objects of a religious nature. I bought a couple of postcards depicting the Holy Virgin with her Babe. Also a couple of stamps.

'I haven't been this way for years,' I said, as the angular *patronne* slipped my cards into a small paper bag. She made no reply. 'I used to know a man here, Raoul Bracante. Is he still in the village?'

She paused and looked at me. '*Connais pas*,' she said, and handed me my modest parcel. I paid and left, with the brassy clang of the bell on the shop door ringing in my ears.

At the bistro across the way I was in better luck. The place was empty and I took a glass of *blanc* at the bar. The *patron* was inclined to chat.

'Tourist?'

'Yes,' I said.

'Come to see Sainte Foy, then?'

'That's right. Magnificent.'

'Spent a fortune on it. They come down from Paris – architects, sculptors, curators, I don't know. They've even got a fellow right now painting some of the new stones – painting them mark you – to make them tone in with the old ones. Never stop spending on it.'

'Worth it,' I said.

'I suppose so. Brings a few tourists up here. But they don't spend much in the village. Your first time here?'

'No,' I said. 'I was here a couple of times a year or two back. Matter of fact, I might look up a fellow I met then. Name is Raoul Bracante.'

'Yes, Bracante's still here. But he's down in Entraygues every day now till nightfall. Got a long job there on a farm they're rebuilding.'

'Where does he live?' I asked, as if I had scarcely any interest in the matter.

'You take the Rodez road out of here and turn off onto a track to the right about two kilometres along. There's a shrine by the roadside just before the turning. Bracante's place is about a kilometre up the track. Stands on its own.'

'Thanks,' I said. 'I might look him up later.'

'He doesn't mix much,' said the *patron*. 'We don't see him in here from one Christmas to the next.'

'Lives alone, you said?'

'Yes, since his wife died. A few years ago now. But he never was one to come in for a drink. Stayed up there in his place, first with his wife, then on his own. They say he sometimes has visitors from Rodez, but that's probably for his work. There's no doubt he does the best roof tiling in these parts.'

'Thanks for the information. And I'll take a sandwich with smoked ham.'

Clutching my sandwich and my postcards of the Holy Virgin, I made my way out to the rue des Ecoles with its great cobblestones and broken-down parapet overhanging the raging Ouche, far below. I sat, shivering a bit, on the parapet, ate the sandwich, and wrote on one of the postcards: 'I am at a beautiful place called Conques and wish you were here.' I signed it with my initials and addressed it to Penny at the office. I posted it in the yellow pillarbox in the village square. Then I made my way back to the car and headed for the house of Raoul Bracony, *alias* Bracante. I reached the place shortly after two, turned the car on the steep and narrow track, and left it facing the way it had come.

It was a typical farm dwelling of the region, built of heavy blocks of local stone and with external steps leading to the living quarters on the first floor. Beneath the steps an open archway gave access to the storage area which took up the ground floor of the house. A large cistern for collecting rainwater stood at one corner, and across the unkempt yard stood the *secadour*, the small outhouse originally intended for the drying of chestnuts when that harvest was an important source of income for the farmers of the Causses region. There was no sign of cultivation and there appeared to be no attached farm or domestic animals around the place.

My bang on the door brought no reply.

I got in easily enough through a first-floor window which had been left on its latch. The ladder to reach it I found in the storage area below. The window gave onto what was evidently the main living room, and once inside I pulled the ladder up behind me. I found myself in a surprisingly comfortable room with a thick rug on the floor and two deep armchairs. There were bookcases against two walls, an old-fashioned enamel stove, round dining table and chairs in a corner and a long, low table piled deep in books and magazines.

Raoul Bracony clearly kept abreast of current affairs, particularly the financial news. He subscribed to the leading French financial weekly. The latest copy was still in its wrapper, addressed to R. Brançon at a *poste restante* number in Rodez. He certainly had a nice range of alliterative names.

I decided to give myself two hours to go over the house, aiming to be back on the Rodez road before the failing winter light brought to an end Bracony's work on the farm roof down in Entraygues. I could always come back tomorrow. The job would have to be done the hard way: without disturbing anything until I was certain that there was something to be found.

So I set to work carefully and systematically in the living room.

On searches of this kind you have to keep an open mind. Once decide that you're looking for this kind of espionage gadgetry and you're likely to miss that kind of gadgetry, which turns out to be the only type on the premises. You may be up against a man who doesn't keep in his home the standard adventure-story goodies: photograhic equipment, code book, radio transmitter, microdot equipment. One solitary sheet of paper, stuffed to the back of a bottom drawer, may be all you'll find – and all you will need to find if it turns out to be a piece of 'white carbon' for the transmission of invisible writing.

But I didn't even find that. Bracony's living room was clean. But it was also odd. In the first place, what was a man of Bracony's background doing with magazines devoted to the stock market? No one could persuade me that that was a typical pursuit for a rural artisan in France. The local bank instead of the sock under the bed, maybe: but not the Bourse. Then again, Bracony appeared to be something of a hi-fi enthusiast. His installation was an expensive Sony model incorporating a tape deck with full recording capability. There was a cabinet containing a couple of dozen recording tapes. They were nearly all unmarked and presumably virgin. I did a spot check on two taken at random and ran them through the playback. The first was blank. The second had been used to record what sounded like a radio programme: it was an Offenbach operetta. Nothing criminal in all that. But not much that was in character either. And there began to come over me the feeling that the house contained secrets, that if only I persisted I would find something, and that what I was uncovering in the living room were the surface signs which pointed to an abnormal reality beneath. I was seized by a fierce desire to abandon caution and start in on the real job – pulling up floorboards, ripping books apart, emptying drawers, shifting furniture – the only way, ultimately, to find what has been professionally hidden.

By four o'clock I had done all I could do in the living quarters: two bedrooms, shower room, kitchen, lumber room and the living room itself. I was convinced that Raoul Bracony was something more than an expert on tiling in the traditional style of the Causses. I would have put big money on finding something decisive in the house. But it was time to leave and I would have to come back the next day. I replaced everything as I'd found it and drove down the track and onto the Rodez road without a hitch.

In Rodez I found a room for the night, ate modestly and well in the cosy restaurant of the hotel, and settled into my bed with my books on the Resistance. I picked on Henri Frenay's account of his extraordinary wartime experiences because it seemed the most readable. But there were over six hundred pages of it. So I browsed. I have a habit, when browsing through a book, of starting at the back. On page 582 my eye was caught by *Annexe No. 5: The Secret Army in France Seen by the Germans, May 1943*. It stated that after the war, in the archives of Hitler's Foreign Office, a twenty-eight page document entitled *Die Armée Secrète in Frankreich* had been found. It bore the signature of Kaltenbrunner, Himmler's deputy, and it had been considered important enough to be passed up to the Fuehrer himself. Page one bore Hitler's initial. I turned to Frenay's index. The entry *Kaltenbrunner* directed me to pp. 323/4. There Frenay described how the report had been sent to him after the end of the war, in the summer of 1945, by Admiral Barjot, and how impressed he was with its accuracy:

> *All this had been pretty accurately analysed by the Gestapo and the Abwehr. These organisations stated in their report that a large part of their information came from a 'confidential informant' (Vertrauensmann) who was a French ex-officer placed at a high level in the Secret Army. I asked myself, and ask myself still, who this traitor in our midst could be. This mystery remains intact.*

I read more of Frenay until, close to one am, I closed the

book, which by then was quite heavily defaced with marginal notes. Then I switched off the light and found it difficult to sleep.

CHAPTER 12

The Search

Driving through the early mist next morning, back along the winding mountain road to Conques, I decided that the issue was no longer whether to pull the place apart, but how soon I could get on with the job. Now or at some future, more propitious time? I couldn't see anything specially propitious about the future, so it had better be now.

I turned off the Conques road up the track to the house and after reaching it, turned the car around as I'd done the day before. Everything was peaceful, it was ten am, and I had most of the day ahead of me. But before wrecking the house I decided to check on the storage area, the cistern and the *secadour*. The first two yielded nothing. I turned to the *secadour*, a squat, circular storehouse built of heavy stone blocks, with a low door and no windows. The door was secured with two iron bars, each pivoted on a massive rod and bolt and secured by a heavy padlock. The padlocks were modern, with thick, sturdy hasps. There was no rust on them. Maybe Bracony kept the tools of his trade in the *secadour* and maybe he kept something else. Finding out would have to wait until I came across a key or a crowbar. I would have to start in the house.

I turned away and started to cross the yard to the main building. I would do what I had done yesterday: use Bracony's ladder from the storage area to enter by the living-room window. I reached the broad stone arch supporting the outside stairway leading to the first floor of the house. As I went under it into the storage area I thought I heard a sound from above – the sound of a step in what would be the living room. I stopped and listened. There was silence. It suddenly struck me that I really was behaving like a bumbling amateur. I hadn't checked the area surrounding the house. I didn't *know* that Bracony was at Entraygues, laying his tiles.

I returned to the yard, went out onto the track and walked up it beyond the house. My footsteps crunched loudly on the broken stone surface and my breath made pale clouds in the chill autumn air. About fifty yards up the track I found a concealed turning into a field. There, invisible from the house, stood a grey Citroën van. Stencilled on its side were the words: *R. BRACONY   Couvreur, Carrelages, à Conques.*

So Bracony was waiting for me and I'd walked straight into it! I lifted the bonnet of the van, helped myself to the distributor head, and closed it again with care. The issue now was overwhelming in its simplicity: should I flush him out, immobilise him in some way and complete my search, or should I make off in my Fiat, my tail between my legs, knowing I'd not get another crack at the house? Common sense said run. But I knew there were secrets in the house. So I crossed the track, scrambled through a gap in the hedge into a ploughed field and made my way round to the back of the house under cover of the thick hedge of hawthorn. I found another gap and got through with some difficulty into the yard. I was behind the *secadour*, shielded from the house but unable to move forward without coming into full view from two of the upstairs windows.

A quick survey showed that Bracony was at neither window. I decided to brazen it out. I stepped from behind the *secadour*, marched across the yard and up the steps to the door of the living quarters. There was no knocker and no bell. I hammered on the heavy wooden door with my fist. The dull thuds hardly echoed within. Nothing stirred. I tried again – twice. If Bracony was there, he must have decided to play it rough – to let me break in and then deal with me. He was bound to have a gun, but then so had I.

For good measure I shouted: 'Anyone there?' No reply came

from the house. I turned and started down the steps and on the last step I trod on a loose stone and stumbled forward, off balance. I never heard the door opening behind me, but as I pitched forward I heard the *whhht* of the bullet past my head, immediately drowned by the crash of the rifle above me. I flung myself round the corner of the stone parapet and into the shelter of the heavy arch. I was out of range and safe for the moment. I checked my .38 and released the safety catch.

One thing was urgent: to stop Bracony telephoning for help if he hadn't already done so. The telephone line was carried overhead, the last link stretching from a pole at the side of the track to a bracket fixed at first-floor level on the outside of the house. From there the wire ran along the wall and in through a hole drilled in the frame of a window. If Bracony decided to stay inside the house no shot from a window could reach me if I placed the ladder against the wall, mounted it and somehow cut the wire. I found a pair of pliers which looked as if they would do the job, slipped them into my pocket, dragged out the ladder, propped it up and mounted it. Cutting the wire proved easy enough, and I was down again and back under the house in a few minutes.

Cut off from the outside world, Bracony would surely lose patience and do something. I didn't know or much care what that might be. It was inactivity that I feared most because that could go on for hours and time was not on my side. I considered the events of the last few minutes. He had aimed at my head, showing the confidence of a practised marksman and foregoing the easier target of the torso. If I hadn't stumbled he would have blown my head off. He had used a rifle despite the close range, which told me it was the only weapon he had. The fact that he was shooting to kill was alarming in more senses than the obvious one. If there's been an intruder in your house and that intruder returns, are you not likely to use your gun either to capture and disarm him, or to wound him, with the object of finding out who he is and what he's after? And isn't this knowledge particularly vital to you if you yourself are up to no good? Certainly. Unless . . . unless you already know who he is and are more interested in eliminating him than in exploring his ideas on topics of the day. Looked at from all the angles available to me, Bracony was behaving like a man who knew he had to kill and knew there was nothing he could learn which would make him change his mind.

So I built on the theory: Bracony knows what I am after. He knows either because he's been tipped off, or because his instinct or his training tells him that an intruder who takes nothing and takes care to disturb virtually nothing is a special case. He decides, very sensibly, that I have to be disposed of. He tries and fails. First time unlucky. Now, of course, he *must* succeed, for he realises that his single rifle shot has told me all I need to know – that he has something that he has to defend. So what will flush him out? The sight or sound of me either getting away or getting into the house. Of course, I can wait until dark, but he knows as well as I do that hanging around all day is the last thing I want to do. *Ergo*: I must break out from beneath the house and in such a way that the advantage shifts from his rifle to my .38. I invested fifteen minutes of precious time in turning the problem inside out and at the end of it I had a plan of sorts.

I remembered that there were two windows on the south side of the house. One led into the bedroom, the other into the bathroom. The distance between them was about six feet. The top of the ladder would reach to a point a couple of feet above the window sills. Sticking close to the wall of the house, I dragged the ladder round to the south side and propped it up between the two windows but closest to the bathroom. Then I shuffled back and selected from the pile of junk at the back of the store room a wooden pole about five feet long. I found a six-inch metal wheel which must have come off an old farm machine and secured it as best I could to the end of the pole, using lengths of garden twine. It looked as if it would hold long enough for my purpose. Then I helped myself to a heavy mallet, and a piece of sacking which I plastered liberally with what looked like axle grease from the bottom of a can. Carrying my assorted and messy paraphernalia, I made my way back to the ladder. There was nothing but silence from the house. Bracony was waiting for me to make the first move. I couldn't blame him. So I was making it.

I climbed slowly to the top of the ladder. My position, arms full of bits and pieces, was precarious and if Bracony had chosen to come outside with his rifle that would have been that. But he didn't. I deposited mallet and sacking carefully on the ledge of the bathroom window immediately to my right. Then, bracing myself as firmly as I could, I swung my home-made flail at the bedroom window on my left with all the force I could muster. The window smashed in with an appropriate sound. The flail went in after it and landed with a crash on the floor within. I was making a lot of useful noise.

Now I had to move fast. I turned my attention to the bathroom window to my right, held the sticky sacking against the centre pane and tapped it as quietly as I could with the mallet. At the third blow the glass cracked and a sizeable bit came away as I pulled the sacking back. It was enough for me to get my hand through and turn the window fastening. I was into the bathroom in maybe fifteen seconds and in almost total silence. Then came my necessary gamble.

With the .38 in my hand, I flung open the bathroom door and stepped through it into the corridor beyond, facing to the left towards the bedroom. My calculation was that Bracony, hearing the hubbub in the bedroom, would assume I'd made my entry into the house that way and would take up position outside the bedroom door, if not inside the room itself, ready to pump a bullet into me the moment I appeared. It would tally with his tactics earlier on. If I was wrong and he was waiting at the end of the corridor, then he would be behind and not in front of me as I came through the bathroom door, facing away from him. And again, that would be that. But I wasn't wrong.

The sound of the bathroom door opening caused him to spin round so that he was almost facing me as I brought my .38 up to eye level and fired twice from a slight crouch. The distance between us was no more than four feet and the energy of the two bullets hitting him in the head rocked him back on his heels and over onto the stone floor with an almighty crash, the rifle flying out of his hands, bouncing off the wall and landing on top of him. He was a very big man, with a mass of tightly curled grey hair and the leather complexion of a countryman. He wore ancient blue denims. One bullet had entered his left eye, travelling upwards into the brain, and the other had smashed through his lower jaw, taking most of his teeth with it as it travelled on and out of the body, presumably through the base of the skull. It looked as if the upper bullet had killed him instantly – too soon, even, for a reflex pull of the finger on the trigger of the rifle.

By the time I had finished the living room it looked as if a troop of cavalry had been through the place. I did the thing strictly according to the routine established in the annexe of the Police College at Hendon where tired coppers who have seen it all run classes for the anonymous gentry sent along by the Section and no questions asked, thank you kindly.

A CID Inspector by the name of Palfreyman had been particularly impressive. 'When a man has something to hide,' he'd told us, 'don't assume he'll hide it on the premises. Where might he hide it?' We dredged up all the improbable hiding places from the depths of our innocent minds and Palfreyman sneered at them one by one until a trainee named, simply, Smith, blurted out: 'What about a left luggage office?'

'Good thinking, lad,' said Palfreyman, brightening. 'So what do you conclude from that?'

'That there may be a ticket somewhere in the house.'

'Good lad, good lad,' said Palfreyman. 'And how do you find a piece of thin paper, two inches by three, hidden – *hidden*, mark you – in someone else's house, eh?'

He didn't wait for an answer, which was as well because we didn't know. 'I'll tell you how you find it, my lads. You find it by tearing the bloody place to effing bloody pieces. No other way.'

Palfreyman's language was a nice compromise between the true demotic and what he considered fit for his social betters to hear. He was a pleasantly out-of-date man and we warmed to him.

'That's why you're interested in every scrap of paper and every effing book in the house,' he said. 'Not just most of the books, but *every* book needs your undivided attention. Off the shelves, fan the pages – *all* the pages: in case of doubt tear off the binding, and into a pile on the floor. And it's hard cheese, isn't it, if the subject happens to be one of your big readers and collects old books, say?' Palfreyman paused to let the awful tedium of such a search sink into our impressionable young minds. 'Then you'll want every drawer emptied and *all* contents minutely examined. Then look inside the hole the drawer came from. What are you looking for? Trouble is, you don't know what you're effing well looking for until you find it, do you now?'

'No,' said Smith, encouraged by the praise he'd been getting.

'Good lad,' said Palfreyman. 'You'll do well, you will. So what is it then – a left luggage ticket, a scrap of paper with an interesting phone number, a single sheet of white carbon, invisible ink in a vinegar bottle, a key at the bottom of a jar of mustard. French mustard at that. Or again, you're looking for the *surface* signs of hidden arms, explosives, transmission gear, photographic equipment, code books – you don't know, it could be any of those or plenty of others. Even porno negs will tell you something about the character who hid 'em.'

We nodded sagely.

'So what signs do you expect to find, leading to stuff like that?' This was easier and we all had a go: loose floorboards, hollow back to a cupboard, a much-used loft, signs of a carpet repeatedly raised and tacked back. And Palfreyman nodded approvingly, with an occasional 'good lad'.

But now I found nothing – nothing at all – in the living room. It was odd all right, but there was nothing there which looked the least bit illegal. What was odd was what I'd already seen the day before: the reading matter, the mass of recording tapes, the expensive Sony tape deck. All that, if you wanted to be highfalutin' about it, was culturally and psychologically off key. But that was all. And the rest of Bracony's living quarters yielded nothing more. The bathroom, toilet and lumber room were clean and there was nothing in the water tanks except water.

There appeared to be no way into the loft. And the bedroom, after I'd stepped carefully over Bracony's great bulk – yielded me nothing, with a single exception. This was a solitary sheet of squared paper which I found lying in the drawer of the bedside table. It was a short list of stocks abbreviated in the manner of the tables to be found in the financial pages of any newspaper. There were eleven of them, with prices and numbers which seemed to indicate the size of purchases or holdings:

Soginter	439 frs	40
Parcor.	1,200	10
Trans. et Ind.	108	50

. . . and so on.

At the top of the sheet there was written *Jules Roberton 261 9898*. I pocketed the paper and stepped into the corridor. Now for Bracony. There aren't many pockets in a set of workman's denims and I went carefully through them all. Small change, a keyring with a key which proved to belong to the front door, the car keys, some bits and pieces – nothing of interest.

So now for the *secadour*, and if my conviction of treasure trove was right, then the treasure had to be in the *secadour* and the keys of the *secadour* with its bolts and padlocks had to be in the house. In which case, I'd missed them. Friend Palfreyman would have been disappointed in me. Smith would have found them.

CHAPTER 13

The Secadour

The *secadour* had been fitted up like a fortress. All the bolts anchoring the system of padlocked bars across the door had been let into solid concrete. The door itself was made of heavy iron plate and everything had been bolted into it by someone who knew what he was doing. I'd found a five-foot iron bar in the yard which I could use as a crowbar, but the thing looked like a joke as I confronted that massive door with its locks, bars, bolts and padlocks. I could get leverage all right by inserting the end between the door and one of the uprights of the fastening system. But when I threw my entire weight against the other end nothing shifted or looked like shifting. Two things were needed: a longer crowbar to provide more leverage, and a greater force applied at its extremity.

Back in the store I found another metal bar, maybe twelve feet long, which looked as if it had once formed part of a heavy gate. I dragged it across the open ground to the *secadour*. By now I was sweating liberally, and the sharp November air had become a welcome relief. The end of the bar could just be inserted behind the closure of the door. I left it there, returned to the Fiat and drove it into the yard. Then I wrapped some sacking firmly round the front bumper and propped up the end of the twelve-foot lever on an empty oil can at the bumper's height from the ground. The risk was that the car would simply succeed in bending the bar before the leverage could prise the fastening away from the door. But what actually happened was a compromise between the various stresses I had set up. As I drove the car fractionally forward against the bar, the lower bolt began to loosen from the door just as the bar itself started to bend. It looked as if the two bits of metal were pretty evenly matched. With a sharp *crrrack* the bolt snapped away just as the bar itself bent through an angle of some twenty degrees.

I got out and examined my handiwork. I needed to prise one more bolt loose. With a lot more sweat and two sore hands I reversed the bar so that the force set up by the car would initially bend it straight again, giving me whatever leverage there was to be had as it moved through a total arc of forty degrees around the true. I managed to wedge the end behind the vertical member on the door fastening, now hanging loose from its upper bolt. Then back to the car and more careful shoving in first until another *crrrrack* announced the sheering of the top bolt. I was nearly there, but not quite. For the door itself was locked, and though the external fastening system lay in ruins, I was now confronted with the massive lock. And it was none of your 'watch me with a hairpin or an American Express card' locks. The throw of the plungers must have been two inches at least.

I couldn't get a fraction of an inch of movement out of the door with my five-foot bar, and the longer bar was too thick to be inserted between the door and its frame. It looked like defeat, until explosives or a bulldozer could be brought into play. But one doesn't travel with such stores and I had no idea how to come by either resource. I might as well have left the padlocks and bars in place and sent for the demolition men from London.

The logical thing to do, no doubt, when defeated, is to stop picking at the problem as if it were an irksome scab and retire for completely fresh thought and action. But hardly anyone ever does that. We go on talking, plucking at a thing verbally, long after we've talked a problem to death. We toy with a container which refuses to open long after we've realised that we should be away somewhere buying a cleat or a five-pound hammer. Not to be outdone, I tugged idiotically at the door, ran my fingers round the keyhole, looked through it into the blackness within, and carefully examined the gap between door and frame. It was when this apparently useless exercise brought me to the base of the door that I noticed the state of the ground for the first time. In that derelict yard, with its uneven, rock-strewn surface, the ground had been carefully levelled and cemented for a distance of about six yards in front of the door. And in the cement two shallow but distinct grooves had been worn, maybe thirty inches apart, as if some object had been repeatedly wheeled in and out of the *secadour*. It looked to me as if the levelling and surfacing had been done quite a few years before: its weathered appearance had led me to miss it until now. There wasn't much doubt: Bracony kept something exceedingly precious in the *secadour* and periodically wheeled it out to take the air. Not far out: just five or six yards, and then, presumably, back again. There were no wheel marks in the softer ground beyond the cemented surface.

But I couldn't get the door open. Keys were out: I hadn't any. Crowbars were out: the job was beyond them. Digging was out: the cement prevented that. Shooting at the thing was out too: even rifle bullets would have bounced off – dangerously. Clearly, the job called for explosives and I had no explosives. So should I try shooting at the lock after all? Pointless. Playing with the problem again. And yet the guns were the only sources of energy I had, apart from the cars. Maybe I could keep driving Bracony's car at it until the door gave way or the car packed up. I reckoned the car would be the first to go. Or I could pull the door off its hinges if there was a way of tethering it to the car, only there was no way. But the guns were a source of energy. Or rather, their cartridges . . .

I grunted a private oath and dashed for the house. I'd already found Bracony's ample store of ammunition in a cupboard in the living room. I now spent ten minutes gathering together various components recollected from the corner of my mind where such lists had been preserved since my last dirty-tricks course at Wendover. A shirt for tearing up; twine; foil, lead sheet or an empty can, with tools to cut and bend the metal; and the cartridges. And matches.

By now I knew the contents of the house so well that finding what I needed was no problem. Putting together an explosive charge of the right size and shape, with the means of detonating it, was a matter of memory, since we'd all been made to spend two hot summer days at the Wendover school pretending to be the IRA on the rampage in Derry.

I bore my dangerous contraption down to the *secadour*. What I needed to do was to blow the door off its hinges. It was a likelier bet than trying to demolish the lock. Furthermore, the gap between the door and frame was wider and deeper on the hinge side. So my first charge would be packed into the gap above and below the lower hinge. I did it all according to the book as I recalled the book, and when the thing was ready I lit my fuse of prepared twine and retired, as they say on the fireworks, to a safe distance, behind the *secadour*. If I were a praying man I would have offered a short prayer. But there was no need. The explosion came dangerously soon, and made a deafening racket. I hoped they did quarrying somewhere in the district.

Through the acrid smoke I could see that I'd remembered pretty well. The lower hinge had been wrenched from its anchorage in the wall, and by a freak of wave pressure theory that I don't pretend to understand, the door had buckled outwards. It still held at the upper hinge.

I repeated the technique in a state of mounting excitement, and again I was rewarded with a fine bang. And this time I was home: as the smoke cleared I saw that the door lay flat on the ground. The *secadour* was about to yield whatever secrets it had.

I really have no idea what I expected to find inside that little building. I'd been so obsessed by the problem of getting in that I hadn't given the matter a thought. The fact that I pulled my gun out of my pocket and advanced with caution didn't mean I thought there was some living creature inside. It was mere routine. If I'd been asked, as a Wendover exercise, to list the probabilities, I suppose I'd have jotted down the usual ironmongery of espionage, because by then my mind had closed around the assumption that whatever Marchand might or might not have been, Bracony was some kind of agent.

But what I saw as I entered the *secadour* was a total surprise. You do not expect, bolts and bars notwithstanding, to be confronted with the gleaming, mystifying presence of high technology in the derelict yard of a French farmhouse high up in the Causses. You do not expect to find an object so advanced in design that you yourself have no immediate recognition of what it is. But the thing confronted me, its metal parts reflecting the dim light which entered the *secadour*.

Culture shock!

I found a switch by the door and the light from a 100-watt bulb in the ceiling illuminated the strange object standing on a trolley in the centre of the little building. Its main feature was a shallow, highly polished dish like a giant silver salver, maybe a couple of yards across and mounted on a structure of beams and struts. Below it was a metal housing with one side left open. Within, I could see plenty of complex circuitry. I knew enough to tell that I was looking at a very sophisticated transmitter of some kind. Your common-or-garden agent's shortwave transmitting equipment, usually fitting neatly into an attaché case, was all very well, but this monster was ridiculous. If messages were sent, they were being sent very far and very privately indeed. I knew I needed help from London.

Now I had to take chances. That no one would come to the Bracony house and see the smashed-in *secadour*. That if they saw it they wouldn't go on to see the smashed windows on the far side of the house. That they wouldn't summon help, break in and find Bracony himself. That whoever was after me from Paris was still floundering round the hills and valleys of the Puy-de-Dôme. I needed twenty-four hours: I couldn't see how to do what needed to be done in less.

I put the distributor head back under the bonnet of Bracony's van and drove it into the yard and up against the *secadour*. It hid the door almost completely. Then I headed the Fiat towards Rodez and stopped at the first *tabac*. I had to call the Embassy since it was now nearly three and I had missed my Bristol standby with Isabel. And it had to be short and sharp because the DST's listening post would pick up the call and in about four minutes – three if they were lucky and I wasn't – they could trace it back through the exchanges, provided the call was still in progress.

'*Ambassade Brittanique*', said the girl.

'Listen carefully, dear. I have a message for Miss Reid-Porter of the Information Department. Tell her Mr Bristol will call her at five and she should be available to take the call. Have you got that?'

'Mr Bristol at five. Thank you.'

' 'Bye,' I said, and hoped the DST weren't smarter than I gave them credit for.

At five I called the Bristol from my hotel and asked them to page Miss Brown. Soon Isabel's unruffled voice came on the line.

'Hi, Brownie,' I said. 'Got your pencil?'

'Yes.'

'One, tell Pabjoy I have to have Harry Sutcliffe here by the very next plane to Toulouse or Marseille or whatever's best and fastest for Rodez, spelt R-o-d-e-z, in the Aveyron. I'll meet him at the airport. Say it's highest speed and very secret. Two, check out the route with Pabjoy and call me back from a public booth in one hour.' I gave her the number of my hotel. 'Three, get Arthur to trace a Jules Roberton at 261 9898. Looks like a Paris number, but if it isn't he'd better try any other cities he can think of that use seven digits. Likely places, I suppose, are Zurich, Geneva, Marseille, Lyon, even London. Got the details?'

'Yes.'

'You're a good girl, Miss Brown.'

'Thanks. And I've some stuff from Arthur on your North African.'

'Good, but it'll have to wait. Don't lose it, dear.'

'I shan't. Call you back.'

I drove to the hotel in Rodez and exactly sixty-five minutes later her call came through. 'The Pabjoy expressed extreme disapproval,' she said. 'Appears Harry's deep in something else and can't be spared. But I wheedled and Pabjoy said you can have him for exactly one day, and do you think the budget's made of elastic?'

'Fine,' I said. 'I wouldn't have expected it any different.'

'You're lucky with the planes, too. He'll fly to Paris tonight and be on the eight am France-Inter flight to Toulouse in the morning. Lands at nine. Good enough for you?'

'Just about.'

'And Arthur has your message. With luck, I'll have a useful answer when you phone next.'

'Be at our trysting place at eleven tomorrow and I'll phone then.'

'I do worry about you, Carey, my sweet.' A hint of feeling had crept into her voice.

'I'd be a bit fed up if you didn't.' And we said goodbye.

Next morning I was in the Fiat at seven and did the 100 miles to Toulouse in under two hours. I hit the rush hour as I came into the town, so that Harry was already waiting for me by the arrival barrier in the crowded concourse of the airport. He was the best radio and electronics man in the Section but he looked like a plumber's mate in his anorak and seedy corduroys.

'Wotcher, Squire,' said Harry in his affected pub lingo. 'Bin up to no good, then?'

'Hallo, Harry,' I said. 'Why no good?'

'Well, the Guv was acting like a bear with a sore arse. Didn't sound at all like a pal of yours.'

'Not a pal of mine,' I said. 'Come on.'

During the run back northwards I filled him in and gave him the best description I could of the contraption in the *secadour*.

'It'll be the only chance we'll get to look at the thing,' I said, 'and you'll have to come away knowing it as if you'd built it yourself. I'll want to know who made it and when, what its capability is and why they couldn't have used an RT44 instead, how it's used, what its likely receiving station is, and of course all the technical gen like frequencies, GHz and the rest of the fancy stuff.'

'And whether the bleeder who built it has an Uncle George living in Tomsk?'

'Quite right,' I said. 'That happens to be the most important question of all.' After that we talked gloomily about the Spurs as far as Albi, where I found a *tabac* with a phone.

Isabel was brisk as ever. 'Easy,' she said. 'Roberton, Jules, is in the Paris directory. He's a stockbroker at forty-eight boulevard des Italiens.'

'Thanks,' I said. 'Harry's arrived and we're on our way.'

We reached the Bracony house soon after midday. My luck had held. No one had been near the place. I drove the Fiat into the yard and nodded towards the *secadour*. 'In there,' I said. 'You'll enjoy yourself.'

Harry climbed out of the car and pushed himself behind Bracony's van and into the *secadour*. I heard a long and expert whistle. Then he reappeared. 'None of my business, like, but why the hell would they have a thing like that out here?'

'It's what I want to know, Harry,' I said. 'How long do you need?'

'Get this van shifted and help me pull it outside and I'll need an hour, perhaps a bit more.'

'You've got your hour,' I said, 'but make it less if you can.'

I moved the van and we rolled the transmitter out into the grey November light.

'She's a beaut,' Harry said. 'We'll soon get to know 'er cunning little ways.' He took a notebook out of his pocket and started jotting in it as he circled the apparatus. From time to time he nodded. Then he whistled tunelessly for a bit.

'Know what it is?' he asked without looking up.

'What?'

'It's a bleedin' ultra-shortwave transmitter fitted with a dish antenna and its own batteries. Independent of the mains. A beaut.'

'And what will it do?'

'Why, send wireless signals. Stands to reason. *But* – and here's the point, Squire – it's designed to send signals over bloody great distances and on a narrow directional beam.'

'So?'

'Well, figure it out for yourself. No point having a powerful job like this if all you want to do is send something out to be picked up in the usual way in Moscow, say, like any of your everyday transmissions.'

'So why all this technology?'

'Because, Squire, *because* they want to transmit as often and as long as they like, knowing for sure that no one can listen in. And there's only one way to do that.'

'Come on, Harry,' I said, 'stop playing silly buggers and come out with it.'

'This 'ere toy,' Harry said, 'is designed for use with a communication satellite. That accounts for your narrow beam and your range. What you get that way is total secrecy because who's to know all this is going on? The message is on a *beam*, see, not being sloshed all over the firmament for any bleeder to pick up. And you get a damn near interference-free signal, as you know from your telly relays from the States.'

He did a lot of writing in his notebook as he poked about inside the base of the transmitter, transcribing figures from dials, checking calibrations and peering closely at the circuitry. Finally he straightened up.

'Think I've got all I can use here,' he said. 'Rest'll have to be dug out back home. Need to talk to a mate or two and check over some papers. T'isn't every day I come across one of these.'

'Fine,' I said. 'By the way, where was it made?'

'That's what foxes me for now,' Harry said. 'You wouldn't expect 'em to screw name plates all over her and they haven't.

But they've done better than that. Every serial number on the components has been filed off. So we'll have to do a bit of detection, won't we?'

He took a Nikon out of his bag and spent the next ten minutes focusing and clicking, getting in as close as he could. 'The assembly will show someone's handwriting. Might match up, say, with some of the Russky hardware the Israelis took off the Syrians last time round.'

'Or it might belong to OTRAG.'

'Doubt it,' Harry said. 'Far as I know, all the German work's in Africa.'

'It could be one of ours, knocked off,' I said.

'Unlikely, Squire, but we won't overlook that either. Matter of fact, I think I'll help myself to a sample or two. Any objections?'

'None.'

Harry unscrewed a number of sub-assemblies and stowed them in his bag. 'Right,' he said, 'I'm through and I could do with a beer.'

Between us we shoved the transmitter back inside and propped up the door to cover the opening.

We were about a mile above Entraygues, driving fast on the twisting road, when we saw another car coming up towards us from the valley, two hairpins away and travelling at least as fast as we were. We passed on a short, straight stretch at a combined speed of something over a hundred miles an hour, so that I had little time to see the occupants of the Mercedes 230. There were four men in the car, and the front passenger was turning round to talk to the two in the back as we passed. I had a glimpse of his thick, black hair. I had no picture of the others.

'Notice any of them?' I asked Harry.

'Nope. Except that the driver looked young and foreign-like. But then you'd expect that, seeing these are foreign parts.'

'You would,' I said. 'Wish I'd got the registration.'

'Hell of a lick, that, up a hill like this,' Harry said. 'Not much like tourists. Mebbe they were on their way through.'

'Can't be,' I said. 'Conques is at the end of this road. There's nothing beyond.'

Harry grunted. 'Guess we got out just in time, then.'

'I was thinking that,' I said. 'Perhaps Bracony did have time to use the phone after all.'

CHAPTER 14

Otto

I was taking no chances at Toulouse airport. Paris was out. The next international flight was an Iberia to Barcelona in twenty minutes and I could make a London connection from there. I used my credit card to buy myself a ticket while Harry booked in for the London flight. As for the Fiat, it would have to look after itself. We kept our distance and when my flight was called I nodded briefly to Harry and trooped out across the apron to the DC9. We were away on schedule for the forty-five-minute flight to Barcelona. I asked the hostess for a timetable, identified a lucky London flight due to take off forty minutes after we landed, and persuaded her to get the captain to radio for a seat.

From London next morning I called Isabel to ask about the Algerians' car and we arranged less cumbersome telephone contact for the duration of my stay. The car, she said, was registered as belonging to the Société Luna of 288 boulevard de Clichy, and a taxi trip had revealed a corroded name plate, a locked door on the third floor and no signs of life. The appropriate archive at the local Mairie gave the Société Luna as having been incorporated in 1952 with four directors whose names meant nothing to me. Isabel said that Arthur was still trying to get something on them. The company described its activities obscurely as 'promotions and presentations'. Also, did I want anything done about Jules Roberton, the stockbroker? I said no, not just now. I'd done some arithmetic, aided by the Bourse listings, in the plane from Barcelona. Bracony's little package of stocks was worth at current values close to £60,000. Not bad from laying roof tiles in the ancient style of the Causses.

That afternoon Andrew Pabjoy was in a singularly difficult mood, which normally meant that he would contradict and upstage one with rather more than his customary zeal. When I came into his office he threw a copy of the *Standard* across his desk. The page-one lead, under the byline of the Political Correspondent, was one of those allusive stories which are written for the dozen people who are already in the know and the further dozen whose suspicions will be hardened by reading it. It must have been gibberish to the remaining million. It spoke of a possible crisis in Anglo-Soviet relations arising from the activities in recent weeks of the British security services. It referred to a visit by the Soviet Ambassador to the Foreign Office, and brought itself, in the sixth paragraph, to utter the dread phrase 'a potential breach of security'. It hinted at the possible recall of certain Soviet diplomats accredited to the Court of St James.

Immediately adjoining this marshmallow of a story was a photograph, taken at Heathrow, of the Independent MP, Anthony Savage, 'seen returning from a holiday in Yugoslavia'. To those dozen target readers, and perhaps their dozen companions, the story and the captioned picture, though separated by eight-point leads, were supposed to be considered together.

I looked up at Pabjoy. 'That shit Killigrew,' he said, 'has been at it again.'

I waited for more.

'It's a bad scene,' he said. 'That little pest goes ferreting around and what does he come up with? Why, this pathetic MP who's still wet behind the ears and thinks Andropov would close down the psychiatric wards if only someone told him about them. He goes off on the grand East European tour – no favouring one shade of red over another – looks in on the Comrades in Warsaw, then on to Moscow where he explains what was wrong with the Fabians before the vodka gets to him, and so on and so forth. Only it turns out that Killigrew has been on to him for the past twelve months and the little twerp has been meeting a couple of Third Secretaries and handing them copies of parliamentary committee meeting minutes, which is all very well provided you don't do it by the third oak from the left through the Robin Gate in Richmond Park, or wherever Russian tradecraft thinks up next.'

'One could say,' I ventured cautiously, 'that Killigrew is only doing his job.'

'One could also say,' Pabjoy remarked sourly, 'that if that's the extent of his job it's about time they reduced the overheads at Special Branch.'

'What's so troublesome in all this for anyone but Mr Savage?'

'Only that the Government will now be obliged to act, since the press is clearly beginning to regard it as its moral duty to tell all. And that means expulsions here, which obliges the Russians to pay us back in the same coin, which means in turn that at least two of my best men will have to be booted out of Moscow and I've no idea, Carey, where I'm to find replacements in our present condition of impoverished incompetence.'

I grunted in a manner calculated to convey a measure of sympathy. 'Why,' Pabjoy was asking, 'cannot these eager beavers in Special Branch leave one alone to conduct one's business in an orderly and civilised fashion? Why can't we stop pretending that when we know a man is a third-grade spy we are promptly obliged to *do* something about it?'

'Why indeed?'

'I shall have to talk to someone on the other side about it,' Pabjoy said, half to himself. 'Maybe to Gennadi. See if I can't contain the damage. It's a whole can of worms that shit Killigrew has opened up here. A whole can of worms.'

With that I left him, and when he called me back to his office a half hour later, Hank Munthe was draped in and around the big armchair.

It took me twenty minutes to give an account of myself, in the course of which I had to bring Hank more fully into the picture, which included the story of Marc Ségur and the trail which had led to Bracony. Andrew Pabjoy did not so much as touch a pencil during my narrative. At the end of it he asked a question.

'What has all that to do with Marchand?'

'Well, Marchand is suspected of belonging to the opposition, Marchand often visited Conques, which was an odd place for a busy politician to go. Bracony lived at Conques and appears to find the telephone inadequate for his communication needs. Marchand and Bracony were in contact in the war. Ergo, we have a prima-facie link between the Minister and the spy.'

'My thinking, Charlie,' Hank said through the stem of his pipe, 'would be that that relationship could be meaningful though we have no present evidence of person to person contact.'

'People have been hanged on thinner evidence,' I said.

'They haven't,' Andrew Pabjoy said. 'Not in Britain.'

'Come on,' I said, feeling irritated, 'are you telling me that you see no connection between Marchand and Bracony?'

'No, I'm telling you that I can't base a report to the Minister on it.'

'And I'm right there with you, Andrew,' Hank Munthe said. 'Looks affirmative, but we need more input.'

'Of course we need more input,' I said. 'That's what I'm doing next – putting in more input.'

'What do you propose?' Andrew Pabjoy asked.

'I'd like to take a look at the Gestapo and SD files from Lyon,' I said. 'Where did your military dump them in the end?' I asked Hank.

'Berlin. The Nazi Document Centre in Zehlendorf. But you know they didn't find much in Barbie's office in Lyon.'

'I don't believe it, but never mind. I need to look at whatever was sent to Zehlendorf.'

'Glad to help, Charlie. I'll get our Berlin Station Officer to meet you and ease things if you let me know when you're flying.'

'Is that still Walter Bailey?'
'Sure is.'
'I know Walter. I'll call him myself when I get in.'
'Sure you wouldn't like him to pick you up at Tegel?'
'Quite sure, thanks. Everyone of any consequence in Berlin knows what Walt does for a living. I'd prefer not to be seen with him in public.'
'Okay,' Hank said. 'But we'd certainly be glad to help identify the equipment. We have pretty good capability in that area.'
'Let's see what Harry has to say. I wouldn't want to have anyone steal his show.'
Pabjoy asked Penny on the intercom to tell Harry to join us. When he was installed Pabjoy asked him if he needed help in identifying the transmitter.
'No thanks,' Harry said.
'Are you sure?'
'Sure.'
'Our American friends have offered their facilities.'
'No thanks.'
There was an awkward pause. Harry thought he should make a gesture. 'In any case,' he said, 'I got friends in US Army Signals. I'll talk to 'em if I need to. And our own Signals people have worked on that kind of hardware.'
'When do you expect to give us a report?'
'Three, four days, I'd say.'
'Well,' Hank said, 'remember my people will be mighty happy to help. Just call us.'
'Thanks,' Harry said on his way out of the room, 'but like I say, I shan't need to.'
After Hank had left, Andrew Pabjoy said: 'Perhaps we should tell Wavre to get someone down to Conques.'
'Either he has already or it's too late,' I said, thinking of the Mercedes on the Entraygues road, 'but I'm sure we should do our duty to a friendly Power.'
'I'll do it later,' Pabjoy said.

That evening I called Otto Feld. 'I have to get back to Paris tomorrow and I'd like the benefit of your insights before I go. Have breakfast with me.'

'It is a disgusting habit, this American thing of a working breakfast. How bad is your problem?'

'Fundamentally disastrous, I shouldn't wonder, but not all that serious.'

'Then I will have breakfast. I will come to you. Please have some bran for me: a little trouble I have down there.'

Over the bran and my eggs, I explained.

'This assignment is as bloody as any other assignment but I've never felt so strongly before that I was on a loser. Not only that, but I have Hank Munthe trying to capture the show.'

'So what can I do about that?'

'Do you think this Marchand affair is a loser?'

'Of course, in the sense that these ridiculous projects never end the way their sponsors expect. A result of some kind, certainly. But the *expected* result? Ridiculous!'

'So what am I wasting my time for?'

'It is your job, no? And who are you, my friend, to expect more job satisfaction than millions of your fellow men, eh?'

'That's all very well, but what I'm talking about isn't exactly job satisfaction. It's three deaths already and maybe more to come. Maybe my own. And at the end of it – what?'

'At the end of it the Prime Minister will have answers which may or may not be true and which may or may not be believed, no? And if you are still here you will receive another assignment of equal stupidity.' He seemed to be enjoying his bran and asked for more coffee.

'Otto, I sometimes wonder if I'm cut out for this job. It isn't a question of nerve, there's nothing wrong with my nerves, not yet anyway. It's just that I sometimes feel I'd like what I do to be *relevant*.'

'And you think counter-intelligence is not relevant?'

'I wouldn't say it to anyone else.'

'Good. They would not understand what you mean. But I

understand. Maybe you are not neurotic enough, Carey. You know, the neurotics, they have a big advantage. If their neurosis is harnessed to the task, then all their energy, their passion, is engaged and they are happy. And they have no doubts, no worries. A neurotic KGB man hates the Americans and his hatred carries him through. Another neurotic may be obsessed with plotting, secrecy, conspiracy: he believes all men are against him. Paranoia. It makes him a very good agent. But you, Carey, you aren't crazy enough for this game. You like women, no?'

'Yes.'

'You like a good *poulet à la crème*?'

'Yes.'

'You are sorry when you kill someone from the opposition?'

'I suppose so.'

Otto wiped his mouth and patted his ample belly. 'Be careful, my friend. This kind of sanity is not good in this job. Now back you go to Paris and put this nonsense out of your head.'

CHAPTER 15

Isabel

I took a tiresome route back into France which involved a flight to Basle, whose airport lies athwart the Franco-Swiss frontier. Instead of emerging through French immigration and customs I chose the Swiss side, hired a Eurocar and crossed the frontier at Huningue on RN69, where the inspection is known to be sloppy. Then I drove to Belfort and took the train to Paris. Isabel was on the platform at the Gare de l'Est in a suede coat the colour of ripe avocado, long floppy boots to match and a velvet beret. The cool austerity melted a little when she saw me and she greeted me to a generous hug and one of her slow smiles. I kissed her.

'Welcome to Paris,' she said, 'where wonderful things happen to you.'

'Nice of you to meet me. In the cold too.' December had come in with a sharp frost. A hostile wind was whipping in off the North European plain. 'Where am I staying?'

'Would you like to stay with me?'

'Yes, please.'

We found her car and were in her studio a half hour later. I always liked being in Isabel's place, which contrasted surprisingly with her classy English manner. The furniture was minimal – one vast armchair, upholstered in a crimson repp, a double divan, a plenitude of cushions and a long-haired white rug on the polished wood floor. On a table – the one authentic touch – serried ranks of framed photographs in which figures bearing the unmistakable high family brow and chiselled county nose were interspersed with faded cabinet ministers and the occasional West End actress. Pride of place, in a silver frame, went to a group which improbably included Lloyd George, Gaby Deslys and the impressive figures of Isabel's maternal grandparents. 'Grandpa had a famous affair with Gaby Deslys,' Isabel would recount. 'He was specially partial to French ladies of the musical stage, you see. It was something about their delicious little ankles – they were very hot on ankles in those days. The family was immensely proud of the fact but Granny always referred to her as "that French creature with the dreadful table manners". It didn't prevent her being received at their place in Cumberland, though family legend has it that she was inclined to have it off with whichever footman seemed to be the youngest at the time. And, on the occasion of the photo, with Lloyd George too, of course.'

I retreated into the mighty armchair while Isabel ground and brewed coffee.

'Tell me all.' We both said it, simultaneously, breathing in the roasted aroma of the coffee and rebuilding by imperceptible gestures and responses our comfortable, familiar intimacy together. We took turns at debriefing each other until all we knew about the Marchand affair was finally held in common.

Later, in bed, we made passionate love to each other.

Next day I held a council of war over lunch with Isabel and Arthur. Arthur had news for me. 'There's something on the Société Luna,' he said. 'It seems to be an all-North African outfit. They're all Ali this or Ben that. I got someone at the Sûreté to run their names through the computer. Seems all four of them have form. GBH, robbery with violence, extortion – stuff like that. The mob, in short. *Le milieu.* I'd say they're running a front for a hit operation. And other stuff like protection, no doubt. But why they're registered as a company I've no idea.'

'Well, they must have turned in a loss for the shareholders on their last venture,' Isabel said.

'Not at all,' I said. 'If there's a contract out on me it's almost certainly still out. So it's only a question of their picking me up again. Only this time it isn't just for the cash. They won't overlook what I did to our friend Ben Ballem.'

'I've something else,' Arthur said. He was filling a battered pipe and puffing doggedly to get the thing alight. I waited, but he was determined to get his pipe going before taking us further into his confidence. At last a decent cloud of tobacco smoke hung around his head and spilled unpleasantly towards us.

'I've had a message from someone I know in the PCF.* They'd like to talk to you.'

'Christ,' I said, 'how do they know about me?'

'No idea. But Robert Tallard – that's the man I know – made it clear the call was a friendly one. You'd be seeing him with another fellow.'

'Which means they know why I'm here.'

'Which is more,' Arthur said wistfully, 'than I know myself.'

'Christ,' I said again.

'What shall I tell him?'

'What's his level?'

'He's only a young man, twenty-eight maybe, but he's on the Central Committee and an associate member of the Political Bureau. He's said to be one of their rising stars.'

'It would have to be in a safe house,' I said, half to myself, 'with tapes available to us and not to them. And first I'd need to know how they know about me and what *they* think I am. I'll provide the location if they come up with the right answers.'

'I'll pass it on,' Arthur said.

'The other thing I shall do is go and have a chat with Artunian's widow. And I'd like you to locate one of the Luna boys for me. I don't know how I'll proceed, but I'd like to know where I can put my hands on him if I want to.'

'That,' Isabel said, 'is asking for bloody trouble.'

'Lady's right, of course,' Arthur said.

* Parti Communiste Français.

'But do it just the same.'

We arranged to meet for dinner at the Dôme in Montparnasse.

I paid off the taxi at the place St Michel and walked along the quai, using the pavement on the river side of the road. The sun was still shining, hanging low in an ice-blue sky. A gusty wind with a sharp edge to it whipped the few remaining leaves along the pavement. The bookstalls were closed. I headed for the old house on the quai Voltaire, reached and passed it without sighting a parked car with an occupant, or a loiterer. No indication that they had the place under surveillance. I crossed the road and made my way back, pressed the door release and hurried past the concierge's *loge* without being seen. Madame Artunian answered my ring, looked puzzled for a moment, and then nodded her recognition. She was dressed in black.

'*Entrez, Monsieur.*' She said it almost as if she had been expecting me, as indeed she may have been. I stepped into the gloomy hall with its heavy furniture and crimson drapes, and she closed the door behind me. A single bulb was alight under a parchment shade.

Madame Artunian led the way into the drawing room where a hundred years ago, so it seemed, I had talked with her husband. She chose a straight-backed chair for herself, and beckoned me to sit opposite her. Once again, I was looking out over the sluggish grey river to the dim golden bulk of the Louvre over on the right bank.

'I have come, Madame, to pay my respects,' I said, 'and to tell you how very sorry I am . . .'

I am not good with the bereaved. Hardly anyone is. And I was responsible for her husband's death. It was a fact of which she might very well be aware herself. But if she was, she betrayed no sign of it.

'Thank you,' she said. 'It is a sad loss for me. Nearly fifty years. A very fine man. A good husband and a gentleman.' She used the English word, since it has no French equivalent.

'I am sorry to call unannounced,' I said, 'but there are reasons. May I ask if the police are . . .'

She guessed at my question, shook her head. 'After the first days they have left me alone,' she said. 'Also the press. I have seen no one but the maid for over a week. They say you get used to that.'

Again the siren of a *bateau-mouche* out on the river punctuated the conversation as it had done on the day I listened to Avram Artunian telling me in his soft, guttural voice why he had never liked André Marchand.

'I am very sorry not to be able to thank your husband for helping me with a matter which we had discussed together. He was most kind.'

'I am sure Avram would be glad to know he had been of service to you. He said he must put you in touch with our good friend Alfred Baum.'

'Indirectly, he did, and Baum was most helpful.'

'Did you meet his wife, Estelle? She is a very good friend of mine.'

'No, I was briefly at his flat but I don't think she was in.'

'You know, they have urged me to close up this place and come to stay with them until I feel better and regain my strength,' Madame Artunian said. 'But I told them I wanted to be here, where Avram was, you understand. And then I couldn't bear to be so far away from the heart of Paris. Being out at Versailles would only increase my depression. You will have seen how long it takes to get there in the train. Or did you go by car, which is certainly worse?'

'Yes, by car,' I said, my mind racing. 'And I thought Baum shows the strain of such a long daily journey.'

'Oh, no, I don't think so,' Madame Artunian said. 'Such a very healthy little man. So chubby, even. A picture of health.'

'Perhaps so,' I said, trying to betray no sign of special interest in this idle afternoon gossip.

'I seem to have mislaid their telephone number,' I said. 'I wonder if I could trouble you for it?'

'Certainly,' she said, and took an address book from the desk in the corner of the room. 'Here, A. Baum, 70784 at Versailles.'

'And the address? I had that written down too.'

She looked in the book. 'Sixty-seven Cité Pasteur.'

'They don't have a place in the rue Etienne Marcel as well?'

'I never heard of one. No, no.'

'I must have been mistaken,' I said.

Madame Artunian offered me tea and I declined. 'I really think I should go now,' I said, getting up. 'I only came to pay my respects and it was good of you to see me at such a time.' And I took my leave.

I walked in the pale afternoon sunshine, keeping to the left bank of the river, past the Institut, the Palais Bourbon and on across the champ de Mars and towards Isabel's studio. As I walked I wrestled with the problem of Baum, the tall sallow man who was short and chubby and who lived in the rue Etienne Marcel in the heart of town, except that his flat was out at Versailles. *Will the real Alfred Baum please stand up?*

I pulled up the collar of my coat against the wind and passed under the iron bridge of the Métro and along the rue de la Convention, cursing the fact that I had no choice: I would have to make the inconvenient journey to Versailles. How right Madame Artunian was about that.

At the studio I had a shower and changed my shirt. When Isabel arrived from the Embassy we drank scotch and water and I told her about my afternoon. Then we drove her Dyane over to Montparnasse and managed to park it like a pram on the pavement outside the Dôme. Arthur was already there, contemplating the remains of a drink and fussing with his pipe. He had chosen a table from which the main entrance of the restaurant and much of the pavement outside could be seen. Behind the *banquette* was a wall of mirror. Isabel refused a seat against the wall and so sat facing the mirror, her back to the restaurant. Arthur and I sat facing her, side by side. We ordered our food from the big menu without a lot of care or attention and settled for the house wine.

'I've just come from having a little chat with Robert Tallard,' Arthur said, 'I told him your conditions. Added that if we found he had a mini-recorder on him the whole deal would be off. He said he understood and agreed. Said he realised you were at some risk in meeting him at all.'

'Who does he think I am?'

'In his foolishness he thinks you are a member of the British Secret Intelligence Service investigating the death of André Marchand because the SIS believes he was a foreign agent.'

I let Comrade Tallard's disarming assertions sink in while the waiter delivered our wine and fooled about with the cutlery.

'What else did Tallard say?'

'That the Party was interested in establishing the truth about Marchand and thought it had a contribution to make.'

'What do you think?'

'I think that the Party is interested in establishing the truth about Marchand and has a contribution to make. I also think the Party sees political dividends if the truth is made public and even a dividend if it isn't. They are not ideologically opposed, you know, to a bit of Anglo-French aggro.'

Isabel nodded. As she looked at us both, her gaze kept slipping past our heads to the mirror behind us, and her eyes refocused as she took in the reflection of the restaurant and the street outside.

'I shall have to see our Station Officer and get the use of the safe house in the rue Debrousse for an hour or two. When can Tallard meet me?'

'He offered ten am tomorrow.'

'Tell him it's OK and I'll meet him and his friend at the pont de l'Alma – on the right bank. You could tell him what I look like. I'll respond when he introduces himself.'

'Right. He's young, as I said, clean-shaven, reddish hair and tall. A good-looking fellow.'

I left the table and went down to the public phone in the basement. In a couple of minutes I had made my arrangements with the SO. When I got back to the table the *crudités* and some smoked sausage had arrived.

As we ate I noticed that Isabel was bothered about something. She kept glancing in the mirror and I could see her gaze sweeping the scene behind her like radar. Once she frowned slightly.

'Give,' I said.

'You know how careful you were when we came out of my place to make sure there was no one hanging about, and we agreed there wasn't anybody. Well, I hope it's just my girlish imagination, but take a peek at the table on your right. The one beyond the door, with a dark guy sitting sideways-on to us. See him?'

'Yes,' I said. 'But he wasn't around when we left your place this evening.'

'Not this evening, but I could swear I saw him when I left for the office this morning. Only then he looked different.'

'In what way different?'

'He was in overalls, leaning into the bonnet of a car across the way. He ducked down when I came out, but I'd swear that's him – the crinkly hair and the macho moustache – no doubt at all. The sallow complexion, too.'

The man in question was busy with his food and did not look towards us. He had a newspaper open on the table next to his plate and he kept his nose down over it.

'Would you say,' I asked Arthur, 'that that young man was a North African?'

'Afraid I would,' Arthur said, 'and I'll take a small bet his newspaper will prove it.'

He got up and made his way to the *toilettes*, making the slight detour necessary to take him past the man's table. As he passed I saw him glance down at the newspaper. Its reader showed no interest in Arthur. When he got back to our table a few minutes later he nodded briefly. 'Arabic,' he said. 'It looks as if you won't need to go chasing after the Luna people. They're chasing after you.'

We ate our food without enthusiasm, playing around with this new problem. 'You know,' Isabel said, 'this means it would be pretty foolish for you to come back to my place.'

'Foolish or not, it's where I'm coming back to. I can look after myself. And in any case, I'd like to have a word with that young man. It's an opportunity.'

'I don't see why you have to rush towards trouble as if it were an oasis in the desert.'

'Never mind why,' I said. 'The real point is that *you* are the one who shouldn't come back. If you get caught in a punch-up there'll be hell to pay at the Embassy. We can't risk it.'

'I'll be OK. I can go to a girlfriend.'

When we had paid the waiter and given our little ticket to the pretty girl who dispensed coats and umbrellas, we stood waiting near the door. The North African had already paid his bill. He remained immersed in his paper. As we left the restaurant I glanced back. For the first time, he had looked up and was getting to his feet. We stood outside for a moment, saying goodbye to Arthur and making practical arrangements. As Isabel climbed into the driving seat of the Dyane and I got in beside her, the North African came out of the restaurant and hurried to a Renault parked a few yards away.

'Drive me to Montparnasse station,' I said, 'and we'd better be clever about it.'

As we drove, I gave Isabel some further instructions. They involved her in a quick return trip to the studio but I reckoned she wouldn't be at risk if she didn't loiter there.

We reached the station with nothing on our tail. I kissed Isabel. 'When I get back from Versailles later tonight,' I said, 'I'll go back to your place. Call me there at one am and if necessary at half-hour intervals until you reach me.'

'Will do.'

'And all being well, I'll come in to see you at the Embassy tomorrow.'

'Fine, my dear. And do be careful.'

We kissed again and I got out of the car and made my way into the big modern booking hall of the station, fumbling for the francs to buy my ticket.

CHAPTER 16

Baum II

When he opened the front door I recognised him at once – the small dapper figure in grey, looking around cautiously as he made his way to Avram Artunian's graveside.

'Monsieur Baum?'

'Yes, Monsieur. Who are you?'

'My name's George Panmure,' I said, using the cover Artunian would have given him. 'Avram Artunian will have mentioned me.'

'Come in. I remember you. You were at the funeral.'

The flat was modest – small, square rooms furnished with rather over-sized furniture which looked as if it had been inherited from some larger family home in the country. Estelle Baum proved to be a comfortable-looking little woman with the anxious, darting manner of a farmyard hen. When Baum introduced me and proposed that we retire to the kitchen to talk, she started tut-tutting and shaking her head so vigorously that she eventually managed to tut and shake herself altogether out of the sitting room, leaving us to settle down among the knitting and two somnolent cats. Soon she returned for the knitting. Baum switched off the TV and offered me a cognac. I took it with a little water. He helped himself and we settled opposite each other in the heavy armchairs.

'I was waiting for you to contact me,' Baum said. 'Avram told me of your mission and sent me a message to expect you, but then nothing happened.'

'I didn't know how to find you discreetly,' I said. 'No doubt he planned to tell me when we met the second time. But someone got to him first.' Baum nodded and waited for me to continue. 'However,' I said, 'I *did* meet you. Or rather, I met someone who passed himself off as you. I met him in your room at the rue des Saussaies.'

Baum raised his bushy eyebrows. It made him look a little like an amiable but astonished hamster. *'Pas possible!'*

'That's what I would have thought, but it certainly happened.'

'What did this man look like?'

I gave the best description I could of the other Baum. The present Baum shook his head. 'I know of no colleague answering to that description.'

'What is more, he took me to his flat in the rue Etienne Marcel.'

'The address means nothing to me. Are you sure you met him in my room?'

'Positive. It had your name on the door, followed by your title: *Chef des Services de Documentation.*'

'I am not *Chef des Services de Documentation*. I am *Directeur de Documentation et Recherches*, and there is no title on my door. Only my name.'

'What is the number of your room?'

'It is room one-sixteen, on the third floor.'

'This was seven-nineteen, on the seventh floor.'

'Monsieur Panmure,' Baum said patiently, as if I had taken leave of my senses, 'I am afraid there is no room seven-nineteen at the Saussaies. There is no seventh floor. The top floor is the sixth and it is used by a different service.'

'But the lift had a button marked seven.'

'Not at the Saussaies.'

'Does the lift have a mirror on the back wall?'

'No.'

'Oh!' I took a long gulp of my cognac.

'You had better tell me everything,' Baum said, 'preferably from the beginning.' He passed me the bottle and I poured myself another drink. The cats stirred and stretched and one of them made a desultory attempt to get to its feet. Defeated by age, sloth, and the warmth of the room, it sank back onto the carpet. Baum gave it a friendly shove in the ribs with his slippered foot.

I started at the beginning and told him most of what I knew – my meetings with Artunian and Albert Chavan, the 'arrest' outside the SEXY-BIZARRE, the affray at the DST, my meeting with the other Baum, the offer of the Auto Ecole Marceau and the car they'd provided for me with its ingenious mods. I included the battle at the Bontemps' house, and for brevity if nothing else I ended my narrative at the point where the car went crashing down the mountainside. Brevity allied to a certain native caution. I said nothing of the death of the North African or the Ségur papers, of Bracony or the house at Conques. Through it all, Baum listened quietly. When I had finished he asked a question.

'Did you get the registration number of the car they used when they picked you up outside the nightclub?'

'I did. I have a memory for things like that. It was 5502 SR 75. Or it may have been 5592.'

'That is a Ministry number. It will be easy to trace.' He reached for the pad and pencil lying on a low table next to his chair and made a note.

'Do you recall the number of the building in the rue Etienne Marcel which is supposed to be my flat?'

'I didn't catch sight of it, but I might pick it out again with a little luck. I don't know.'

'Please try to do that tomorrow.'

'I will.'

'Give me physical descriptions of the men who beat you up.'

I did my best and as I talked he made notes.

'Their dress?'

I told him what I could. I'd had a particularly close look at their footwear.

'Did either of them address the other by name?'

'If they did, I never heard them.'

'What was your impression of them?'

'They were pros,' I said. 'They knew where to hit and how hard. They were expressionless, bored and technically competent. Must have done jobs like that plenty of times. Definitely pros.'

'Please describe the apartment of the man who called himself Baum.'

I flogged my memory. After all, I'd seen it under trying conditions. But there were one or two features that I'd kept a grip on. 'He drank Black Label scotch,' I said. 'An expensive drink in France. The apartment itself was nothing special. The only thing I ought to say – very tentatively, you understand – is that he did not walk into the place altogether like a man entering his own home. I couldn't swear to it, mind, but he handled the unlocking of the front door with just a shade of hesitation. But I wouldn't make too much of that.'

'Did he *say* it was his apartment?'

'I think he referred to it as "my place". And he offered me plasters and stuff for my cuts, which seemed to indicate that he knew his way to the bathroom cabinet.'

'Was it your impression that the place was regularly lived in?'

'That, or it had been beautifully set up for me. There was mail on a table in the hall, and a man's hat and umbrella on a stand. In the room where we talked I remember a plate with grape pips on it. I'd say lived in.'

'Let's return to what you imagined to be our offices in the rue des Saussaies. When you climbed out of the window did you see any neighbouring buildings?'

'Yes – that is, I saw the top of a building across the way, but I can't say I can recall any features. I couldn't see down into the street because of the parapet.'

'Any characteristics that you can recall? Any details of the construction or the materials used?'

'The building opposite was in brick, not stone. And it was

taller than the one I was in. Otherwise, I couldn't have seen it from my crawling position behind the parapet.'

'Eight stories?'

'I suppose so.'

'You realise that all the buildings opposite us in the rue des Saussaies are in stone?'

'If you say so.'

'And I scarcely need tell you that we do not use the Auto Ecole Marceau.'

'I am not surprised.'

'What else? Please think hard.'

'I caught sight of the Eiffel Tower. Rather near, I'd say not more than a kilometre away. Perhaps less. It didn't strike me at the time, of course, but I'm sure now that I was a good bit nearer to the Eiffel Tower than I would have been at the rue des Saussaies.'

'Was it beyond the brick building?'

'Yes, it appeared to be exactly opposite me across the road.'

'So that the road you were in, if your judgment is correct, was running at right angles to a line radiating from the Eiffel Tower?'

'At right angles or close to it.'

'We won't be able to rely on your estimate of a kilometre. Judging the distance of an object seen in the sky is even more difficult than over water.'

'I must agree.'

'Anything else?'

I racked my brains. 'Yes, one thing. The building must have been very close to a Métro line. One could feel the rumble of passing trains down in the garage. When I was waiting in the boot of the car I passed some of the time by plotting in my mind the frequency of the trains, just for something to do. I know how to count in seconds. It gave me a train every seventy or ninety seconds.'

Baum was taking notes. 'The frequency of trains on the Paris

Métro system varies from line to line,' he said. 'We may be able to identify the line you were on. It's worth trying.'

'There's another thing,' I said. 'That's my impression of the route we took in the car. Difficult to tell from inside the boot, but being at the back end of the vehicle, over the rear axle, you get a strong lateral sway when the car turns. I'd say we went up a circular ramp and straight out onto the road. After what I took to be a smooth spiral action upwards, the car stopped and I heard traffic noises for the first time. Then there was a slight bump – presumably the kerb. We turned right onto the road and very soon the car turned right again.' I paused and thought for a moment. 'My God,' I said, 'that should have tipped me off. You can't turn right out of the DST offices into the rue des Saussaies. It's one-way in the other direction!'

'Perfectly correct,' Baum said drily, making his notes. 'I don't suppose you noticed the direction of the sun when you were on the roof?'

'No sun,' I said. 'Just early morning mist or fog.'

'Ah, a pity. Any unusual noise or smells?' The man was thorough.

'No,' I said. 'Just the early traffic in the street below.'

Baum looked up at me. 'You reckoned it was about eight am. How much traffic?'

'Pretty frequent cars. Maybe one every few seconds.'

'I would conclude from what you say that you were not in a purely residential street, but in an artery carrying a certain amount of through traffic. Do you think it was a one-way street?'

'I have no way of telling. The traffic noises weren't really that specific.'

'A pity. It would have helped to reduce the range of possibilities. But at least we know that traffic passes frequently when you stand facing an eight-storey modern brick building in a certain street a kilometre or so from the Eiffel Tower, running at right angles to a radius from the Tower, and over or very close to a Métro line with a morning train frequency of about seventy seconds. Furthermore, we know that the building we are looking for has an underground garage with access down a circular ramp from the street, over a low kerb.'

He paused and tapped his pencil on the note pad. 'Anything more?'

'I think that's all.'

'Right. We will work on what we have.' He got up from his chair. 'We'll have coffee now. Estelle must have gone to bed but she'll have left a pot on the stove.'

Out in the kitchen we sat at the square table with its tomato-red plastic cloth. We sipped strong black coffee. I gave Baum what I had on the Société Luna, inventing a way of acquiring the information which omitted the use of a corpse. I still said nothing about Bracony and his space-age gadgetry at Conques. There was time enough for that. And for my Communist Party contacts. But I asked him what he could find out about the account of one R. Brançon with Jules Roberton, stockbroker, of 48 boulevard des Italiens. His bushy eyebrows went up but I offered no details and he didn't press me. He made a note.

'I am impressed,' he said, 'by the *trouble* these people are taking. They use Ministry cars – or at any rate, Ministry number plates. They create a fair replica of part of the DST premises. They stage an elaborate charade – a fake escape – for you, simply so that you can encounter under convincing circumstances a man masquerading as me. Then there's the business of the doctored car – both troublesome and expensive. We have, first, intimidation, then mystification, followed by attempted elimination. A complex procedure, almost a Gothic tale, and organised without regard to cost.'

'What doesn't make sense,' I said, 'is that they didn't finish me off when I was in their hands. Instead, they send me out in a lethal car and then send a posse of incompetent North African bandits after me as well.'

Baum grunted. 'It's as if something happened very soon after they beat you up to make them change their minds about you.

Whatever it was, it shifted them from a policy of threats and intimidation to a policy of murder.'

'Any guesses?'

'I do not normally guess. But let me say that it does not bear the imprint of an official French operation. The resources are too extensive and the style is wrong. Soviet? Possibly, I don't know, though again the Soviets are usually willing to spend on personnel rather than on hardware. They deploy people – plenty of them. But the KGB has budgeting problems, just like the services here.' He chuckled at the parallel. 'And now we must locate the false Saussaies and I will also take a look at these Luna people for you.'

'Can you also let me see André Marchand's file at the DST?'

Baum whistled softly through his teeth. 'I wonder,' he said, 'if your people would do the equivalent for me should I ever need it?'

'Certainly,' I lied.

Before answering he got up, fetched the red enamel coffee pot and refilled our cups. He fell back heavily in his chair and looked hard at me. 'No,' he said, 'I cannot let you see the file. I am surprised that you should think I would. But I will check it again myself and talk to you about it. That is the best I can do.'

'What was your own opinion of André Marchand?' I asked.

'I never met him, beyond brief handshakes and the exchange of pleasantries when he made an occasional round of the department. But of all the ministers we headed to, he was the most interested in the DST's work. By far. He often called for top-secret files. He even did that a couple of times when he was at other ministries and no longer had anything to do with us.'

'Did you supply them?'

'I supplied the minimum. Where I considered something to be highly sensitive – totally confidential to the department – I substituted dummy dossiers. One cannot trust politicians, you know.'

'Did you conclude that he was a security risk?'

'I did.'

'Did you act on that belief?'

'I did not, beyond withholding the files where I could.'

'Why not?'

'I had no hard evidence and I decided against pressing for positive vetting of Marchand, which would necessarily involve questioning him, always supposing I could persuade the Director to act – and that is a big supposition.'

'What would Marchand have done?'

'In my judgment he would effectively have destroyed the department. Your old-boy network, I think you call it, protected your Kim Philby for years. Don't imagine we do not have comparable networks of influence here. We do. They are peculiarly unscrupulous. The DST heads to a political department, the Ministry of the Interior. It is therefore vulnerable to manipulation. I put the preservation of the DST first.'

'At the price of leaving a suspected agent in the Cabinet?'

Baum looked hard at me and took a sip of cognac. 'Isn't it a very simple equation? Let us suppose you have an agent of the other side in the Government. He is transmitting confidential and damaging information. Most of it is political. Some will be technical and therefore more important – arms specifications, the location of installations and stuff like that – but ministers do not often get their hands on that kind of material. Or if they do, they have only a limited ability to remove and copy it. After all, politicians deal primarily with policies. The papers they take home are policy papers. And so, if a minister is working for the other side, most of what he will betray is in that sphere. Damaging, certainly: extremely damaging. But that is only one side of the equation. Now consider the other side. It is made up, in essence, of the intelligence and counter-intelligence services of the nation. And here you come to the *realities* of state power. For if a foreign power manages to subvert the secret services it has in fact subverted the State itself. And then there is no bottom to the chasm which opens before you. That is why you British were at far greater risk with a Philby – a bureaucrat in intelligence – than we ever were with our great public figure – Minister of this and that – André Marchand. In any case we were not dealing with a really determined man.'

'Can you explain that?'

'There was a hesitation, an indecision in his pattern of behaviour. That is why he never became Prime Minister. I think this was because his work as an agent, if agent he was, depended on duress rather than political conviction. Perhaps he was trying to keep the thing within some kind of limits. Not that that makes him a hero – just a run-of-the-mill spy, recruited under pressure and ultimately worn down by the years of risk and moral squalor in which he was forced to live. In that, if I am right, he was the antithesis of your convinced ideologist, your Philby.'

'I see that.'

'Then you will also understand that if I could see no *certain* way of mounting a successful investigation of André Marchand, I could only leave him where he was and take what steps I could to protect the DST.'

I sat pondering this lesson in Gallic *Realpolitik* and suddenly realised I had a train to catch. We spent five minutes making arrangements for further meetings. Then I took my leave and caught by twenty seconds the last train back to Paris. It was just before one am when we pulled into the Gare Montparnasse.

At 1.20 the taxi deposited me a hundred yards short of Isabel's building. The street was deserted. I let myself in through the heavy street door, using the key Isabel had lent me, and felt my way up the four flights to her floor, silently and without using the stair lights. Her door was the last of four along a short corridor leading from the lift and stairwell. I approached it like a footpad and managed to find it in the pitch blackness. I ran my index finger carefully along the gap between the top of the door and the frame. A few inches from the hinge side my finger encountered the matchstick Isabel had put in place after we parted in Montparnasse. I had asked her to place it at the handle side and Isabel was not a girl to be asked one thing only to do another. They must have been wise to that simple and ancient device but a bit sloppy in reconstructing it.

I pushed the tip of my key into the lock and eased it very slowly against the tumblers, virtually without a sound. I turned it carefully to the point where the bolt was fully retracted into the lock housing, and with the fingers of my other hand pressed the door gently inwards until it was fractionally open. I flattened myself against the wall and gave it a violent shove inwards with my outstretched hand. I had no idea what, if anything, to expect.

The explosion lifted me off my feet and deposited me flat on the floor. The blast must have bounced off the wall opposite, catching me with plenty of force still left in it. Secondary noises mingled with the terrific bang – the crash as the door ripped off its hinges and hit the floor; the clatter of falling glass and plaster; the splintering of furniture. Whitish smoke billowed out and filled the corridor and I choked as it reached my lungs. I realised at once that the noise in that confined space had deafened me, and I remember thinking *bang go my eardrums*. As I pulled myself upright the word *plastique* flashed into my mind – the explosive material used by the OAS terror groups in their campaign against the French Government in North Africa and later in France itself. A typical device for a North African hit organisation.

Then everything moved fast. First, Isabel's phone rang (very distantly, it seemed) and I felt my way past the door which was lying across the tiny hall, through the smoke and debris to where I remembered the instrument standing at the far side of the living room. Gusts of cold night air were sweeping in through the gaping window frames. It looked as if most of the blast had gone inwards into the studio. The other way, and it would certainly have done for my lungs. It was Isabel's call as planned.

'Listen carefully. They've blown up your place. You'd better get over here fast. I'm leaving if I can get out of the building without being questioned, but it'll be dodgy.' My voice sounded distant and didn't belong to me. I imagine I was shouting into the mouthpiece. I rang off and felt my way back through the wrecked room. Fortunately, there was no one in the corridor yet, but I could hear voices in the building and someone had turned on the lights on the stairs. I sprinted for the stairwell and took the stairs two at a time up to the floor above. As I arrived on the landing, a couple in their dressing gowns were coming down from the next floor up. I hoped they hadn't seen me coming up.

'What on earth was that?'

'An explosion, I think,' I said. 'I was just going out when I heard it. Must be the next floor down.'

We went down the remaining stairs together. By then doors had opened on Isabel's corridor and people in night attire were coming up from the floors below. Fortunately there were two men in their street clothes: it made me less conspicuous in mine. I joined the growing crowd filling the corridor. Someone tried to put on the lights in Isabel's place but the explosion had smashed the bulbs.

'Who lives here?' a young man asked.

'It's the English girl,' someone said.

A man with a torch pushed through the crowd and went into the studio. I heard his shout: 'It's all right, there was no one here.'

'What happened, what happened?' an old lady shouted in my ear.

'Explosion,' I said. 'Probably gas.'

'The gas stove blew up,' I heard her shout to someone else. The news passed round among the spectators. Someone was telephoning the fire service from the apartment opposite. I called the lift and descended to the ground floor, where the concierge was coming out of her *loge*, sleepy-eyed and ready for a little Neapolitan hysteria.

'*Che cosa succede?*' she shrieked at me, grabbing at the lapel of my coat. She was wearing a man's raincoat over a nightdress with a fetching decolleté. The coat flapped open to reveal a splendid bosom, not fully under control.

'I'm getting the police,' I said. *'La Polizia!'*

'*Madonna mia!*' she shrieked, and clutching the gaberdine across her breasts, made for the lift.

The street appeared deserted, but as I turned left towards the rue de la Convention, a car which had been parked across the way, maybe fifty yards beyond me, pulled away from the kerb and moved fast into the main road. Its lights were off and in the dim yellow of the street lighting I saw neither the car's registration number nor the driver's face. Nor did I have any means of knowing whether he had seen and recognised me.

CHAPTER 17

Robert Tallard

The wind beat harshly across the bridge, driving a flurry of early snow before it and cutting unkindly into one's extremities. The temperature had dropped far enough for a thin dapple of snow to lie unmelted on roadway and parapets. Upriver I could just see the comforting outline of the Eiffel Tower. Through the turbulence of the snowflakes it looked just like one of those models set in plastic globes which you shake to create the selfsame effect of a snow shower. The sky, a sullen grey, had turned the river to gunmetal and gave the promise of more snow to come.

I spotted the two PCF men as they emerged from the Alma Métro station on the far side of the place de l'Alma and started to cross towards me. The younger – presumably Robert Tallard – was tall and thin, with an angular white face and a shock of ginger hair. His companion was a stocky figure, a man in his sixties, red-faced, greying, sturdy. Both wore tan leather jackets. They walked vigorously across the place, their shoulders hunched against the cold. They must have decided I was their man – indeed, there was no one else standing about – for they marched straight up to me and the younger extended his hand and said, 'I am Robert Tallard.'

'I'm Parrot,' I said.

'This is our good comrade, Etienne Reynal.'

We shook hands. The fierce grip on my cold hand was painful. Reynal nodded and said nothing.

'I have a suitable place near here,' I said. 'We can walk.'

It took us five minutes to reach the flat in the rue Debrousse. The SO had fixed everything as agreed between us and I noted the hi-fi loudspeaker in the corner of the living room which should contain the live voice-activated mike, wired to recording equipment tucked into some distant cupboard. The two men looked around appraisingly as if they too were trying to guess where a microphone might be. I'd got them to hang their jackets in the hall and there were no tell-tale bulges in their cheap suits. It looked as if they were respecting the no-recording deal.

The two sat down side by side on the long sofa and I pulled up an armchair to face them. Tallard at once took over, talking in a low, steady voice with the hard consonants of the northern working class.

'We are authorised by our Party to talk with you on this matter, Monsieur Parrot. I am a member of the Central Committee of our Party and I am here at the request of the Political Bureau. Etienne is the Regional Organiser for the CGT* in the central region of France.'

Reynal nodded briefly. He was rolling a cigarette in yellow paper, using a little machine and teasing the tobacco out of an ancient pouch on his lap.

'I will tell you why we sought a meeting,' Tallard said. 'It is our understanding that you wish to establish whether or not André Marchand had illicit connections with a foreign power. We further assume you will receive no assistance in this from the French authorities. Indeed, it seems likely that the opposite will be the case, since they can have no interest in revealing that he had been a traitor in wartime and a foreign agent. We, on the other hand, have no such reluctance. We are therefore interested in making available to you the information in our possession, particularly relating to Marchand's wartime activity.'

He paused. I said nothing. 'You may know that the purge of

*Confédération Générale du Travail: the Communist led trade union federation.

collaborators and wartime traitors in our country was far from complete. Many who should have been brought to trial enjoyed a certain protection – the protection of money, influence or complicity. Changing political circumstances since the war have in many cases made prosecution unattractive to the various governments of the day. Today, more than three decades after the end of the war, we still have important data on public personalities and others. It is data that we usually cannot and would not use at this late date, but from time to time an opportunity presents itself of doing an act of popular justice, of exposing the truth.'

And (I reflected) of exercising a little political blackmail here and there. I said nothing.

'In the case of André Marchand,' Tallard was saying, 'we believe our data may prove useful in establishing the truth about his role during and since the war.'

'I will naturally be asking you why you have never used the data yourselves and why your Party was positively hostile to an exposure of Marchand back in the early fifties.'

'The answer is very simple,' Tallard said. 'You will know that it does not suffice to make charges or even to offer documentary proofs. In political cases of this kind one has first of all to assess the balance of forces, both in political life proper and also in the State's prosecuting departments, the press and among the judiciary. We do not think a case of collaboration with or without subsequent espionage can be looked at in isolation, on its merits alone. And so the view of our Party was that the political climate did not permit a *successful* prosecution of André Marchand at that time.'

This was hogwash but I let it go. If Marchand had been a collaborator and an agent and the Communist Party knew it and did nothing about it, it had to be because Communist Parties do not, of their nature, initiate hunts for agents of the KGB, even when those agents have been inherited from the Gestapo.

'Now, however,' Tallard was saying in his low, reasonable

voice, 'the situation is different and we believe it has become possible to make the truth known. The Party considered you should hear it from a comrade who took part in the relevant events. That is why Etienne is with us.'

I was struck by the way this articulate and intelligent young man invested that abstraction, *the Party*, with a will, an opinion, a reasoning power and ultimately a personality of its own. Very dangerous, it seemed to me. It used to be, 'The Lord moves me . . .' now it was, 'The Party considers . . .' I couldn't lay my finger on the difference.

I turned to Reynal, stolidly smoking, his big workman's hands folded across his belly. Until now he had not uttered a word. His voice turned out to be a harsh and guttural Auvergnat. He talked in short, unadorned sentences.

Yes, he had known André Marchand in the Resistance in Lyon. That was from late 1942. Marchand had national responsibilities in the liaison and documentation services but his base was in Lyon and he had also worked in the Aveyron department. He had first joined the Resistance there. A good militant, Reynal said. His army background had taught him discipline, order. He showed courage and energy. A good clandestine worker. Politically he was a progressive Catholic, anti-Communist.

Also in the group at that time was one Raoul Bracony. On the night of 28 December 1942 Bracony visited the surgery of a Dr Janet, a fellow member of the network, with details of comrades to be contacted in a certain matter – it no longer mattered what. He was in the waiting room among the doctor's patients, waiting to see him, when agents of the German SD and thugs from the French *milice* surrounded the building and beat their way in, brandishing their revolvers. Bracony managed to swallow the incriminating paper he was carrying and pretended to be a patient awaiting a consultation. Everyone – Dr Janet and his family and assistant, and all the patients – was hauled off to SD headquarters and immediately subjected to questioning. It was Bracony's hard luck, Reynal said, that the first patient to be interrogated was a local contractor to the German occupying forces. He had noticed Bracony swallow the paper and no doubt hoping to do himself some good with the Germans, denounced him to the Major in charge of the incident. The Major's name was Klaus Barbie.

They thrust a spoon down his throat and made him vomit. The gastric juices had not completely erased the writing on the scrap of paper. It was enough for them to conclude that there was useful information to be extracted from him. 'He wasn't tortured,' Reynal said. 'It wasn't necessary. They must have described their methods to him, or maybe they showed him one of our comrades who'd had three or four days of *baignoire* and beatings about the face and genitals. Anyway, it was enough. He talked. Far more than he needed to. He must have given them everything he knew, and he knew a lot – names, addresses, responsibilities . . .

'Usually, if one of us was forced to give something, we'd keep it to a minimum – try to tell them what they already knew. People are weak. They can't always stand the pain. But Bracony *collaborated*. He changed sides. You must understand the difference. And we know he changed sides because later he was seen leading the *milice* gangs to our people's places. Anyway, he turned up a couple of days later, claiming he'd fooled the SD into believing he was just one of Dr Janet's patients.'

Reynal's voice droned on, hard, impassive. 'Our good friend Dr Janet died in Fresnes prison from injuries received during interrogation. They ruptured his spleen and drove two of his ribs into a lung. Then they left him without medical care, waiting for the coma. By then, the prison doctor was helpless, as he was meant to be. Janet's wife didn't return from Ravensbruck. I blame myself for what happened later: there was something unsatisfactory about Bracony's manner after his release. I put it down to shock. It was deceit.'

Bracony's defection, Reynal said, eventually decimated the network in Lyon. There were fifteen arrests. And among those 'given' to the SD by Bracony was André Marchand. His apartment was raided at the end of January 1943, while he was away on secret business. Or so he said. But they had discovered much later that in fact the Germans had found him at home.

'The SD and the Gestapo always had a problem,' Reynal said. 'If they wanted to "turn" someone, they either had to return him to his network badly and convincingly damaged, with an equally convincing escape story; or they had to persuade him to collaborate in double-quick time so that his friends wouldn't miss him – would never know he'd been in German hands at all. And it usually wasn't easy to scare someone into changing sides that fast. But Barbie did it with Marchand.'

'How?' I asked.

'Through a woman. Marchand was besotted with her. I warned him to be careful because she was apolitical and far too beautiful for safety. A peach. And she was just as crazy about him. It led him to take risks in order to be with her. I warned him but he wouldn't listen. It was stronger than him. Bracony knew it was the way to get Marchand and he must have put Barbie up to it. Anyway, they picked up the girl and when they brought in Marchand, Barbie confronted him with her, there in his office.'

'How do you know this?'

'She told us later.'

'Go on.'

'Barbie was clever. He had the girl taken away before he put his proposition to Marchand. Like that she wouldn't know he had betrayed for her sake. He could claim he'd fooled them. Though I've always reckoned she knew what had happened: she was a woman, after all. They have intuition. But she always denied it. Anyway, Barbie must have told Marchand what they'd do to the girl. I won't turn your stomach with details of what they did to some of our young women, but it must have been enough to break Marchand. Don't forget, he was mad about her. We shouldn't judge him harshly *at that stage*.'

'Why only at that stage?'

'Because it was always possible for a comrade who had been caught and released to disappear to avoid working for the Germans. We fitted them up with papers and hid them away somewhere. But Marchand never did that. He rejoined his comrades, seemed to redouble his efforts, and it's from then on that he should be judged. Clearly, they weren't using him for rank-and-file betrayals the way they used Bracony. I expect they saw him as a sleeper – someone who would rise in the Resistance and provide information on the leadership – the big stuff. That's why the SD and the Gestapo squabbled over who would have him. The Gestapo won.'

I was reminded of the Kaltenbrunner document of 1943, quoted in Henri Frenay's book. A confidential informant in *Combat's* Secret Army, it had said.

'As you may know,' Tallard was saying, 'André Marchand had become a member of the national leadership late in 1942.'

'Why has Bracony never been arrested?'

'We lost sight of him. There was a warrant out for years but he was never found.'

'And André Marchand?'

'He went on to do great things in the Resistance, as everyone knows. But he was also working for the Gestapo, as we now know.'

'What's your evidence for that?'

'Firstly, the girl confirmed the meeting in Barbie's office.'

'Is she still alive?'

'I don't know.'

'What is her name?'

'Anny Lecourt. I believe she worked as a secretary for Marchand for some years after the war.'

'Can you describe her?'

'As I say, very beautiful,' Reynal said. 'You know – a peach, classy. Black hair, fine figure, like I say, beautiful.'

'Any distinguishing features you can remember?'

'Well, she had splendid eyes. A kind of deep blue, almost violet. And she had a birthmark on her neck. She was self-conscious about it and always wore stuff like little scarves or high collars to hide it.'

Anny Lecourt: Anny Dupuy. Dark hair. Striking blue eyes. Postwar work for Marchand. I hoped my expression was noncommital.

'We have an affidavit from a man called Johannes Muller. He was Klaus Barbie's assistant. He was present at Marchand's interrogation.'

'An affidavit from an SD man isn't very strong stuff.'

'We can put you in touch with Muller,' Tallard said. 'He lives in Cologne. He'll talk to you. He has a thing about telling the truth – about lies being punished in hell. He also thinks he got an unjust twenty-year sentence.' He took a clip of papers from an inside pocket. 'Those are photocopies. You are welcome to keep them.'

I turned to the crux of the matter. 'Tell me,' I said, 'why you think Marchand became an agent after the war?'

Robert Tallard scratched his mop of ginger curls and stretched his spindly legs out before him. 'There are many facts,' he said. 'In the first place, the SD records from Lyon disappeared. They were the only major SD archives in the whole of France to be missing.'

'Who took them?' I knew but I put the question.

'The Americans. Their special units occupied the SD and Gestapo headquarters ahead of the local Resistance groups. When our people got there they found the filing cabinets empty. Barbie, as everyone knows now, signed on with the Americans. It would be natural enough for him to find other recruits for their intelligence services.'

'What else?'

'Bracony was tried *in absentia*. At the trial all mention by witnesses of André Marchand was ruled out of order by the presiding judge. This, in 1946, was highly irregular.'

'All this,' I said, 'really adds up to very little.'

'It is circumstantial,' Tallard agreed. 'Nevertheless, we believe Marchand was working for the Americans.'

'What if I conclude Marchand was working for the Soviets?'

'If you come to that conclusion, faulty as it is, and decide to say nothing publicly in order to preserve Anglo-French and indeed Anglo-Soviet relations, that will have no political effect for us one way or the other. If you allow the press to report that Marchand was a Russian agent, true or false, you will readily see that it will do more harm to his Party than to ours. What would be damaging to us would be a *Communist* minister who was a Russian agent. But a minister from any other party . . . ?' He shrugged and allowed himself a brief smile. 'But then, of course, he is more likely to have been an American agent. Such a revelation, of course, can in no way harm our Party.' It was neat stuff.

'Anything further?' I asked.

'I think not,' Tallard said.

'Thank you,' I said. We got up, shook hands, and I showed them out.

'Keep a dupe of the tape and log it,' I told the SO on the phone after they'd gone. 'I'll pick up the master later this week.'

CHAPTER 18

Boudin aux Pommes de Reinette

On the way to see Baum II I walked the length of the rue Etienne Marcel but I couldn't find Baum I's apartment. I located a 300-yard stretch between the rue Montorgueil and the rue de Turbigo which probably contained the building, but in my roughed-up condition I must have lost my powers of observation. I couldn't recall a single landmark among the shops and apartment entrances. I had had no reason at the time to look for landmarks.

I met Baum II at a *bistro* he'd chosen near the Châtelet. He ordered the *boudin aux pommes de reinette* for both of us. Then he pulled a notebook out of his pocket and consulted it. 'You were to check the rue Etienne Marcel,' he said.

'I did. It's a total blank. I must have been in shock.'

'Never mind, we'll return to it if necessary. I have two reliable men working on the rest of your story.'

'Have you got anything?'

'Let's take things in their proper order.' Baum tucked the red-checked napkin into his collar and attacked the *boudin*, which had just arrived. He took a mighty draught of the wine and pulled a handful of bread off the *baguette*. He ate like a good Frenchman.

'We have something,' he said between mouthfuls, 'on the Auto Ecole . . . Marceau.' The words came in short bursts, interspersed with the chewing and swallowing. 'They're well known to the police. The owner . . . Corsican named Panelli . . . plenty of form . . . bank jobs, extortion, stuff like that . . .

extensive connections in the *milieu*. Right man for a job like that doctored car of yours. God, this *boudin* is good.'

'It is,' I said.

'I eat here when I want to be undisturbed. Georges . . . an old mate of mine from the Service . . . complete discretion. Hey, Georges, we can use some more wine!' Georges, in his blue-striped bib and chef's cap, brought the wine himself and uncorked it. His wife sat at the till like a broody hen in her black silk, tight across big bosom and thighs.

'My friend Panmure,' Baum said, mopping at his mouth with the check napkin and tearing off more bread. 'Georges Dumay . . . outstanding cook. Not a bad operative either, in his day – ha, ha!'

Georges offered me an immense paw. 'English?'

'Yes.'

'I know the English. I was in London twice on personal security, first time with Big Charles and then with Pompidou. And back here I was on the detail which looked after your Winston Churchill on his last visit to Paris.'

'There's a great man,' Baum said, his mouth full.

'On that trip he was stewed all the time,' Georges said with a grin. 'Carried it magnificently. A great man all right.' And he retreated to the tiny kitchen behind the *zinc*.

'I had one of my men round to the stockbroker Roberton this morning,' Baum said. 'He passed himself off as police – financial section – checking your Brançon's taxable income . . . Came away with this list of share transactions.' He handed me a sheet of paper. 'Steady purchases over the years . . . Roberton said his client . . . good judge of the market . . . rarely went wrong . . . Is it what you want?'

'Exactly,' I said. 'Thanks.'

'I also spent an hour this morning with the Marchand file. Here, have some more of this *boudin*.' He piled it on my plate and helped himself to more pieces of the blood sausage and browned apple rings. 'Georges, the *boudin*'s as good as ever!'

Georges came back to the table. 'Next time I'll do it *au style*

Flamand,' he said. 'That's good too. I make a *marmelade* of the apples, with currants and sultanas, done to a rich bronze and the consistency of a good jam. It goes well with the *boudin*.'

Baum turned to me. 'Yes, I renewed acquaintance with the Marchand file. A file I've spent some unhappy hours with over the years.' He paused, took time eating. 'I have to tell you first of all that the file had been tampered with. Four documents are missing. I know that because we number them consecutively and keep an index pasted inside the folder. Two of my colleagues have access to the dossiers of Government personalities and one of those is the *patron*, our friend Wavre. It doesn't matter who broke up the file – he would be under orders from higher up, whoever he was. I don't recall exactly the contents of the missing sheets. They were all security reports on Marchand as he moved into various Government posts. They were dated 1949, 1951, 1958 and 1963, and must have been taken within the last month. You have certainly stirred up a hornets' nest.'

'So we're blocked on that one,' I said.

'No,' Baum said, 'not blocked . . . just a small delay. I always anticipated . . . something like this. As I said before, who can trust politicians . . . ? And our department heads up, perforce, to a succession of them . . . So I take my little precautions.' His conversation was again in conflict with the progress of his meal. 'Tonight I'll check . . . be able to talk tomorrow. But don't expect . . . anything . . . sensational.' He was wiping the last of the sauce from his plate with pieces of bread. 'What interests me most particularly,' he was saying, 'is your building, the false-Saussaies. My other man has started on that. I think we'll be hearing something by tomorrow. Then you must go out to look for eight-storey brick buildings with views of the Eiffel Tower.' He chuckled at the prospect.

'Now, what can *you* tell *me*?' The intelligent eyes twinkled almost mischievously as they looked straight into mine. Either it was a ploy to persuade me to be truthful, or he already knew something about the mayhem of the night before. Since I was the one who stood to gain most from mutual confidence, I decided to play it straight. I told him of the Algerian at the Dôme, the explosion, the car in Isabel's street afterwards.

'This man in the restaurant,' Baum said, 'would you be able to identify him?'

'With moustache and current hair style, yes. Without, probably not.'

'I'll show you some mug shots and also some surveillance shots. I expect they will lead us back to the boys at Luna.' Baum paused, picking delicately at his teeth with a wooden toothpick, his hand cupped politely round his mouth. 'What we need, of course, is to trace backwards from Luna, from the Auto Ecole Marceau, back to whoever contracted with them on your account. We need, in short, to lean on them.'

'I need a day in Germany and one in London,' I said. 'How would it be if I did that in the next forty-eight hours?'

'About right,' Baum said. 'It would give me time to pinpoint the building, as far as we can. And to make a few more enquiries in the North African community.'

A splendid Roquefort had arrived and was living up to its promise.

'Don't come back in through Charles de Gaulle or Orly,' Baum was saying. 'I'd prefer you to come in by road from Belgium on the N365. It crosses the frontier at Erguelines. I can arrange for you to have no trouble there.' He wrote something in his notebook.

'Tell me,' I said, 'can Albert Chavan be useful in all this? You know Artunian put me on to him.'

'I was a little surprised,' Baum said. 'He's a great character, a useful route into the *milieu*. But in a matter like this, even your own grandmother is scarcely to be trusted.'

'Do you distrust him?'

'I distrust everyone. I distrust you. It's the habit of a lifetime.'

'That's no answer.'

'I think Albert Chavan can be useful. As I say, he knows

everyone in the *milieu*. Both sides respect him. You'll always find an intermediary like that between the law and the underworld. But don't forget that above all, he's a crooked businessman nowadays. He does things, ultimately, for money like any Mafioso. And if the other side feels like spending . . .' He shrugged. 'Also remember that's where they jumped you. So someone there is likely to tip them off if you go back.'

I thought of the sad-sack North African bouncer in his oversized trench coat and Chavan's tame hoodlums with their swagger, their silence and plastered hair. There was something about the hair . . .

Baum interrupted my thoughts. 'By the way, who is Brançon?'

'I'll tell you that,' I said, 'when I get back.'

'And another thing,' Baum said. 'We ran a check on Jules Roberton himself. Just routine.'

'Find anything?'

'Not much really. But just in case you're interested at all, you might as well have his political history. In the *Jeunesses Communistes* at his *lycée* in Grenoble; a member of a Trotskyist cell at the Sorbonne; and now in an extreme right-wing nationalist group, *Action de la France*. An odd political progression, that, and pretty rapid for a man still in his thirties.'

'Anything else on him?'

'Nothing else. But don't forget to tell me who his friend Brançon is.'

The first newspapers to reach the street with coverage of the explosion were that afternoon's *France Soir* and *Le Monde*. To my relief, the story didn't make page one in either of them. Good! I'd landed Isabel in enough trouble without the benefit of a French press campaign. Fortunately, they hadn't got hold of the Embassy angle yet. In both cases, a near-identical account spoke of an explosion, cause unknown, with no casualties.

'Do you *have* to file it?' I asked Arthur later that afternoon in the bar of the Scribe.

'I do. The UP office will file because Isabel's British and the police are now saying it's *plastique* and they're treating it as attempted murder. They had an inspector questioning Isabel for most of the morning. So how can I not file?'

'Keep it low key,' I said. 'She'll be in all kinds of trouble.'

'Do my best,' Arthur said, 'but I'll look like a fool tomorrow. If it's a thin day for news this will get onto most of the front pages on both sides of the Channel.'

'Oh, Christ,' I said. 'It's all we need.'

'How did it go with Robert Tallard?' Arthur asked, trying to change the subject.

'Useful,' I said. 'They've given me details of a man in Cologne who really does interest me.'

'When are you off then?'

'Tomorrow. Cologne first, then London. A couple of days.'

'What did you make of Tallard and his motives?'

'Your friend Tallard has no motives. "Our Party" has motives. It also has views, requirements, knowledge, objectives, responsibilities and I daresay a preference for stewed figs. These characters simply don't *exist* in their own right. They're extensions of the will of "the Party". It's weird.'

Later Isabel rescued my belongings from the debris and brought them to me at the rather seedy hotel I'd found on the Left Bank. There was a good deal of dust in my shaving tackle.

'I shan't stay,' she said. 'My friend is expecting me. I've moved in with her till my lodging problems are sorted out. Take care.'

We kissed rather tenderly and she was gone.

I turned to Tallard's document. There was a one-page biography of Johannes Muller, a three-page account of his trial, including a lot of detail on his singularly repellent maltreatment of prisoners, and some hints on how to handle him: 'If he is evasive, treat him harshly. We have found that he responds. He has two obsessions: his religion and his belief that he is the victim of a miscarriage of justice. You may present yourself as coming from Reynal. You could suggest a "deal" whereby you would intercede for him at the International Court of Justice. Naturally, you would in fact do no such thing.'

I pondered all this for a while. Then I phoned Arthur. Later he called me back with what I wanted: a list of the names of the members of the International Court of Justice at The Hague.

CHAPTER 19

Johannes Muller

From my hotel in Cologne I called the Berlin Station Officer and asked him to call me back on a safe line. A half hour later I was telling him what interested me at Zehlendorf* and told him to call me with the information that evening. Cologne was blanketed in early snow – the spires of the cathedral sticking into the grey December air like two black fingers through a white counterpane. The trams clanged and clattered about the place and pedestrians shuffled cautiously on the compacted snow.

There were few taxis about. The doorman blew ineffectually on his whistle to ensure that when something turned up he'd get a suitable reward for the event. An erect little man with a military bearing came out of the hotel and waited beside me. I was mildly struck by the coincidence: he had been a couple of rows back on the Lufthansa flight from Paris. I nodded, but he showed no sign of recognising me. Two taxis pulled up almost together and deposited their fares. The doorman held the door of the first one, waving me in as if he had towed the thing there for my use.

'Where are you going?' he asked, his other hand extended receptively. I told him.

* The Nazi Document Centre in the Berlin suburb of Zehlendorf contains the records of the 10.7 million members of Hitler's National Socialist Party, the files on 600,000 SS officers and on the membership of the SA, and many other Third Reich documents from within Germany and from the occupied countries. It is administered the US State Department and funded by the West German Government. It handles close to 50,000 information requests a year.

'Leopoldstrasse thirty-four, *schnell!*' he barked at the taxi driver and slammed the door on me. The military man stood on the kerb, waiting to be shown into the next taxi. As my vehicle pulled away, I heard the door of the next one slam in turn. Then I switched my mind to the matter in hand. I decided to exercise my rusty German on the driver.

'What's the area we're going to like?'

'Lousy. Worst part of Cologne. Lot of street crime. Some taxis wouldn't take you. What's your business there?'

'I have a man to see.'

We had passed the vast complex of the Messe Halle exhibition centre and were travelling past the dirty brick of factory walls and the yellow lights of mean food shops. The side streets were lined with dismal apartment blocks. There were few people about. Leopoldstrasse 34 proved to be a block like the others. Dark red brick, square windows, steeply pitched roof designed to shed the snow. Outside on the pavement the snow barely covered a line of dustbins, a broken bicycle wheel, a pile of rags and waste paper. Two youths in check donkey jackets stood at the door, sulking at the weather or at life itself.

I asked the likeliest of the youths: 'Does Johannes Muller live here?'

He looked at me without interest. *'Ich weisse nicht.'*

I asked his companion: 'Do you know?'

'Der Alte im dritten Stock hinten.' They returned to their gloomy survey of the street.

Inside I plunged straight into murk and the stench of poverty – different in every country but always unmistakable. Here it was the eternal German cabbage, boiling behind doors, floor by floor. Cabbage and rotting refuse, and urine, cats and disinfectant. Yet the hall and stairs were newly scrubbed. God alone knew what decay lay hidden behind the battered apartment doors. On the third floor I counted four doors. There were no name plates. I chose one which led to the back of the building. It had no bell or knocker. I banged with my fist. There was shuffling on the other side, then silence. Someone had come to the door and lacked the courage, the energy perhaps, to answer it. I banged again. This time there was a scratching sound on the door and then the metallic grind of a bolt disengaging from its socket. The door opened two inches releasing a geriatric odour of sweat and stale bedclothes. I caught the outline of a head of white hair, scarcely more than four feet from the floor. The tiny creature peered at me, saying nothing. Its sex was uncertain.

'Does Herr Muller live here?'

'Neben an.'

The door slammed shut and the bolt ground back home. I banged on the next door and footsteps sounded on the floorboards within.

'Wer ist da?' It was an old man's voice, cracked and hoarse.

'I have come to see you, Herr Muller.'

'Warum?'

'About your case.'

'Wer sind sie?'

'Reynal sent me.'

There was a pause. Then the latch of the door was pulled back and I was beckoned into the near-darkness of a small hall. The front door closed behind me and Muller opened a further door. '*Kommen sie herein*,' he said, leading the way.

The room was threadbare but clean. Warm air came from a round enamel stove in one corner but not enough to make the place comfortable. Next to it was a narrow bed. Opposite stood a dresser with a gas ring and a few pots and plates. A big square table in the centre of the room was maybe a foot deep in papers, including folders and files of various colours and legal documents trailing tape. A small space had been cleared and here Johannes Muller had been writing, a fat reference work lying open next to the lined paper half covered in minute script. A brass crucifix lay on the open book, holding the pages back. He nodded me to one of the hard-backed kitchen chairs and took another for himself on the far side of the table.

'*Ja?*' the old-man's voice was querulous. He sat stiff on his chair, the watery blue eyes staring distrustfully from the deep sockets, desiccated skin stretched tight over the hairless skull and face. He wore an old grey cardigan, patched with leather at the cuffs and elbows, over an equally old and grey collarless shirt, held at the neckband with a bone stud.

'Reynal gave me your address. He told me about your campaign. I also am interested in Klaus Barbie.'

'Justice must be done. The Book says "an eye for an eye". The truth must be told.'

'I am interested in the truth.'

'At my trial they never heard the truth. I was the scapegoat because Barbie had friends in high places.'

'Reynal told me. He also showed me your affidavit on the Marchand case.'

'How does a man like Barbie disappear – poof, like that – off the face of the earth?' The harsh voice carried on, ignoring me, serving the old man's fixed idea. 'How does he do that without friends, without connivance? He doesn't! No one could. I was there when the Americans came and I can tell you.'

'Yes, yes, we all know that now.'

The voice took on the hectoring tone that goes with an over-rehearsed speech. The old man had lived with his private version of the events of the war for over thirty years and was word perfect in his obsession. 'I say nothing – Americans, French, British, I know nothing. But Barbie had money, plenty of money. He knew how to turn his wartime duties into cash. And with money, you can make a fool of justice. Our Lord drove the moneylenders from the temple. Consider that! Consider why He had to do it!'

For punctuation, he slapped a mottled hand onto the pile of documents before him on the table. I couldn't pull my gaze back from the hand to the watery eyes. The hands of torturers are exactly the same as the hands of surgeons and poets. Perhaps the eyes differ.

'Do you remember André Marchand?'

He was not to be deterred. 'I served twenty years. I was not guilty. I acted under orders, as any man must in wartime – like your British tommies in Ireland and the GIs in Vietnam. Where is the difference, eh? I served twenty years because they decided not to find Barbie. *I served his sentence.* My trial was illegal under the Geneva Convention and my sentence was therefore a crime against humanity.'

I looked at the hand, almost devoid of flesh, hitting at the documents.

'I would like to talk to you about the Marchand and Bracony cases.'

The hand came up in a gesture of impatience, waving me aside. 'I am an old man. I am almost eighty. I have survived twenty years of a harsh, inhuman prison regime in maximum security only because my faith has sustained me. My appeal has been with the International Court of Justice at The Hague since March of last year. I have their acknowledgment – I have correspondence here.' He reached for a thin buff folder, proof that the official world outside had taken cognisance of Johannes Muller, torturer, some of whose victims had managed ridiculously to survive. Proof that lawyers and officials were studying his legal arguments, his citations of protocol, statute and precedent, solemnly deciding whether Europe had perhaps got a little impatient, a little rough with the Johannes Mullers.

'Reynal thought I might help your case forward at The Hague,' I said. 'I have a connection with the Vice-President of the Court.'

'Deesman?' He was as well informed as I was.

'Yes, Hugo Deesman. But in return, I need help from you.'

Now he was listening and the eyes seemed to focus properly on me for the first time.

'What is your connection with Deesman?'

'He adjudicated in a case I was involved in a few years ago. I prepared submissions and gave evidence.'

'A human rights case?'

'No, a technical matter between governments. We became quite friendly, Deesman and I.'

The pale eyes were on me, distrust and hope chasing each other.

'How do I know you aren't lying?'

'You cannot know. You have to trust me. Otherwise we can't do business.'

There was a long pause. 'How long have you known Reynal?'

'A short time,' I said. 'How long have you known him?'

'He first came to me in November of last year. I don't know how he found me. He wouldn't say.'

Another pause. 'Well, Muller,' I said. 'Do we do business?'

The old man shrugged. 'I have nothing left to lose. Tell me what you want.'

'I have seen your affidavit on the Marchand case,' I said. 'Do you remember it?'

'Of course I remember it. Barbie had this reputation for never forgetting a face or a fact. It's what made him deadly in interrogation. But actually he had a lousy memory. It was always my memory that he used. That is why I attended interrogations. And you should know that unlike the Gestapo, the Sicherheitsdienst section of the Abwehr did not use violent methods in interrogation. It was an honourable service of the Reich.'

The old man was using a general truth to cover the monstrous exception of the Lyon SD and no doubt quite a few others. I did not let myself be drawn. 'You swore in your affidavit that you were controlling Marchand from early in 1943, when he fell into your hands.'

'Correct.'

'If he belonged to the Abwehr, to you, how did the Gestapo get into the act?'

'You must understand, Abwehr officers considered the Gestapo scum, the dregs of society. But Barbie was a strong National Socialist, with a four-digit Party card. That dates his membership card to the early days. He did not share our view of Gestapo personnel and later he strongly favoured the arrest of our chief, the Admiral. So when the high-ups at Gestapo headquarters in Paris heard of Marchand's arrest and decided to take him over, Barbie agreed. You must remember that by 1943 the Gestapo had pretty well absorbed our functions.'

'What happened then?'

'SS General Oberg himself came down from Paris and a meeting with Marchand was arranged. Dr Knochen, the chief of the Gestapo in France, was there too.'

'Do you know of the Kaltenbrunner report of May 1943?'

'Yes. Barbie was shown part of it and he told me about it.'

'Do you know that it mentioned an informant high up in the Secret Army?'

'Yes. All the senior men in Paris believed it was Marchand. They didn't have anyone else in *Combat* at that level.'

'What was Marchand's cryptonym?'

'*Fledermaus.* Barbie and I gave it to him. Barbie liked Strauss, Lehǎr, that sort of music. So we gave him *Fledermaus*. It was appropriate: a bat works in the dark.' The old man's voice cracked in a hoarse cackle but the face did not laugh.

'Would the facts of Marchand's arrest be in your archives in Lyon?'

'Of course. In exact detail. It was my responsibility. The files were accurate.' He was proud of his competence.

'Where are the files?'

'How should I know? They disappeared.'

'And you didn't keep copies of a few choice items like this – you know, insurance for the future?'

The old man snorted. 'I didn't. But Barbie did. Perhaps it's *because* he kept copies that no one was interested in finding him for all those years.'

'Now the case of Bracony. Do you confirm that he was turned by Barbie?'

'By me. And I never laid a finger on him.' He was proud of the achievement.

'Muller, you're a bloody fool!' I barked it out in the most colloquial German I could muster. *'Sie sind ein Vollidiot!'*

The old man stiffened and began to rise from his chair.

'Sit down!' I yelled at him.

'What is this? Why am I a fool? Why do you shout?'

'You expect me to speak for you at The Hague, and in return you give me all this crap. You don't know where the files are. You don't know what Barbie did with them. You don't know this. You never knew that. Do you take me for an idiot, eh, Muller? D'you think I don't realise every Nazi swine like you pleads lost files?'

He sat silent, a hand plucking at a sleeve of his cardigan. A twitch had developed in the nerve at the corner of his left eye. I pressed on. 'You're a liar, Muller, and the Lord God will punish you. You expect help and all you give in return is shit – stuff I know already.' I got up and started buttoning my coat.

'Wait a minute, wait a minute,' Muller said. 'No need to get angry. I'm an old man. Maybe my memory isn't always as good as it used to be. Sit, sit. What was it that you wanted? Let's see what we can work out together, you and I.'

'One can't do business with shit like you, Muller. You've learned nothing. You can't drop the habits of a lifetime.'

'Maybe, maybe. We are all sinners. I pray, but I am a weak sinner.' The voice trembled, muttered.

'Never mind your bloody sins, let's hear the facts!' and I brought my fist down on the table. The tic was now continuous and the watery eyes refused to meet mine.

'Please,' he said, 'please, I am an old man, nearly eighty, I cannot deal with people's anger after the years of prison.'

'You make me sick,' I said.

The silence was a long one. 'Please,' he said again, 'let us try once more. I need your help at The Hague. They no longer answer my letters, you see. There's been silence for four months. I will do what is necessary to earn your help. If Reynal sent you, I trust you.'

'Now then,' I said, 'let's start again. What did you keep from the files?'

'Not much. Very little. I . . .'

'Answer my question, damn you! And if I decide you're lying I'll tear the bloody room apart to find the stuff myself.'

'I kept micros of some documents. I realise it was against regulations. I shouldn't have done it.'

'Which documents?'

'Marchand's signed statement. And Bracony's. The signatures were our hold on them.'

'What else?'

A slight hesitation. A wave of the skinny hand. 'Come on,' I barked at him. 'I warn you, Muller, I'm not known for my patience with idiots.'

'No, no. I was about to say . . . I, I also kept . . . just a small thing, you know, from the last days before the defeat . . . a micro of a Minute from Paris. A copy of a report in Marchand's hand on certain London plans for the attack on Paris.'

'What else?'

'I swear, nothing else.'

'Why didn't you use any of this?'

'I tried. It was made clear to me at my trial that the prosecutor would demand the death penalty – and would get it – if I incriminated anyone else.'

'Give me the stuff.'

Muller got up stiffly and moved out of the room. I glanced at the papers on the table. They all related to his trial and the appeal to The Hague. He was gone for five minutes and I guessed he was extracting what I wanted from all the microfilm he must have taken out of France with him and stashed away through his years in prison. When he came back he was carrying three pieces of 35-mm film. They were blank save for a dot about a millimetre square in the centre of each and a mark in ink in a corner. I took them.

'If you're fooling me, Muller,' I said, 'I'll come back here and shove your head into that stove.'

'You're too hard with me,' he said. 'You are so hostile yet you claim you will help me. I don't understand it.'

'Then you're a fool,' I told him. 'I'm not helping you, I'm

closing a deal with you. In return for this stuff I'm interceding for you with Justice Deesman. That's all. As far as I'm concerned, you can go to hell, affidavits, crucifix and all.'

'I understand.' The tic was subsiding. He had returned to his seat and was searching through a pile of documents. 'Here,' he said, 'you must take this. A copy of my submission to the Court. Please read it before you see Justice Deesman. I am a victim, you understand. I did nothing wrong . . . just my duty, like any man . . . there were lies about me, you understand . . . it is all in there. Read it, please.'

I got up. 'I'll be in touch,' I said.

He offered the fleshless, mottled hand. I had no wish to take it. I walked past him, out and down the stone stairs. Outside the building I threw the heavy folder into the first of the dustbins and walked carefully towards the main road, where I could hear trams. It was snowing hard and the familiar smell of the Ruhr, the smell of soft coal, was carried on the freezing air. As I turned the corner and made for the nearest tram stop, I thought I saw a short, erect figure standing in the doorway of an ironmonger's shop on the far side of the street. I couldn't be sure.

The Berlin Station Officer's call came through at eight.

'I had a dekko,' he said. He was that type.

'Yes?'

'No dice – Johnnie in charge was good as gold but he couldn't oblige.'

'Nothing?'

'Zero. *Rien-du-tout.* All taken out, old sport.'

'Did he say when?'

'That's what's a bit rum. He looked up the register for me. Nice feller, like I said. And the stuff was signed out last week. Tuesday, eleven ack emma if you want to be precise.'

'Who signed for it?'

'One Walter Bailey, giving US Army HQ as his address.'

'Oh,' I said.

'What was that, old sport?'

'Nothing.'

'Well, as I say, it was decidedly rum. Not only because the stuff had gone only last week, but because people usually just copy what's there. They've got a couple of photocopiers handy. Only this Johnnie had taken the originals. It appears US Army can do that with a suitably signed chit.'

'And Walter Bailey had a suitably signed chit.'

'Could assume that, old boy. Place is stuffed with Yanks and Krauts. You're not going to get past that lot without a suitably signed chit.'

'I suppose not. You wouldn't know who signed it?'

'Thought of that, but again, no dice. It must have satisfied the duty officer at the time. He didn't make a note of it.'

'All right, thanks.'

'Any time. Glad to help.'

It looked as if Hank Munthe or someone like him was getting competitive. Why else would they take the original dossiers on Barbie and Johannes Muller?

Later I went downstairs for a coffee and a hamburger. My military friend was studying magazines at the paper stand in the hall. He did not look up as I passed him, but a few moments later in the coffee shop, as I turned to summon a reluctant waiter, I saw him sitting alone behind me. He had bought a copy of *Paris Match* and seemed to be absorbed in it.

Next morning at the airport he was nowhere to be seen.

CHAPTER 20

Marisat, Anik & Molniya

I sat myself down in Harry's cubbyhole at the end of the corridor and let my eyes wander over his pinups. Then I lit a cigarette and waited. Harry was not above creating a bit of suspense.

'What we 'ave 'ere,' he said with deliberate slowness and laying on the cockney, 'is in fact amazin'. Very odd. Oddest thing I ever come across.' He shuffled papers among the mess on the desk and spread out, fanwise, the blowups of the photos he'd taken at Conques. He'd had some sections magnified and areas had been ringed in red felt-tip. On one side of the desk stood the components he'd brought back. They'd been broken down into their various parts. He pulled to the top of the pile a picture of the transmitter. 'That,' he said, 'is a mobile radio transmitter with a one-and-a-half-metre dish antenna, designed to send radio signals via satellite to distant points.'

'So you said at Conques.'

'It transmits, for your information, in the C-band, which is SHF or super-high frequency to you. Your actual frequency is in the four to six GigaHertz range.'

'Does this technical stuff matter?'

'It matters if you want to know what this job was there for, what its likely target was and who put it there. Its technical nature governs the tasks it can perform.' Harry counted off his points on his fingers. 'One, the dish gives you narrow-beam capability – mebbe a beam of around thirty degrees arc. And narrow beam gives you security, since no one can steal your signal unless he's operating within the beam. And of course, if you direct your beam where you want it, 'e can't very well be, can 'e?'

'I've got that.'

'Two, you'll be transmitting like I said in the C-band at four to six GigaHertz because you need to send your signal over a long distance with top-class quality and minimum interference. Put that together with the nature of your dish and you've only one answer: transmission via a communication satellite, like I said.'

'Got that too,' I said.

'Three, with equipment like this you'd never be able to locate one of your common or garden satellites in low orbit, of which there's bloody hundreds up there now. It'd be over and gone before you'd 'ad a chance to give it the time of day. Couldn't never lock on to it, see? Conclusion: this lad was serving a geostationary satellite in synchronous orbit a bit over twenty-two thousand miles up. They're the ones that stay put.'

'Got that too,' I said.

'Now look here at this picture,' Harry said. He pushed across the desk a close-up of what looked like a tape deck built into the body of the transmitter. 'What do you reckon that is?'

'A tape deck,' I said.

'Too bloody right,' Harry said gleefully. He was warming to his subject. 'And that gives me me fourth point. This transmitter was designed to take an input of audio-frequency signals – that is, voice on tape – and from other stuff I've got here I've established that it shifted the input to radio frequencies in the usual way for this class of operation. Then they're ready for transmission, right?'

He showed me a picture, marked in red, of what looked like a hi-fi tuner-amplifier without its casing.

'Now, it would work like this, see. Your tape, recorded at normal speed in any tape recorder, would feed through here at a terrific lick, to save transmitting time and power and to limit your time on the air so that interception's harder, and the transmitter would be squirting the fast signal on this narrow beam straight at the satellite.'

'All right,' I said, 'and what can you conclude about the satellite itself and what it does with the stuff coming up to it?'

'Well, let's make a couple of assumptions,' Harry said. 'Let's assume first that the high security of the system so far lets 'em send up their signals *en clair* – speeded up, like I said, but no messing about with hours of encoding and all that jazz. Then let's suppose a cypher-codifier capability in the satellite itself which will pick up your *en clair* signals and do two things with 'em. First, translate 'em into a digital or analogue code of your choice – that's numbers and intervals in place of impulses which correspond to the human voice or the bleedin' "Marseillaise" or whatever they're sending up. Second, store the signals in the computer memory aboard the satellite. Not transmit 'em, right, but store 'em.'

'Fair assumptions,' I said, 'if you're telling me that's what this type of satellite can do.'

'It can,' Harry said. 'Sounds clever but there's nothing to it. And now I'll tell you *why* you want your message first coded and then stored.' Harry paused, enjoying the way he was revealing layers of his story like the seven veils.

'Do that, Harry,' I said.

'Well, you see, whereas your signal *up* to your satellite is on a narrow beam and therefore safe, see, your retransmission from satellite to ground station can't be a beam job, not in the present state of the art, according to mates of mine who know about these matters. Which means the satellite will be spilling your message all over the district once it starts transmitting. So that you need coding, see, for security. And then your second level of security comes when you decide you want to pick your message out of the satellite's memory store. 'Cos to get at it, you need to interrogate the bugger by means of a command signal, and only that command will make him spew out what he's got on board. So that anyone eavesdropping has two hurdles to get over: he needs to know the command signal, then he needs to decode what he picks up. Not easy, that. Not easy at all.'

'Who made the equipment?' I asked.

'Now here, Guv, is where your magical mystery tour starts. As you know, we didn't find name plates on the job itself. Well now, I've had the components and sub-assemblies looked at, and there's a good thirty serial numbers that have been filed off. Not only that, but they've been careful to dig deep enough into the metal to rout out the impacted areas which might have shown up some of the numerals on the electron equipment they have nowadays. A very thorough bit of work. So we got no joy there.'

'So what did you do?'

'I showed the pictures and a description of the transmitter to a few mates of mine. Asked 'em who, in their judgment, made the job. Whether they've seen anything like it in the journals, the military specs, NASA* reports, bulletins from the makers such as TRW in California or Hughes Aircraft, or in the stuff the intelligence people cobble together on the Russkies.'

'Are these friends of yours people who really know?'

'They are,' Harry said. 'There's a boffin at the RSRE** who helped develop the SGT4 Compack man-portable terminal. That was done with Marconi Space and Defence Systems, and I've got a mate there too. Then I spent a quid or two of HMG's cash on a call to a feller in the Canadian Signals. They worked with the Yanks on NORAD's*** Space Detection and Tracking System. Very knowledgable, he is. And I know a Yank whose name's nobody's business, who can get at the records in Washington and a few other places any time I want. So they're people who know, right?'

'And what do they say?'

'All say the same thing. First, the style of the assemblies, the handwriting if you care to put it that way, is unmistakable. It's

* National Aeronautical and Space Administration.
** Royal Signals and Radar Establishment of the Ministry of Defence.
*** North America Defense System.

American. The finish, the standard of circuitry, the little technical tricks and so on – all American. Nothing like what the Russkies do.'

Harry paused, enjoying the effect he was making. I said nothing.

'Then the overall design is clearly a development of the SGT4. My pal at the RSRE says a junior draughtsman and a couple of chargehands could have taken the SGT4 to this stage in six months, and that's topside. So you see, what we have 'ere, Guv, is a bit of flamin' Yank equipment.'

'Could it have been stolen?'

'Well, anything *can* be nicked. But if it was nicked, why didn't we ever hear about it on the Joint Committee?'

'Do they sell this kind of stuff to other countries?'

'Mebbe, I don't know.'

'What about the Germans in OTRAG?'

'Far as anyone knows, they're only working on rocketry – how to deliver payloads into space cheap for third-world governments with more money than sense. No one's ever accused 'em of working on telemetry and radio.'

'Was this transmitter beamed to one of the existing multipurpose satellites, sharing it with other civilian or military transmitters? Or was it beamed to a satellite of its own?'

Harry fished into the papers on his desk and pulled out a photostat. It showed a sketch of the globe with an elipse drawn round it. There were dots drawn at irregular intervals along the eliptical line. Each dot had been named: Marisat 3, Intelsat IV F1, Cosmos 775, Anik 1, 2 and 3, Molniya 1S and so on. There were thirty-nine of these labelled dots.

'This,' said Harry, 'is a sketch of your most valuable bit of real estate in the world, except that it's over twenty-two thousand miles up. It shows what's up in geostationary orbit. Each dot's a satellite, see? To avoid interference with each other's signals, they have to be four degrees apart, and their positioning depends on the origin and destination of the signals. So that if you wanted to slot in another one over the USA to handle signals between, say, Ottawa and Washington, you'd be hard put to do it because there's hardly any space left there. Whereas you'd find a bit of room over the Atlantic, say, or further round over the Pacific. In all, there's twenty-seven payloads in deep space belonging to the Yanks right now, twenty-five for the Russkies and two for the Krauts. They're not all shown on this particular diagram but you get the idea.'

'And all of them are known, plotted, recorded regularly?'

'Right. Watched and plotted by the Yanks at the NORAD Space Center at Cheyenne Mountain, Colorado, and by the other side wherever it is they have their control centre.'

'And their purpose is known to both sides?'

'Sure. Most of it's for commercial communications and scientific research, anyway.'

'But if the Conques transmitter was working to its own satellite, then that satellite has to be up there somewhere, *not* on the published records and tracking reports.'

'Right.'

'And it must be known to *both* sides. One side couldn't own it without the other knowing. So if we suppose it's an American job, we have to assume that the Americans are not reporting its existence, and for some reason of their own the Russians aren't either?'

'Yes, well, you see, the Russkies have never put out reports on satellites, their own or anyone else's, so you wouldn't never get *confirmation* from them that they'd spotted it. But spot it they certainly have.'

'Whereas, if it's a Russian satellite, the Americans would certainly keep an eye on it and publish their data?'

'Right again. They always publish, bless 'em.'

'But it would be true to say that whoever owns it, the other side has no means of knowing what it's actually *doing*?'

'Well, they can guess from the weight and orbit, and they can use intelligence methods. But the satellite itself won't tell 'em nothing.'

'Could the Ministry of Defence locate and track it?'

'Fylingdales has the capability but they're really part of the Ballistic Missile Early Warning System and I can't see the nobs at NATO letting 'em get on to much else. We usually rely on the Cheyenne digests. No point in doing the job twice.'

'Why should the transmitter be working to its own satellite, anyway?'

'Security, Guv. If they was using a channel on one of the known satellites there'd be no security at the receiving end. So what'd be the point of shoving a transmitter like this into an awkward bloody place in the French mountains?'

'All of which shows you how to find out who Bracony was talking to,' I said.

Harry frowned. 'You mean search the launching and tracking records?'

'That's right.'

'Christ! I'll need help.'

'You can have George Roberts and his ferrets for a week.'

'Okay,' Harry said with a deep sigh. 'I know what to do.'

As I got up to go, Harry let out a yelp. 'Hell, I nearly forgot. There was another thing and I don't know if it's significant or not.' He was shuffling the prints, found the one he wanted and threw it on top of the pile.

'That's a shot of the tape deck in the transmitter,' he said. 'It's been modified. You wouldn't know it but you can take my word for it. See the pair of spindles there? They take the tape spools for transmission, right?'

'If you say so.'

'But look over 'ere. What do you see?'

'Looks like another pair of spindles.'

'Right. And they have to be there to take a second tape cassette. A recording tape, see? So while your original tape is feeding its signals into the gut of the transmitter, it can also be feeding the second cassette. Making a dupe, in fact. So whoever was transmitting could also take a copy for 'is own purposes. Mebbe he had to return the original each time and wanted a copy for his private collection.'

'Maybe, except that there were no recorded tapes in the house.'

'Well, that's your problem, Guv, not mine,' Harry said. 'I'll be getting on with the rest of it.'

Pabjoy was absent. You could always feel his absence from the office: people made jokes about him and took tiny liberties with their lunch hour.

'Where is he?' I asked Penny.

'I booked him to Stockholm, but it doesn't really tell you anything.'

'When is he back?'

'He didn't say, but all the signs point to one of his wilder trips.'

'Explain, please.'

'Well, I can always tell when it's one of those. He calls for all his passports from the safe and fusses for hours over which one to take. Then he fusses some more over his appointments diary. He'll book a three-day trip somewhere and clear his diary for two weeks ahead. Then he leaves elaborate instructions about not contacting him. And a couple of months later his credit cards tend to give the game away. He's not really your most security-minded person, you know.'

'Anyway, if he does get back in the measurable future, tell him I've seen Harry and we should have something comprehensive for him in a week.'

'Will do.'

I caught my flight to Brussels later that afternoon.

CHAPTER 21

6 Rue Bezout

At the Hertz desk at Brussels airport I picked up a car and settled to the long journey south. I stopped for a *gaufre* and some coffee at Nivelles, and pushed on down the motorway to Charleroi. Then it got complicated because I had to cross the frontier where Baum had told me to, and that meant wrestling the car over ice on the lousy Belgian secondary roads to reach the frontier south of Merbes-le-Château. There was nothing immediately ahead of me at the barrier, so that the pallid youth in his creaseless uniform had me all to himself. He sauntered over from the hut on the French side and thrust out a hand. *'Vos papiers.'*

He didn't look at me at all until he had my passport open at the page with the mug shot stuck to it. Then he stared shrewdly from under the peak of his cap like he'd seen them do it on the movies. He flipped through the rest of the passport and paused for a quiet read at the page carrying an Iraqi visa. I wished it wasn't in there: too exotic and, being in Arabic script, too challenging for a young man like this. He wandered right round the car and back to my window.

'Any foreign currency?'

'About four hundred Belgian francs.'

'Where are you going?'

'Paris.'

'The purpose of your journey.' He said it the way the French police say it: not as a question so much as a statement of what one is about to tell them. Asking a question implies weakness:

the questioner wants something he hasn't got. Making a statement, on the other hand, implies superiority: *you* will now tell me what I require to know. These random philosophical thoughts made their way unbidden through my mind as I waited for the young man to decide whether he would call out the guard. If this was Baum's way of getting me in unnoticed, I fancied I'd have been better advised to get myself processed like anyone else at Charles de Gaulle.

'Business,' I said.

Suddenly he got bored. '*Passez*,' he said without looking at me. It was the way they waved them through at Warner Brothers.

I reached Paris stiff and weary in mid-afternoon and booked in at the same hotel. It was in the rue de Fleurus, near the Luxembourg. I called Isabel from a *tabac* down the street. We arranged to meet for dinner. I found a kiosk and bought all the newspapers I could find. Back in my room I settled to a miserable read.

The lads had made a meal of Isabel's *plastique*. As Arthur feared, it had been a thin news day and Isabel was there, looking lovely, on most of the front pages. She had played dumb. No, she had *no* idea who could have done such a boring thing. No, she hadn't an enemy in the world. No, she didn't *have* a lover. No, really, it was an awful bore but she hadn't. Really.

I lay on the bed and slept for an hour. When I awoke it was time to meet Isabel. Over dinner, I told her about Muller. 'The microfilm should sew it up,' I said. 'He has to be the key. He's Tallard's main source. I don't think I've been fooled.'

When the coffee came Isabel said: 'I'd like to come up to your room in a minute and make love on your hotel bed.'

'Like a whore.'

'That's exactly it. I'm wearing stockings and I'll keep them on.'

Later, we did that, and everything else seemed very far away.

Baum came to my hotel next morning at ten. He had with him a red-faced young man whom he introduced as Jean. 'My assistant,' he said. 'You may talk freely.'

Jean was carrying a large briefcase. I sat them down on the two chairs and installed myself on the bed. The tiny room was crowded. Baum clicked his fingers in the direction of the briefcase and Jean extracted a buff envelope. Baum removed a clutch of photographs and handed them to me.

I looked. They were all North Africans – some hairy, some not; some in mug shots, some taken at street demonstrations. I studied them carefully and shook my head.

Baum sighed. 'Never mind. It would have been sheer luck anyway.' He shrugged. 'We have checked on the car in which you were abducted. The number is in the Ministry's series but hadn't been issued. So they were registration plates put together by someone who knew about such things.'

'That's two blanks this morning,' I said. 'Maybe it isn't our day.'

'Wait,' Baum said. 'Things get better.' He clicked his fingers again.

Jean extracted a folded map of Paris and a file from the briefcase. He spread the map on the bed and took a sheet of paper from the file. 'I think we have been able to make some progress,' he said. 'First, I obtained the train schedules from the headquarters of the Métro and I will return to that in a moment. Then, allowing for a margin of error in your judgment of your distance from the Eiffel Tower, I drew a circle with its centre on the Tower and a radius equivalent to just over one and a half kilometres, not one kilometre as you estimated. What interests us are those sections of the Métro lines which fall within the circle but no nearer to the Tower than, say, eight hundred metres. So I drew another circle with a radius of eight hundred metres, and it's the area between the two circles that we have to look at.'

He smoothed the map on the bed. 'I have assumed that in a basement you would probably hear the sound of passing trains within twenty-five metres on either side of a Métro line. For safety, I have increased that to thirty metres, so that we are interested in a band sixty metres wide along any Métro lines which fall between our two circles.'

'Which lines?' Baum asked.

'The traffic manager at the Métro headquarters at the quai Bercy was helpful and has good records. We excluded the Etoile-Nation line – that's line six – where train frequency is too low at that time of day, and also the line which runs above ground between our circles. It leaves us with Balard-Créteil, Sèvres-Montreuil and Auteuil-Gare d'Austerlitz. That's lines eight, nine and ten. I have shaded on the map a path sixty metres wide along the route of those three lines between our concentric circles. As you probably know, Monsieur, the Paris Métro lines all follow main roads, so we have in fact drawn a broad band along seven main thoroughfares in the seventh, eighth, ninth, fifteenth and sixteenth *arrondissements*, covering a distance of about four and a half kilometres in all. That is a manageable area for a rapid house-to-house operation.'

I looked closely at the map. The shaded bands were mostly on the left bank of the river to the south and east of the Eiffel Tower. There was also some shading in the exclusive residential areas of the 9th and 16th *arrondissements* north of the river. Even cut down to these areas, the search looked pretty daunting.

'Next,' Jean was saying, 'I eliminated those streets which run, broadly speaking, towards the Tower. I have therefore shaded in red all the streets running into our seven main roads and meeting this definition. There are forty-nine of them along the four kilometres or so we are concerned with. In our field work we will ignore those which have no through traffic, since you heard frequent cars around eight am.'

'I have a man who started this morning,' Baum said. 'He is doing it on foot, which is the only way in our Paris traffic conditions. Jean here will join him now.'

'We'll need the rest of today and tomorrow.' Jean collected his map and papers.

'Right, off you go. Good lad.' And Baum waved him out. Then he turned to me. His eyes were twinkling. 'How did you get on in Cologne?'

I had told him I was going to Germany. I hadn't mentioned Cologne. 'All right,' I said. 'Didn't the Major report to you?'

Baum looked puzzled for a moment. Then he burst out laughing, the bushy brows working up and down. 'He's not a Major,' he said, 'but I agree he looks like a military type.'

'Why are you having me tailed – and with such subtlety?'

'I'm keeping an eye on you because I think your life is still in danger and you do not take sufficient care of it. I am also interested to know what you were doing in Cologne in the midst of our pressing problems here in Paris. Who, for instance, lives at Leopoldstrasse thirty-four?'

'A man called Muller.'

'All Germans are called Muller.'

'Johannes Muller, of the Lyon SD under Barbie.'

'I never thought he was still alive.'

'Well, he is, and I saw him and he talked. And I have some microfilm which I invite you to view with me if you can suggest somewhere quiet with the necessary equipment.'

'We will go to the *Archives Nationales*,' Baum said briskly. 'I have my car downstairs. And on the way you can tell me about R. Brançon.'

As we drove north to cross the Seine by the pont Neuf I told Baum about Brançon, changing everything save his address – poste restante, Rodez – lest the stockbroker had already mentioned it to Baum's men. Brançon's name, I said, had been given to me by Andrew Pabjoy. So had the name of Roberton, the stockbroker. I had no idea where he'd got them. I didn't even know if they were connected with the Marchand enquiry. It was one of the problems with Pabjoy, I said. He pushed need-to-know to ridiculous lengths. A neurosis.

Baum watched the traffic and said nothing until we reached

the national archives. 'I hope,' he said flatly, as he pulled into a lucky parking space and switched off the ignition, 'that we have a relationship of mutual confidence.'

'We do,' I said.

At the enquiry desk he asked for the microfilm record of an Annexe to the Treaty of Rome. 'It will give us a viewer and a booth,' he said. When we were installed before the viewing console I pulled the three bits of film from my pocket and handed one marked J1 to Baum. We were confronted on the screen by the image of a sheet of paper with less than a hundred words written on it, followed by two signatures. Baum adjusted the focus and the writing acquired definition. The paper was the letterheading of the *Sicherheitsdienst* Section IV of the Abwehr in Lyon.

I, André Marchand, acknowledge my co-operation with the services of the Third Reich in maintaining law and order in the occupied territory of France and in identifying and bringing to justice agents of the London Gaullists and other illegal and terrorist organisations.

Signed without duress and of my own free will on this 19 January, 1943 at 1600 hrs in the office of the Abwehr.

André Marchand
Klaus Barbie (witness)

Baum grunted. 'I know that handwriting and the signature. It looks genuine. Let's see the other.'

The second microfilm, marked J2, showed a similar declaration by Raoul Bracony. The third was the memo from Gestapo headquarters in Paris. It gave the text of a secret communiqué from General Leclerc, commanding the French army with the Allied invasion forces, to the Resistance leadership within the capital. It was dated 2 July 1944. The memo gave the source as *Fledermaus*.

'Marchand's cryptonym with the Gestapo,' I said. 'Muller says he and Barbie chose it. According to him, General Oberg himself took Marchand over. It looks likely that Marchand was the *Vertrauensmann*, the confidential informant, of Kaltenbrunner's report to the Fuehrer.'

Baum said nothing until we were outside the building again. 'You have established,' he said at last, 'that André Marchand was an agent of the Gestapo. Nothing in the missing sheets from his file at the DST is worth quoting by the side of what we've just seen. I rule out forgery because so much circumstantial evidence points back to those microfilms. But, my friend, you have not established that Marchand was an agent of a foreign power *after* the war. I believe he was and so do you. But our opinions are valueless. What we have just seen is history – interesting, no doubt, but still history. Perhaps if we find the people who are pursuing you they will lead us to some kind of answer.'

It might be asked at this point why I did not take Baum into my confidence over Bracony. Here, surely, was the missing link in our chain. For there was evidence that Marchand continued his contact with Bracony into the postwar period. Why else should he constantly go off to Conques on his own? But if I told Baum about Bracony and the *secadour* and my role as a hunter (and killer) of spies on French territory, he was entitled to retreat into his official position as a high-ranking official of the DST and to object formally and with force. He would, at that point, almost certainly have to take the whole thing back to Wavre, and we'd have trouble at ministerial level. I'd had a close enough shave with him over R. Brançon, and he hadn't for one moment believed my story. I reckoned I had to keep him away from Bracony until all possibility of error had vanished.

After lunch I telephoned Anny Dupuy at the number she had given me. There was no reply. I tried again twice during the afternoon and again in the evening at seven and at nine. I checked the directory. She was listed at 6 rue Bezout, over near the porte d'Orléans. I had been trying the right number. At ten there was still no reply and I had the line checked. Something told me I was wasting my time. I found rue Bezout on my street map and went in search of a taxi. I paid him off nearby and walked the last couple of hundred yards. Number 6 was a modest, old-fashioned apartment building. I decided to try to find Anny Dupuy's apartment without the help of the concierge.

I worked my way up the building. There were two flats on each floor. Most of the twelve doors had names on them. I didn't find Dupuy. From the first of the nameless doors, on the second floor, came the cheerful sounds of family strife. The second unmarked door was on the floor above. I rang the bell. Soon there were footsteps and the sound of a bolt being pulled. The door was opened by a middle-aged man in a dressing gown. He was black. Behind him hovered his equally African wife.

'I'm sorry,' I said. 'I was looking for Mr Janson.'

'You have come to the wrong door. Our name is Obi. I do not know a Janson.'

I went up to the fifth floor and rang at the last unmarked door. The bell echoed through the apartment and nothing happened. I examined the door. Paint and slivers of wood had been chipped away near the lock. The small areas of bare wood were clean: the forcing job was very recent. It had been expertly done. I pressed the door but it held firm. There was a heavy mat hard up against the door at its base. In the absurd hope that there might be a key beneath it, I lifted it away and it was then, from the gap beneath the door, that the sweet, familiar smell reached me. I bent down and forced myself to breathe in near the draught of warm air coming through the gap. There wasn't the slightest doubt about it.

I used my shoulder against the door but there was no movement. I had no choice but to take a chance with the neighbours. I took a run across the landing and hit the door with my full weight. The previous damage must have been hastily patched up because the door gave beneath my first assault with a sharp crack. Inside it was black and I groped for a switch. The light revealed a small, bare hall. There was a pile of coats on the floor beneath a rack. The stench of death was overpowering.

I retreated to the landing, took the deepest breath I could and returned to the flat, pushing the front door closed behind me. I found my way through the living room and got a window open before I had to take another breath. There were three more doors in the hall and two of them were open. One revealed a small kitchen and the other led to a bathroom. I put on more lights. There was total chaos in the place, with cushions and upholstery ripped open, every movable object strewn on the floor, furniture overturned and even packets of foodstuffs opened and the contents flung about the kitchen. The door of the refrigerator was open, the pilot light shining dimly within. The kitchen tap was dripping.

I opened the kitchen window, trying to organise some kind of draught and, I suppose, playing for time before I came to the last door and found what I was going to find. In the bathroom everything had been thrown into the bath – all except a pink toothbrush still hanging in its holder above the sink. There were pills all over the floor. I soaked my handkerchief under the tap, wrung it out and tied it over my nose and mouth. I found some eau de cologne and dabbed it on the handkerchief and on my face. Then I opened the bedroom door and switched on the light.

Anny Dupuy lay on her back on the floor. She was fully dressed. One leg was bent back awkwardly beneath her body. A towel had been forced into her mouth and, seemingly, down her throat. There was no telling at a glance exactly how she had died, but whoever had done it had given himself nearly two weeks' start over me or anyone else who was interested in what Anny Dupuy might have to say. The face was mottled and puffed and only the black hair reminded me of the living woman I had talked to, embattled and angry and craving her drinks, at the Colisée. I steeled myself to come closer and examined her neck. On the left side was a darker blotch, the size of a large coin. I had not seen it when we met. It must have been covered by the little chiffon scarf.

The bedroom had received the same treatment as the rest of the apartment. The contents of drawers and cupboards were heaped in piles on the floor. The bed had been stripped and the mattress gutted. Flock from the duvet started moving across the floor as the draught from outside disturbed the foetid air of the room. If Anny Dupuy had had anything more to tell me, it was too late. And if she had possessed anything that could interest me, it was clearly too late for that too.

I picked up a cloth and went round the place wiping my prints off everything I'd touched. I closed the doors and windows and put out the lights. The latch on the front door was done for, so I jammed it with a wedge of paper, wiped off the outside, and made my way out of the building. I had a large cognac at the nearest bar that I dared to use and found my way back to my hotel by Métro. Despite the eau de cologne the dreadful odour from the bedroom clung to my clothes.

Next morning I phoned the Préfecture de Police of the 4th *arrondissement*, introduced myself as Mr Dupont of 6 rue Bezout, and told them they ought to take a look at the fifth floor right because the lady hadn't been seen lately and there was a nasty smell spreading through the building.

I was hardly off the phone when Isabel came through.

'This phone's OK,' she said. 'I'm afraid I have another of those tiresome messages from Andrew. He says Hank will be in Paris today and will you meet him in the bar of the Hotel Continental at five.'

'Thanks,' I said, 'I'll be there.'

When I reached the bar of the Continental, Hank Munthe was already installed in a deep armchair, watching over what turned out to be a Bristol Cream on the rocks. I ordered a scotch and water.

'It's great to see you, Charlie,' he said. 'I had to see my

people at the Embassy, so I thought I'd bring myself up to date on the Marchand thing.'

'By all means, Hank,' I said.

'So how's progress?'

'Slow,' I said.

'I'm sorry to hear that.'

'Made slower by a number of strange happenings.'

'You don't say?'

'I do say.'

'Such as?' Hank was sharing out his attention evenly between the customers in the bar and me. I'd noticed before that it was never possible to win his undivided attention in a public place. It was as if he expected an armed assault at any moment.

'Such as the irritating propensity of documents to disappear just when I am about to consult them.'

Hank was examining two men who had come to the entrance of the bar and had immediately turned away. One of them was short, erect: possibly an officer in mufti. Familiar.

'You were saying,' Hank said vaguely.

'Documents,' I said. 'Disappearing. Suddenly.'

'Oh, where was that?'

'Zehlendorf,' I said. 'Also at the DST, but let's talk about Zehlendorf.'

'You mean the Document Centre?'

'I do, Hank, I do.'

'Oh.' He paused. 'Which documents, Charlie?'

I told him. 'Walt Bailey signed for them only last week,' I said. 'I thought I was the one on this case but I may have heard it wrong.'

'You are, Charlie, you most certainly are. I can't think what Walt is up to, the son of a gun.'

'I can,' I said. 'Very precisely.'

Hank emptied his glass and signalled the waiter for more drinks. It gave him time to think.

'No instructions from me, old buddy,' he said. His eyes twinkled with insincerity. A friendly hand extended to pat my forearm. 'If Berlin is on to this case they've certainly forgotten to copy me in on that fact as of now. So that you and I both have gotten our toes trodden on.' It was good but not good enough.

'That's a lot of bull, Hank,' I said. 'You can do better. Try again.'

'It's a fact, Charlie,' he said, his eyes wandering again as people moved at a nearby table. 'You can't always keep the local Residents off a case when they hear on the office grapevine that it's a hot potato. London and Paris have been advised but maybe Langley forgot to copy in Berlin.' He made it sound like an administrative hiccup in somebody's office.

'Hank,' I said, 'you are an unmitigated rogue. Amiable, I grant you, but a rogue. You must get off my tail, my good friend, and if you don't do so I simply won't report anything worth hearing to London and you'll be left out there in the dark. Furthermore, that would be a pity because it is my solemn belief that what we have here is what our friend Andrew would call a *situation*.'

For the first time, the eyes came to rest squarely on mine and the twinkle wasn't there. 'You mean that, Charlie?'

'I do.'

'Care to tell me?'

'No, Hank, I wouldn't.'

'Oh, I see.' He drank his frozen sherry, allowing some of the liquor to drip onto his tie. 'When can we get together on this, then?'

'When I'm ready,' I said. 'When what I have will stand up to scrutiny. When you call your damned Residents to heel and let me get on with it.'

'I see what you mean, Charlie. I'll put something on telex this evening.'

'Good thinking,' I said, 'and for God's sake make it secure. This whole thing leaks like a sieve already. We don't need any more holes punched in it.'

'Sure, sure, Charlie.' He was soothing what he took to be my ruffled feelings. 'Sure, we'll keep it under wraps.' He paused. 'What's your next move?'

'I don't know, but I hope to be in London next week.'

'That's great. We'll get together there.'

'All right,' I said as I got up to go, 'and thanks for the drinks.'

As I emerged into the main foyer of the hotel, the military man and his friend were walking slowly between the armchairs. I glanced back. Hank Munthe was searching vaguely through his pockets for a pen with which to sign the bill, ignoring the one proffered by the waiter.

CHAPTER 22

Avenue de la Motte-Picquet

'Tell me first,' Baum said, 'about your American friend of yesterday.' We were again in my poky hotel room. Jean was expected with his maps.

'I saw your men,' I said.

'They followed your American friend later. It was a piece of initiative on their part. Who did you say he was?'

'I didn't say but I am very willing to tell you. He's Hank Munthe of the CIA. You must know him.'

'Of course, but my men didn't. He's booked in at the Continental as Horace Crossley. What is he doing here?'

'Trying to capture this investigation, and I don't know if that's personal ambition or a directive from above.'

Baum frowned. 'Our American friends have energy and they have great resources. Unfortunately, they lack finesse. How can you inculcate finesse in farm boys from Kansas?'

'Hank is from Texas.'

'Perhaps worse. The CIA recruits in the backwoods to ensure political naïveté and thus loyalty to certain very simple principles. What they get, of course, is parochialism. By the time their men reach Europe they have the irreversible mental attitudes of insurance salesmen from Galveston or Kansas City.'

'Hank is more dangerous than he is incompetent,' I said. 'Unfortunately, he believes that the objectives of the CIA are all imperatives. He's the most unscrupulous fellow I ever met in my life. I don't know why he didn't join the KGB.'

'I don't like the way he is spending his time in Paris.'

'Tell me more.'

'The picture, unfortunately, is incomplete. Yesterday, after meeting you he travelled by taxi and crossed the river at the pont de Grenelle, after which my men lost him in our damned Paris traffic. But they got the number of the taxi and we expect to trace the driver today.'

'I can see nothing sinister in that,' I said. 'Some very nice people live on the Left Bank.'

'Wait,' Baum said. 'My men knew he was staying at the Continental, so they went back and waited for him there. They picked him up again about an hour later and just before midnight he went out again. That time they had more luck.'

'Where did he go?'

'To the SEXY-BIZARRE in the rue Victor Massé. He stayed there for over an hour, most of it in Albert Chavan's office.'

'After I'd told him to lay off, too,' I said.

'One cannot tell the CIA to lay off. One has simply to divert their attention.'

At that point Jean arrived. He was still shivering from the cold outside. He looked miserable.

'Well, young man?' Baum said.

'No luck. Luc and I have covered every possibility within our formula, all of it on foot. We have failed to find the arrangement of buildings in the brief. We found stone buildings with ramps leading down to underground garages, and we found brick buildings of eight storeys, but we never found one opposite the other – not if we observe all the additional requirements.'

'Check your map,' Baum said. 'Make sure you missed nothing.'

'I've done that twice,' Jean said. 'I was up at dawn today, going over the whole thing from the start. If my brief is right, my conclusions are right.'

Baum turned to me. 'Somewhere, my friend, there is a mistake. I suggest you now go over the ground yourself. You may spot something these young men have missed.'

'I have prepared here,' Jean said, 'a list of the streets worth looking at. Of the forty-nine streets I marked originally, eleven can be excluded. Here is a list of the remaining thirty-eight. They are all possibilities. And here is a fresh map with only those thirty-eight streets marked in red. You will only need to examine the first thirty metres or so of each street on one or both sides of the main artery. Unfortunately, they are distributed pretty evenly along the four kilometres of avenues which we identified.'

'I'd better get on with it,' I said. 'I can't see any other way. I wasn't hallucinating, so the damned buildings have to be somewhere.'

'I have also listed the buildings with drive-in garages,' Jean said. 'We checked the inner courtyards in case your impression of coming straight off the ramp onto the pavement was wrong. The list shows all buildings which we know to have a ramp down to a garage. The ones marked with a star had gates or doors which made it impossible for us to check without making enquiries.'

I took the map and the bits of paper and they left me.

I tramped all afternoon against the chill east wind, starting north of the river along the three wealthy thoroughfares marked on Jean's map. I could find nothing remotely resembling my layout. It eliminated seven of the thirty-eight streets on the list – thirty-one to go. But it also convinced me that my guess of a kilometre from the Eiffel Tower was not far off the mark.

I took a taxi down to the avenue Emile Zola, south of the river, and started again. At each of the buildings listed by Jean as having garage ramps, or closed doors which might lead to ramps, I stopped and stared disconsolately at whatever stood opposite. It was never in brick. I checked all the turnings off the avenue Emile Zola and was finished with the rue du Commerce as well by the time dusk was falling. Nothing looked even faintly possible. I had dinner alone in a small place near the Luxembourg, and all through the meal I prodded my memory, relived in particular that grotesque journey along the parapet in the breaking light of the dawn. And nowhere could I fault my recollection.

I was back on the job at nine next morning, shouldering my way through the last of the rush-hour crowds. I started near the great crescent of the UNESCO building and worked my way north up the avenue de Suffren. Jean had listed four possibilities and none of them was any good. It left the avenue de la Motte-Picquet: about a kilometre and a bit, with seven possibilities on the list. The wind had sharpened since the day before and now had a savage bite to it. I put up my coat collar and wished I had gloves. I found all seven of Jean's 'possibles' and they were all hopeless. I finished up at the top end of the avenue, frozen and disconsolate, and over a *crème* at a decently heated café went over the whole thing for the tenth time. I decided that I simply didn't know what to do next. Either Jean was wrong or I was wrong. Or we were both wrong, maybe compounding each other's mistake. Yet there was symmetry and logic in everything we had done. Maybe a little too much deductive logic. What about some lateral thinking for a change? I suddenly felt the need to bring Isabel's more impressionistic and imaginative mind to bear on the problem. I broke my own rules and called her office from the café.

'I need your undivided attention over dinner. Can you manage it?'

'Yes, I'd like it.'

'Good. I'll pick you up at eight.'

I left the café and picked my way past the roadworks with their red and white pedestrian barriers which were creating traffic diversions in the avenue and the intersecting boulevard. I found a taxi at last and from my hotel I called Baum. 'No luck,' I said.

'What do you propose?'

'I don't know yet, but I'll tell you in the morning. If necessary, I'll go over every inch of the ground again, including everything your men rejected.'

'By the way,' Baum was speaking carefully and his tone was flat. 'You remember our interest in tracing a taxi?'

'I do.'

'Well, we got hold of him last night. He remembered the fare. He was told to drive to the boulevard de la Tour-Maubourg. You may know, it runs along the side of the Invalides. At a point opposite the Invalides museum his fare stopped him and got out. That's all the driver could tell us. I mention it because, who knows, we may all be looking for the same place.'

'I can't imagine why he'd be after what we're after,' I said.

'Nor can I. But I would draw your attention to the fact that he alighted close to the point where the boulevard crosses the avenue de la Motte-Picquet, which I believe is one of the thoroughfares which interest us.'

'It is,' I said, 'but I don't see it.' But it was not strictly true.

I collected Isabel at eight and we ate at a place a few doors down the street. While we waited for our food I explained everything. She heard me through in silence and after I'd finished, her silence persisted while we were served. 'The trouble is,' she said at last, 'you are all certain you are right. You're certain about what you saw. Baum's men are certain about their method of looking for it. You are asking third parties like me to believe that both sides are right.'

'Yes.'

'Well, instead of saying the obvious thing, which is that one of you must be wrong, let's go along with all this certainty. So that *you* were right when you saw what you saw, and the fuzz was right when it checked up. *Ergo*, something must have changed in the interim.'

'You mean someone came along and pulled one of our buildings down, quick like?'

'That's it.'

'Or shifted the Métro a bit to the left.'

'Or the Eiffel Tower a bit to the right.'

'Ha, ha.'

'Ha, ha. But I'm serious. Now then, what can have changed in three weeks? The Métro schedules?'

'No, that was checked.'

'I can't think of anything else. It's your turn.'

'Nor can I.'

'Oh, well,' Isabel said. 'It seemed a good idea at the time.'

We finished our meal gloomily, throwing foolish suggestions at each other with no success.

I went back next morning to the big intersection of the boulevard de la Tour-Maubourg with the avenue de la Motte-Picquet. I stood where Hank Munthe must have alighted from his taxi in the boulevard and then made my way south and round the corner into the avenue. I had to follow pedestrian walkways which had been created round the roadworks. The diverted traffic nosed its way down the avenue and emerged into unfamiliar side streets. What could have changed in three weeks? As I tried to avoid the ridges of mud from the diggings I kept coming back to Isabel's idea. Not the Métro, not the buildings, not the Eiffel Tower. The traffic? Obviously, the traffic. The large filled-in areas in the avenue showed that there had been recent diversions which had since given way to new traffic patterns. I decided on a close examination of every side street giving on to the avenue.

One thing was clear. In the recent past large holes had been dug in the avenue in such positions that the intersection with the boulevard must have been wholly out of commission for a while. Which meant that the traffic travelling north up the avenue and wanting to turn into the boulevard could only do so if the one-way system in one of the side streets had been reversed to take the traffic flow. This gave me three streets to look at which were not on Jean's list. The first two offered nothing. The third was rue Duvivier, a short, quiet street running north out of the avenue and normally leading nowhere in particular. In the rue Duvivier, near the corner of the avenue, was an office block of indeterminate age. It was built in stone.

The carriageway leading to the inner courtyard was closed off with big metal doors. The kerb had been nearly flattened to the level of the roadway to allow cars to pass over the pavement. It looked promising, except that the building opposite was also in stone. And once again on this strange Odyssey of mine I did the illogical thing. Instead of shrugging my shoulders and moving on, I hung around and worried at the problem. Perhaps it was because I now had nowhere else to go and couldn't face the hours of tramping back over the routes taken by Baum's young men. So I crossed and recrossed the road. I looked at the large engraved plaque in the entrance of the office building. The ground and first four floors were occupied by an outcrop of the Ministry of Public Works. Below the Ministry on the plaque I read:

Société Sofranal
Gallenburg, Hunt Inc., Houston
Commodity Brokers, Petroleum products, Petrochemicals
Enquiries: 5th floor.

I stood outside the building and looked across the road at the modern block opposite. It was built in solid dressed stone. All of it. I looked up to prove the point to myself. And at the sixth storey I found at last what I'd been looking for. They had, at some stage, added two more storeys to the building. In yellow brick.

I went into the office building and presented myself to the commissionaire.

'I'm looking for the Association of Actuaries. I believe they are on the seventh floor.'

'Not here, they aren't.'

'Who occupies the seventh floor, then?'

'Sofranal. They have the top three floors.'

'But isn't this number six rue Duvivier?'

'No, it's number four.'

'Sorry, wrong building.' I made for the door and before

reaching it, turned with an afterthought. 'Does this building have a garage?'

'Why do you ask?'

'I'm looking for office space round here myself and thought I might ask Sofranal if they have anything to spare. But I'd need off-street parking.'

'We have underground parking,' the commissionaire said. 'It's shared between Sofranal and the Ministry.'

'Thanks,' I said, 'I think I'll go up and have a word with the receptionist.'

'That's the fifth,' the commissionaire said.

In the lift I pressed the button marked seven. The inside of the lift brought back to me a good part of the misery of the night when I'd travelled up on the floor with my two thugs. I was now certain that I was in the same lift. When it reached the seventh floor, the door opened. The landing was dimly lit, as if the floor was not in constant use. It was light enough for me to recognise the grey paint and panelled doors. This was certainly where they'd brought me. I walked down the corridor. The door number and name plate had been removed from the door leading into Baum I's office. I looked inside. It was exactly as I had seen it before. I returned to the lift and pressed the ground-floor button. Halfway down I pressed the STOP button and killed a couple of minutes doing nothing. When I finally reached the ground floor, the commissionaire was waiting for me.

'Where have you been? The receptionist at Sofranal says no one has been up to see her.'

'I didn't go up,' I said. 'I've been inspecting the car parking instead. I'll write in. Thanks for your help.' I made for the door.

'Hey, come back here a minute,' the commissionaire called after me. But I was out in the street by the time he reached for his telephone.

I called Baum from the café in the avenue and gave him the news, including the text of Sofranal's inscription in the lobby of the building.

'We need to hold a conference, you and I,' he said. 'Let us do that tomorrow morning. By that time I will have checked on this Société Sofranal. The name, by the way, strikes a chord in my memory. Dim, but a chord none the less.' We fixed our meeting and I emerged once more into the bitter weather of the avenue.

Baum bustled into my room next morning, the frosty air clinging to his coat. He settled himself and pulled papers out of a pocket. 'Let us deal first of all,' he said, 'with the Société Sofranal, in association with Gallenburg, Hunt Incorporated, of Houston, Texas. I said the name struck a chord, and having made enquiries and examined a couple of files I can tell you the chord has become a sinister little tune.'

'Who are they?'

'They are specialists in barter deals, three-cornered trading, anything requiring fancy footwork in the trade between the Communist bloc and the West. We know them because we believe they regularly break the US State Department's embargo arrangements.'

'You mean the strategic list?'

'Yes. If Poland wants US radar spares, for instance, which are on the list, Sofranal will find someone in Italy – a front, you understand – to place an order. The goods will acquire false certificates of origin by the time they are trans-shipped in Genoa, and someone will mess about with the bills of lading too, if need be. Then they go on to Poland as, say, circuit-breakers of Italian manufacture. That's one way of doing it. There are others.'

'Who runs this outfit?'

'A character calling himself Ion Radescu, alias Ramon Lupescu, alias Boris Simianski. As Simianski he served seven of ten years for wartime collaboration and expropriation of Jewish property. You know the type – stateless and speaking six languages, none of them properly, though I daresay he could rob you in all of them. There's a lot of shit left lying about in Europe, you know.'

'A front or the boss man?'

'We think he's a front. Their offices belong to a Swiss holding company called Sofranal (Suisse) SA, and the US firm Gallenburg, Hunt owns forty per cent of the French company. When we last looked at Sofranal we enquired through our joint committee with the CIA about Gallenburg, Hunt. The CIA had nothing much on them – private company, trading profitably, books in order, one hundred and thirty-seven employees, four directors – more like a credit rating from a bank than a security report. So that we really know nothing about the American end.'

'And the Swiss?'

'Just a holding company with its registered office at a perfectly respectable legal partnership in Zurich and its bank account at the Crédit Suisse shrouded in the usual Swiss secrecy.'

'Whose side do you think they're on?'

'No way of telling. It suits the Russian bloc to get their hands on strategic goods. But it often suits the Americans to provide them. The strategic list is mainly designed to keep the Russia-haters in the Congress quiet. It has nothing to do with national security and even less with the real aims of Western policy.'

'Could Sofranal be a front for the KGB?'

'It could. But if it is, we should all resign at the DST because we didn't know it.'

'More likely to be a freelance outfit, then?'

'Possible.' He paused and scratched his head. 'I've been thinking about what we do next. I think we need to pull in a number of people for interrogation, but before we do that we have to identify the ones that interest us. So I propose to keep the Sofranal building under surveillance for as long as is needed to collect a useful photo file from which I hope you will identify some people for us to talk to. We'll pull in everyone we can from the Auto Ecole Marceau and Luna at the same time.'

'But Wavre will eat you for breakfast,' I said.

Baum chuckled. 'The *patron* will be in Gabon next week,' he said, 'on an official visit. Meanwhile, I am in charge here. So we will be settling our little business to everyone's satisfaction, and though I am sure Wavre would forbid our investigation if he knew of it, he will be very happy with the results. That, or I am in trouble.'

CHAPTER 23

(703) 351–1100

At Smith Square on the Monday I found Harry in high good humour. 'We've bin 'ard at it,' he said, 'and we're ready to talk. George may be a right twerp – he *is* a right twerp – but he certainly does a day's work. A great grafter.'

'Right,' I said, 'we'll make it this afternoon. Meanwhile I'll bring A.P. up to date on what you've already given me.'

I did that in Andrew Pabjoy's office over a cheese roll and a cup of Penny's coffee. He made no comment, but when I'd finished he said: 'The rest of it had better be good. The Foreign Secretary wants to see us at six.'

'George is making the presentation,' I said as we trooped into the conference room after lunch. The place smelt foully of stale tobacco and whoever was paid to clear away the teacups from the previous day had not cleared away the teacups. A document marked VERY SECRET – NOT FOR CIRCULATION in fourteen-point caps lay, abandoned, on the long baize-covered table. The ashtrays were full.

There was a good deal of clatter and fuss with cups, chairs and electric leads and plugs before we were finally settled, with a three-foot projection screen balanced on the far end of the table. Pabjoy was in the only chair with arms, directly facing the screen.

'Well then, let's go,' he said.

George Roberts was a brisk and pressing young man with yellow hair and a poor complexion – a redbrick product with a brain like a buzz-saw and utterly without charm. His First in statistics from somewhere like Birmingham was no accident at all: he had a major talent for quantitative research and analysis. He had never heard of intuition.

'I propose,' said George Roberts matter of factly, 'to project data onto the screen where I consider it useful. No doubt Mr Sutcliffe may wish to add a comment of his own from time to time and I trust he'll feel free to do so.'

'I will 'an all,' Harry said.

'Very well then,' said George, 'let us first redefine the assignment. We were instructed to seek an answer to the question: can we establish the presence of a communication satellite parked in a synchronous geostationary orbit for the purpose of receiving and retransmitting signals from a transmitter situated at Conques in south-western France. Further, what conclusions can be drawn as to the control of the satellite and its ground receiving station. That, as I understand it, was our assignment.'

'It was,' said Pabjoy. 'It didn't need restating.'

'Let us first of all consider our environment.' He pressed a button and a chart appeared on the screen. It was headed: OBJECTS IN SPACE – JULY 1981. Below were some figures. 'My table shows that in July 1981 there were 4,847 objects orbiting the earth, of which 988 were effective payloads, with a further 6,779 items previously identified and since decayed. My source is NORAD. Apart from satellites, such debris as rocket stages, tether cables, de-spin weights and even bits of metal are tracked and recorded in computer memory banks. The point I wish to make is that there is a great deal of material being tracked at present by the principal powers, with only the USA and USSR maintaining a full picture.'

He pressed the button and a new chart appeared: SUMMARY LOG OF SPACE LAUNCHES 1957–81. Below it were columns headed NAME, INTERNATIONAL DESIGNATION, PROJECT DIRECTION, LAUNCH DATA, INITIAL ORBITAL DATA and STATUS.

'The chart of which we see a section here is regularly updated at the US Army's NORAD Space Centre at Cheyenne Mountain. It provides data on every launching from whatever base, and thereafter keeps track of the object launched. Let us take an instance at random – say here – the Kosmos 21, launched by the USSR on eleventh November 1967 from their site at Tyuratam.' George pointed to the line on the chart with a stick. 'We have the orbital data – period, perigee, apogee and inclination – which can be read there, and then we have under STATUS the entry: "Decayed fourteenth November 1967, unannounced payload."'

'A bust, that one,' said Harry. George Roberts ignored him.

'Or consider this line.' He pointed to an entry further down the chart. 'Relay 2, launched by NASA on twenty-first January 1968, from ETR – that's the Eastern Test Range. Launch vehicle was a Delta rocket, payload one hundred and seventy-two kilograms, orbital data as shown, and status: "In orbit, communication satellite, experiments conducted until September 1968." That would now be dead equipment and it will re-enter the atmosphere and burn up, if it hasn't done so already.'

'Aren't we getting too much detail?'

'No, Sir, with respect,' said Arthur. 'My object is to show that the Americans, and no doubt the Soviets, have useful data on everything that goes up.'

'Can't they miss something sometimes?'

'They say they never miss anything. I cannot judge that claim, but I am bound to say the technology is well established.'

'And what if the Americans launch something themselves and choose not to report it?' I asked.

George appeared shocked. He was the kind of young man who would accept as fact what the US Army told him was fact.

'That seems improbable,' he said. 'It would invalidate the entire reporting system.'

'Go on,' Pabjoy said. 'I am inclined to agree.'

'Well, Sir, our examination of the Cheyenne reports was our

point of departure in this investigation, and I am only reporting now on anomalies which were subsequently confirmed as significant.'

'By what subsequent means?'

'Intelligence,' George replied, deadpan.

'Go on.'

'May I draw your attention to this entry with launch date fourteenth February 1968.' He pointed to a line on the chart. 'You will see firstly that in the NAME column the entry reads "None". That is not unique but it is highly unusual in the light of the entry under PROJECT DIRECTION, which reads "NASA". Now, unnamed satellites are the rule rather than the exception where they are directed by the US Air Force or Navy. But it is not usual where the direction is NASA. Indeed, you will observe that *all* other NASA launches on this chart bear names – Ranger, Beacon, Explorer, Tiros, and so on. This reflects the fact that all NASA projects are commercial or scientific, of course, and it was this minor anomaly which first alerted us to the fourteenth February entry.'

George moved his stick along the entry on the chart. 'You will note the technical details. An Atlas-Agena B rocket which you will know has the capability to lift a substantial payload into a distant orbit.'

We nodded though we knew no such thing.

'The weight is given as one hundred and twenty kilograms, which I understand is a typical payload for a communication satellite. But the initial orbital data – the description of the orbit aimed at – which should be in the next column, is missing. This, Sir, is because the satellite is reported in the last column as having failed to orbit, with the comment: "Insufficient third stage thrust." We are to conclude that it disintegrated or burned up, and we would not have doubted the veracity of the statement were it not for the suspicion aroused by the lack of a name.'

'So what did you do?'

'We had the NASA files checked for failures to orbit –

FTOs, Sir, in the jargon. It is, of course, unclassified information.'

'And?'

'There is no record of an FTO on or near fourteenth February 1968. Indeed, there is no record *at NASA* of any kind of launch within a month on either side of that date.' George Roberts' face was as expressionless as if he had been establishing that four minus three equalled one. His interest in facts left no room in his mind for anything else. Certainly not for a sense of drama.

'We then directed our enquiries to the two military sponsors of satellites: the Air Force branch of the US Army, and the US Navy, since these are the only other US agencies in the business of satellite sponsorship and control.' He paused, not for dramatic effect but to blow his nose.

'And what did you find there?'

'According to the records, neither the Air Force nor the Navy had had a launch on that date, and nothing resembling this item started appearing on their monthly box-score lists.'

'From which,' Andrew Pabjoy said, 'you concluded that it was a no-go situation – that no launch had in fact taken place?'

'Well, Sir, that was our first conclusion. But Mr Sutcliffe has a friend, Sir, who is well placed to, er, examine the records at the Eastern and Western Test Ranges, and we asked him to check. He reported that there was indeed a launch from ETR on that date. And even the movement of stores and personnel, which are recorded separately, of course, tended to confirm it. I think we have to assume a launch.'

'So we have a launch disclaimed by the three agencies who control between them all the US space projects?'

'So it seemed at that point in our enquiries, Sir. But our informant in Washington happened to mention that the Air Force was known to have handed one of its projects to another agency once the satellite was in orbit.'

'Which agency?'

'A body calling itself the Eastern Space Agency – ESA. It doesn't appear to be listed anywhere in the records of the space-flight community. Nothing at NASA. Nothing in the catalogues of the Superintendant of Documents at the US Government Printing Office in Washington. "Not known" at Cheyenne Mountain. We even checked at the Marshall and Goddard Space Flight Centers and at the MIT Lincoln Laboratory's deep-space tracking station at Millstone Hill in Massachussetts. We thought it was a likely facility to be controlling the satellite. But they'd never heard of it.'

'But tell me,' Pabjoy interrupted. 'Why do we need such complications? Why couldn't they have put up their satellite, placed it under Army or Navy control, and simply reported it in the usual way on the Cheyenne printouts which I understand are widely circulated? They don't need to report what it actually does.'

'That is what we would expect them to do,' George replied. 'It is precisely their failure to do so which seemed significant to us. You see, the detection and tracking system is a worldwide network of radars, cameras and radio receivers, located in such places as Greenland, Ascension Island, New Zealand and the UK, as well as the USA itself. About twenty thousand readings a day are fed back to the computer at Cheyenne, and they'll have had to modify the computer program to exclude the readings which relate to the satellite we are concerned with. It must be turning up continually in thousands of readings from the tracking stations around the world, and they've gone to the trouble of filleting it out of the program. It appears to show a very great desire for security.'

Pabjoy grunted. George Roberts blew his nose again. He appeared to have a cold in the head.

'I will return, if I may, to the ESA. We came to feel that the answer to our problem was tied up with this body, and so we set out to locate and identify it, Sir, while respecting of course the general rules governing our intelligence activities on the territory of the USA.'

'And why was I not informed that this cloak and dagger stuff was going on?'

Harry shifted uncomfortably in his chair and George Roberts looked mildly surprised. 'I understand, Sir,' he said, 'that Mr Sutcliffe had the necessary authority to make these enquiries.'

'No sweat,' Harry said with a failed laugh. 'I 'ave me contacts, I ask 'em a question or two, it's up to them whether they answer me or not. That don't break no rules on this side. And I can always do 'em a service in return sometime.'

'Can you now?' said Pabjoy.

There was a heavy silence which no one chose to break. Pabjoy nodded to George Roberts.

'As I said, we believe we have identified ESA. Curiously enough, its existence can be deduced from published sources, as is so often the case in the United States, where publication seems to be the first reaction to any new development. We at first distrusted our findings precisely because they were arrived at so easily.'

'Let us have the findings,' Pabjoy said. 'I will make my own assessment of credibility.'

George pressed his button. On the screen appeared a photograph of part of a control room. A console complete with TV displays could be seen on the left. The right-hand third of the picture was taken up by part of a wall on which several notices had been posted. A caption beneath the picture read: VIEW OF CENTRAL CONTROL ROOM, GODDARD SPACE FLIGHT CENTER. Below could be seen part of two columns of print. 'This,' George was saying, 'is a photograph of a page from *Space*, the information sheet put out by the Office of Public Affairs at Goddard. I would incidentally draw your attention to the fact that the Goddard Space Flight Center is located at Greenbelt, Maryland, which is thirteen miles north of Washington DC. This has its significance, as I shall demonstrate in a moment.'

He pressed the button again. Now we saw a heavily magnified section of the wall from the previous picture. The entire area was taken up by a notice. It was headed: FLIGHT MANAGE-

MENT CONTACTS. The lines of type below the heading were blurred and difficult to read. One line had been marked on the transparency in red.

'This appears to be a list of names and telephone numbers of individuals to be contacted in the event of queries arising on any of the space programmes in which Goddard is involved. You will see under NASA three names with phone numbers, marked respectively *Comsat*, *Intelsat* and *Marisat*, all of which are NASA programmes – that is, satellites launched by Goddard and under NASA's management. But the following line, which I have marked in red, is headed ESA. The S is not clear but we have confirmed it under strong magnification. Similarly, we have done detailed work on the type which appears under this heading.'

He pressed the button and a single line of powerfully magnified typewriter face appeared on the screen. Parts of letters which were too blurred to be recognisable had been delicately filled in with red ink. One or two letters and numerals were missing completely. The line read:

R. Cocker Jr. 703- 51-110 Ext. 1461

I recognised the mutilated number and leant towards Pabjoy. 'It's Langley's main switchboard,' I said. 'They must be crazy.' I meant the CIA, not George and Harry. I don't know whether Pabjoy understood it that way round.

'That is the telephone number of the Central Intelligence Agency,'* George Roberts was saying through his catarrh. 'I'm afraid the Americans' devotion to the media has breached their security as usual. It is, if I may say so, a curious parallel to the Tass agency photo which betrayed the Soviet tracking network to us in 1974.'**

* The actual number of the CIA is (703) 351 1100.

** On 4 December 1974 Tass released a picture in Moscow showing a control room in an unnamed space establishment. On the wall was a map of the USSR. Under strong magnification, Western intelligence analysts were able to decipher a series of locations with codes and names which had been marked on the map and which other evidence identified as space tracking stations.

'Confirmatory evidence?' Pabjoy's voice was flat.

'We have a certain amount of confirmatory evidence, Sir, and we also have some data which appear significant on the possible content of the ESA programme. But first I would draw your attention to the fact that we are dealing here with Goddard, which is a few miles only from the CIA at Langley, Virginia, whereas from the nature of the launching and its assumed content we would have expected control to be with the Marshall Space Flight Center at Huntsville, Alabama, where most of the geosynchronous work is done.'

He paused and pressed the button. The screen showed part of a magazine news story. The heading read: NOW YOU SEE IT, NOW YOU DON'T.

'This,' George said, 'is a cutting from the US magazine *Aviation Week and Space Technology* of tenth May 1968. I would like to read out the first part of the article.' He cleared his throat: '"A spokesman at NASA headquarters has refused to comment on the mysterious disappearance from the records of a satellite launched on 14 February last and referred this reporter to the Army at Cheyenne Mountain. But Public Affairs at the Colorado facility stated that the launch appeared to have taken place as recorded on the daily log, and had presumably failed since it no longer figured on subsequent logs. Questioned, he stated that no satellite dating from 14 February was being currently tracked. This reporter then asked the NASA spokesman to comment on the Army's statement. A 'no comment' reply was given. Enquiries at Marshall and Goddard Space Flight Centers produced identical replies to the effect that all launches were as reported at the time."

'The rest of the article need not concern us,' George said. 'What I have read out tends to confirm the confusion between the agencies concerned – a confusion arising from the unortho-

---

These were at Yevpatoria, Tbilisi, Dzhusaly, Kolpashevo, Ulan Ude, Ussuriysk and Petropavlovsk. Certain overly cynical Russia-watchers regarded the whole thing as a subtle bit of KGB disinformation. They made no allowance for the incompetence factor.

dox manner in which the origin and control of the programme was reported.'

'It's pretty thin stuff so far,' Pabjoy said. 'I can't see a link between this launching and the French end of the story. Even if everything you've said is accurate, all you may have stumbled on is an attempt to hide from the opposition a new space surveillance or communication facility. I'm not saying it's the most elegant piece of deception I have come across, but nor can I see that it has anything to do with us.'

Again, George Roberts appeared entirely unperturbed by the cold douche with which Pabjoy was greeting his detective work. He dabbed at his nose. 'We did not expect to convince you on the evidence presented so far. But in order to take the investigation to a conclusion we need your authorisation for the next stage. We have technical data from the French equipment which tells us precisely what the installation and settings aboard the satellite must be. We therefore need to ascertain whether the fourteenth February 1968 launch had those characteristics.'

'Do you have any way of finding out?'

'We do,' Harry said.

'I don't want to know what you have. I want to know that it cannot blow up in our faces.'

'No way, Guv,' Harry said.

Pabjoy looked at him long and hard. 'How long do you need?'

'Mebbe two, three days.'

'You have clearance.'

As we stretched our legs and started to move out of the room I caught a broad wink from Harry. It betokened one of his tricky games of hide and seek. I did not respond.

'I think,' Andrew Pabjoy said to me as we made our way down the corridor, 'that at this point in time there is little purpose in bringing friend Hank into the picture. I wouldn't care to upset him needlessly.'

'Nor would I,' I said.

'I don't like that young man Roberts,' Pabjoy said pensively. 'He lacks respect.'

'May I offer you gentlemen a little sherry?' the Foreign Secretary enquired. 'It is suitably dry and very good, part of a modest gift from a visitation of Spaniards who were here yesterday raising bloody hell about Gibraltar. As if I can move a rock that size.' He chuckled. He clearly enjoyed his job.

The pinstriped Vivian circulated with glasses and a bottle. 'No, thank you,' Killigrew said.

'I have been subjected to a good deal of aggravation today,' the Foreign Secretary was saying. 'There is nothing like the Third World, you know, for aggravation. We all support doing more for the Third World. It's just a bloody shame it can't be done by post, that's all. So now let us turn to the problem of our own impossible continent, and I hope you haven't more aggravation in store for me.' He took a sip of his sherry and looked cheerfully round the room. All the sparkle was travelling in one direction. 'Well, Andrew,' he said, 'what have you got?'

'Not a great deal yet, Foreign Secretary. We have some leads but we need a little more time.'

'How much more time?'

'Say until next week, possibly a shade more.'

Killigrew fidgeted, looked as if he was about to speak, thought better of it.

'A pity, Andrew,' the Foreign Secretary said. 'You see, I am actually being harassed by the Prime Minister. Now, I yield to no one, mark you, in my admiration for the Prime Minister, but that does not prevent me saying that patience is not the PM's strongest suit. Drive, perhaps, and forcefulness, yes. But patience, no. And I can tell you, gentlemen, that the PM is driving me barmy about this Marchand business. You see, the PM simply does not understand why our services cannot come up within a reasonable space of time with a simple answer to a simple question. The need for discretion, don't you see, is something which interests me, but doesn't in the least interest the PM. And why should it? Prime Ministers have other fish to fry, do they not? So you see, gentlemen, I am under a lot of pressure.' He sipped again. No one cared to plug the gap in the monologue. The Foreign Secretary looked at each of us in turn with his amiable and decidedly cunning gaze.

'Well, Danvers,' he was addressing the KGB type, 'do you have any bright ideas?'

'No, Foreign Secretary.' The wizened Danvers retreated behind his sherry glass. He didn't seem to care a great deal.

'Commander?'

'Nothing this end, Sir,' Killigrew said.

'So what can I do to help, gentlemen?'

'There is one thing, Sir,' I said.

Killigrew bristled in my direction. It was the first time he had acknowledged my existence. KGB swivelled round towards me, sharing Killigrew's discovery.

'Yes, Carey,' the Foreign Secretary said, 'what is it?'

'I think it might help if we could get a sight of the minutes of the meetings Marchand attended here in London.'

The Foreign Secretary scratched his head. 'H'm,' he said. Then he said it again. 'H'm. Difficult, that. Your department, Danvers. Do we get full minutes?'

'Only decisions,' Danvers could see awkward international complications ahead and didn't like it.

'I thought as much. Well, Danvers, you'll have to do the necessary. Clear it first with NATO security without telling 'em what you want it for.'

Danvers said nothing. It was impossible to tell whether he would do it or assassinate the Foreign Secretary.

'What else, gentlemen?' The Foreign Secretary's normal Welsh ebullience had finally been squashed out of him by these lugubrious security types.

'Do you think,' he asked, 'on what you have so far, that the outcome is going to be . . . startling, troublesome?' His eyes were pleading with Pabjoy to say no. Pabjoy obliged.

'I don't think you need worry, Foreign Secretary,' he said.

'All right, I'll tell the PM you aren't quite ready but don't expect any nasty surprises. Is that a fair précis of your views, Andrew?'

'Perfectly fair,' Pabjoy said.

'Good. Vivian here will let you know when we have the stuff from NATO.'

Out in Whitehall I asked Pabjoy why he'd prejudged our findings as innocuous, and wasn't it a shade risky in view of the fact that they were in fact dynamite.

'No risk at all, Carey,' he said. 'Don't confuse your findings with our report. There is likely to be an almighty gap between them. Of course, *we* need to know what went on, but the Foreign Secretary doesn't and knows he doesn't. Goddamn it, the man's been signalling us all along that he doesn't want to hear anything more disturbing than the time of day. But *we*, Carey, we need to know. And above all, we need to be seen to be looking.'

'So why not just tell him now that all's well?'

'Too easy, Carey. If they don't sweat they'll get no sense of relief when we turn the heat off. No, we'll take another week over it.'

I didn't press the point. It was, after all, politics.

I was in Pabjoy's office on the Thursday when Harry announced he was ready to report.

'Come in now,' Pabjoy said. We sat in silence waiting for Harry to appear. Pabjoy was at work with a 2H on one of his yellow pads. I smoked. For once, Harry came straight to the point.

'It's them,' he said.

He spread typed sheets of flimsy on Pabjoy's desk. 'First, here's the transmission data from the French transmitter. It tells you your wavelength, frequency, power output, and – very important, this – the correlatives for finding the receiver, which is your satellite.'

Pabjoy and I looked solemnly at Harry's meaningless numbers.

'That lot tells us the location of the receiving satellite – period, perigee, apogee and inclination, see – and its reception characteristics. Only a particular receiver in a particular parking lot could pick up what the French job was sending out, right?'

Pabjoy nodded.

'Now look,' Harry said, substituting another sheet. 'This is what my American mate got me off the launch records for 1968 at Goddard. It gives two things: nature of payload and intended orbit. You'll see for yourselves, payload characteristics match what I got off the French job and so does the orbit.'

'How reliable?' Pabjoy asked.

'Copper-bottomed,' Harry said. 'How could he guess what the other sheet had on it?'

Andrew Pabjoy sat silent for a few moments, drawing lines. Then he seemed to come to some sort of decision. 'Tell me,' he said, 'what would the Russians need in order to break into the communication system between France and the USA, assuming for a moment it's what you claim it to be?'

'Well,' Harry said cautiously, 'they'd need first of all to locate the satellite, which they could do easy enough by normal tracking techniques. Then they'd need a mighty powerful reason for the effort they'd have to put into eavesdropping on it. In other words, they'd have to know that what they'd located was worth investing a fair bit 'o time and roubles in *before* they started work on it. It'd mean getting hold of the code which unlocks the computer memory to release the message. Once they had that, it'd be easy enough to pick up and record whatever was in the memory bank, but they'd have to decrypt it afterwards. How tough that would be, I don't know.'

'Once the satellite has been commanded to spew out a message,' I said, 'is that message lost for good?'

'Thought of that,' Harry said. 'Checked it. There's a device to restore the message to the memory in case the transmission or recording fails. Then the next message up from the transmitter erases the one before.'

'So that the opposition could steal messages and leave them for the Americans to pick up in turn, or vice versa?'

'Sure.'

'Which means they could eavesdrop pretty well indefinitely without leaving their footprints.'

'Dead right, Guv.'

'What makes you think the Russians have the know-how for this kind of thing?' Pabjoy asked.

Harry chose his words with care. 'They'd be doing it one of two ways: from a tracking station on the ground or from a satellite of their own in some suitable orbit. There's nothing in the technology in the first place that we don't have, so I reckon they have it too. As to interception in space, they're reckoned to be ahead of the Yanks there. I'm told there's a lot of worry in Washington about the Soviet space interceptor programme.'

Pabjoy nodded. 'Thanks, Harry,' he said. 'That's all we need.'

When Harry had left he turned to me. 'We still can't demonstrate that Marchand had anything to do with all this.'

'He had,' I said. 'The evidence may all be circumstantial so far, but it's very strong circumstantial evidence. We have the fact that Bracony was an agent, with the probability that he belonged to Hank or someone very much like him. But whether that's all Bracony was or whether he was doubling in some way, we have the further fact that Marchand went scooting off to Conques of all improbable places whenever he had the chance. Put that together with what the PCF people and Muller had to say about those two during the occupation, and you certainly have something.'

Pabjoy didn't seem to be listening. A 2H was tracing the outline of a big square box. 'The transmissions were neat,' he was saying, almost to himself. 'Nothing on paper, so no dead-letter drops, no meetings of any kind. Everything based on Marchand's famous memory for detail. All very neat, except that it had to include a Bracony. And that was the weak link. That, and whoever was controlling him.' He was working carefully on his box. 'I think,' he said suddenly, 'that you can exclude Harry's fantasies of Soviet interception of the signals in space. Life is rarely that complicated. And in any case, I don't think we'll need such exotic explanations. If there was a leak to the Soviets, there were easier ways.'

CHAPTER 24

Chez Drouant

Paris, the indomitable old tart, was primping for Christmas. She wore thousands of fairy lights like so many cheap diamonds in the snow-white filigree of the trees of the Champs Elysées. Around the British Embassy in the faubourg St Honoré the luxury shops achieved their annual blend of the exquisite and the faintly vulgar. The Ministry of Fine Arts had lit up, in perfect taste, the great buildings by Mansart, Gabriel and Antoine. In the pastry shops chocolate yule logs were everywhere and Dior was offering mink-lined cat baskets for people who had everything, including a cat.

I hired a Renault at the airport and drove it to the hotel in the rue de Fleurus, happily unaware that I was in process of making the most disastrous move of my life. After all, I had no way of knowing.

At the hotel I called Isabel and suggested supper.

'A rather venerable aunt has drifted into town. I have to see to her, but I can be with you by nine.'

'Fine,' I said. Then I called Baum. 'You can come to my office,' he said. 'Remember, it's on the third floor, not the seventh. Ha, ha! Come right away.'

I took a cab to the rue des Saussaies, where parking was always impossible. I was sent up to Baum's room. He had dozens of prints of photographs in neat piles on his desk.

'Sit here, my friend,' he said, 'and see what you can recognise in this lot.'

I worked carefully through the pictures, pile by pile. Among the North Africans I could still find nothing. But I had better luck with Sofranal.

'We installed a camera across the way, on the first floor,' Baum said. 'We also used a van. I think we have shots of everyone working in the building: those are the people who arrived and left at regular office hours. There's a separate collection of shots of visitors. An interesting one, that. We'll come to it later.'

The DST's photographic people had put in a lot of overtime, snapping men and women as they emerged from the building. Halfway through the pile I found myself looking at a figure in raincoat and dark hat, tall and slightly stooping.

'That,' I said. 'is your *dopplegänger*, the other Baum.'

Baum took the picture from me and placed it on the blotter in front of him. Soon I stopped shuffling the prints again. I was looking at a stocky figure, hatless, wearing what appeared to be a car coat.

'One of the enforcers,' I said. 'No doubt about it.'

Baum took the print.

I failed to find the second thug. Baum cleared away the discarded prints and put the last pile before me. 'Those appear to be visitors to the building,' he said. 'Tell me what you find.'

On the top of the pile lay an unmistakable photograph of Albert Chavan. The big, florid figure was pulling the door closed behind him, looking almost directly into the camera lens.

Baum was smiling. 'I thought that would intrigue you,' he said. 'It intrigues me.'

Halfway down the pile I stopped. Lying before me was the photograph of an untidy-looking figure in a loud check topcoat. In his hand was a Russian-style fur hat. He was looking vaguely up the road to his left. The fair hair was cut close to the big skull. The features, unmistakably, were those of Hank Munthe.

I looked up at Baum. He was smiling slightly, his eyes watching me carefully from beneath the bushy brows. 'Oh dear,' I said. 'This is the point at which the spaghetti hits the fan.'

'An appropriate Americanism.'

'I have a lot to tell you,' I said, 'and much of it leads to this picture.'

'I hope it will include an account of what has been happening down at Conques.'

'It will,' I said, 'among other things.'

There was nothing more in the pile of prints before me. Baum called for coffee, and after a severe, middle-aged secretary had brought it, he settled back in his chair and waved a chubby hand in my direction.

'I prefer not to talk here,' I said.

Baum's eyebrows moved up a couple of notches. 'So little confidence?'

'Nothing to do with you or your good faith,' I said, 'but a tape is a tape. It can always end up on the wrong deck.'

'I will not pretend there are no microphones here,' Baum said, 'and even though they are switched off there is no reason why you should take my word for it.'

'It's nearly twelve,' I said. 'We could talk over lunch. May I invite you to Drouant? I think it will be a celebration in its rather macabre way.'

We exchanged trivialities in the car on the way to the restaurant: though the driver kept his eyes on the road, his ears appeared to be of normal size. Installed in the handsome old dining room, we ordered the *pâté de perdreau en croûte* and the house's famous fillets of sole. I sought Baum's advice on the wine and he chose a Vouvray.

Waiters hovered over us, adjusting the napery and shuffling knives and forks. The bottle, dripping from the ice bucket, was solemnly presented and subjected to the ritual violation of the cork.

'On our expenses, of course,' Baum was saying, 'we cannot eat at Drouant.'

'On our expenses,' I said, 'we cannot eat at Drouant either.'

Through the meal, with interruptions for service, I took Baum back through the whole saga, round by round, filling in my earlier reticences and working my way finally to Harry's revelations and Pabjoy's speculation. I had no authority whatever for bringing a member of a foreign service into our confidence, but then nor had Baum for helping me. He listened in silence, doing justice to the marvellous food but missing nothing of the narrative.

'I can add a few points,' Baum said when the coffee arrived. 'Let us take the Conques story first. Following a thoughtful call from our friend Pabjoy in London the other day, we got a man down to the Bracony place. He found nothing – no corpse, certainly no radio transmitter. He reported the place had been broken into and was in a mess, but that was all. While he was down there I got him to check R. Brançon's box in the poste restante at Rodez. There were six uncollected items, five of them newspapers. The sixth was a letter posted in Paris, giving a lot of family news which carries no conviction whatever. Our lab has come up with nothing on it yet, but we may still get a break.' He took a sip of coffee.

'Now, there is one person in all this whom you appear to regard as marginal but who interests me perhaps more than anyone else, and that is your stockbroker of the slightly odd political background, Jules Roberton.'

'What's so interesting about him?'

'In the first place, we already have a modest political dossier on him. I must tell you that in more than thirty years in counter-intelligence I doubt if I have seen much more than half a dozen agents who were not already on our files, who were totally clean. Wavre always says that what matters in this work is the archives because sooner or later you'd find your man in there somewhere.'

'It's true, of course. If our records hadn't been in such a filthy mess we'd have put our finger on Philby's early membership of the Communist Party and he'd never have got into the Service at all.'

'The case of Philby is interesting. Consider his political progress from the Communists to the Anglo-German Fellowship, the extreme right. It was contrived of course. And so, I suspect, are Roberton's moves, first leftwards from the PCF to the Trotskyists, and then far over to the right, to the *Action de la France*. The lunatic fringe of French reactionary politics – a thick soup of royalists, Petainists and former supporters of the prewar *Action Française*. Such a political progression – left, further left, far right – is either neurotic or contrived. I must assume the latter. And now he turns out to be in contact over a number of years with the agent Bracony. I think we will have a little talk with Mr Roberton.'

'And what about Albert Chavan, everyone's good friend?'

'I think one of Albert's men killed Avram Artunian. I think the car you saw on the Entraygues Road, heading for Conques, was one of his. Which means that his people had the task of cleaning up the Bracony house; called in, just like furniture removers. Chavan, by the way, owns two Mercedes.'

'That makes Chavan something of a key figure in the story, receiving Hank Munthe at his place, and visiting Sofranal, possibly at the same time as Hank.'

'Possibly, I don't know. It would make sense for Munthe to use Chavan as an intermediary to organise the rough stuff – to be paymaster for the Luna people and the Auto Ecole Marceau. A strange man, Chavan. I had a word with him at Avram's funeral. He was deeply moved. They had been pretty close for twenty-five years. I can only conclude that Albert was given no choice when it came to eliminating Avram.'

'Will you pull him in?'

'I will, though I don't hope for much. He was too long on our side of the fence to be taken in by our little stratagems.'

'Who else?'

'Radescu from Sofranal, plus the two you identified if we can lay our hands on them. From the Auto Ecole Marceau we'll pick up whoever looks likely. And there's the Luna mob too – Ben Rifka, Salek and Ben Ballem. We have an address at eighty-eight rue St Denis where it seems some of them hang out. That street's full of illegal immigrants.'

'When is it for?'

'I'll have everything ready by late tomorrow – addresses checked, my team briefed, a scenario for the interrogations and all the rest. We shall make simultaneous arrests at six am the following morning.'

I was back at the hotel by six and was asleep on my bed when the phone rang. It was Isabel, exactly on time, in the lobby, but as the lift wheezed to a halt on the ground floor, the ancient concierge beckoned me.

'Telephone for Monsieur Carey.'

'Who wants me?'

He enquired. 'A Monsieur Baum.'

There was only the concierge's own phone. I decided I'd best take the call back in my room. I handed Isabel my car keys. I realised later that I hardly looked at her.

'Be a dear,' I said, 'it's the white Renault 5, maybe four cars down to the left. You could be warming it up. I shan't be long.'

She smiled, took the keys, and pulled the fur collar of her coat round her throat. I took the lift up to my room.

Baum's voice was apologetic. 'When we were together I completely forgot to mention that I'd like you to be with me when we bring these fellows in.'

'No problem.'

'Make it six thirty, then, in my office.'

'I'll be there.'

It was at the precise moment I put the receiver down that I heard the explosion. From my room it was a muffled bang, as if some vast object had fallen to the ground, followed by the familiar tinkling sound of shattering glass. The windows rattled in their frames and downstairs something crashed to the floor. It is a very curious thing, but whereas until then I had had no sense of impending catastrophe, at the very moment of hearing the bang I knew exactly what had happened. And with the knowledge came a sickening wave of self-disgust and remorse, and a feeling, too, of total professional incompetence.

I leapt for the door and took the stairs in a series of dangerous leaps. When I reached what was left of the car there were already people out in the usually deserted street and others at their windows. Black smoke was billowing into the icy night air as petrol flamed in the roadway. There were bits of twisted metal everywhere. There was glass. Intense heat from the fire was preventing anyone from getting closer than twenty feet or so. I knew it was hopeless and I will not, cannot describe what the explosion had done to Isabel.

I remember weeping and cursing, and then yelling at a hapless bystander to send for the police. Of the formalities with the police I no longer recall anything at all. But for some reason one image remains with me: the look of sheer horror on the face of the young ambulanceman as he and his mate struggled to lift Isabel's shattered body onto a stretcher. 'There, there, my lad,' the other man said. 'You can get used to anything in this job.' And they pulled the sheet over what had once been her beautiful and aristocratic face.

No 88 rue St Denis proved to be one of those crazily leaning buildings which in any other city would long since have fallen down if no enterprising developer had not already thought of pushing it over and putting up something more profitable. But successive waves of poverty-stricken immigrants willing to sleep six or more to a room had made such squalid tenements profitable enough to save for another year and then another . . . At street level there was a *porno* movie house. Above, and reached through an unsecured street door, a dank corridor and a narrow stairwell, were the upper floors. They consisted entirely of flats and single rooms. The pervading odour was of obscure spices and endlessly boiling mutton.

I had spent some time looking at the desolate pile from across the road. It was just after midnight and I had finished with the police. Three cognacs, neat and in too rapid succession, had steadied my nerves though they had not, I suppose, improved my judgment. But human physiology is a funny thing: I could not stop crying. And so I had stood across the street from No 88 rue St Denis, the tears streaming down my face and my hand resting on the familiar contour of the .38 in my overcoat pocket.

Looking back now, I find it quite impossible to describe my state of mind. Perhaps I was, momentarily, unhinged . . . crazy. Certainly, my normally rational thought processes had been suspended. I was not only about to break the law: I was about to break several of the most sacred rules of the Section, to say nothing of the Sixth Commandment. I do not believe in vigilante law. I do not subscribe to the concept of an eye for an eye. I am not a bloodthirsty man. And yet I stood and wept and fingered my .38 as if it were the only friend I had in the world.

It never struck me that I should long since have phoned Alfred Baum to tell him what had happened. Nor did it occur to me that to erupt into a building full of illegal North African immigrants in order to mete out rough justice to one or more of their number was not merely foolhardy: it was insane. I was, I say, temporarily out of my mind. But within my insanity I was lucid – never more so – and wary as a cat. Thus, I suppose, are many murders carried out. Be that as it may, I eased the safety catch of the gun in my pocket, crossed the deserted street and pushed in through the cracked and blistered door.

The Arabs of the Maghreb are, fortunately, noisy people. They shout a lot. They play their wailing, endlessly lovelorn music at full volume, and they go late to bed. From the dimly lit landings, the building was a cacophony. I could not have wished for better. I had to take my chances, so I knocked hard on the first door I came to. It was answered after a while by a solemn-faced, overweight girl. She was wearing a red dressing gown and she looked sleepy.

'Oui?'

'Where does Mahmoud Ben Rifka live?'

She looked at me in the way illegals have: they expect no good of strangers.

'Connais pas.'

I smiled and pulled a 100-franc note from my pocket. I held it up by a corner.'

'I bet you do.'

'He's shit,' the girl said, reaching for the note. 'Second floor left.' Her hand closed over the note, crumpling it. Then she shut the door in my face. I banged on it again and it opened promptly.

'If he's shit,' I said, 'maybe you'll help me. He owes me money. If he knows it's me he won't open up.'

'What's that got to do with me?'

I pulled another 100-franc note from my pocket. It was what seemed to motivate her. 'If you were to call to him through the door, perhaps he'd open it. You know, say it's a friend enquiring for him.'

Her gaze travelled from my face to the note and back again. Greed and caution fought their way across her eyes.

'He'd beat me up when he found out. He hit my mother. Broke her nose with his fist. Over fifteen francs, that was.'

'Wouldn't you like to see him paid back?'

'Who'd pay him back?' She had sized me up and decided I'd be no match for Mahmoud upstairs.

'I think I can trust you,' I said, trying a smile. 'It isn't a debt. I'm from the border police. Immigration.'

The girl suddenly looked frightened. 'Our papers are in order,' she said. 'We have our *carte* from the police. I can show you.'

'I'm not interested in you and your mother,' I said, 'though I might be if you won't co-operate. I'm interested in Ben Rifka.'

'How do I know you're police anyway?' She was a village girl but they aren't fools in villages.

I took a chance. 'Can you read?' I asked.

She shook her head.

'Well, here's the warrant, if you're so particular.' I had an official-looking document in my pocket. It had been stamped and signed. There were scrolls at the top with some gothic-looking type. It was the unused prescription which Isabel had got for me when I'd been beaten up. I tend to leave bits and pieces like that in my pockets. I took it out now and showed it to the girl. She gazed at it solemnly.

'A warrant,' I said.

'Are you going to take him away?'

'Yes.'

'Will he come back?'

'He'll be on the streets of Casablanca within the week.'

It seemed to decide her. 'Serve the bastard right,' she said. 'The lousy bastard. My mother's in pain all day.' She took the second note, crumpled it and thrust it into a pocket. Then she pushed past me and started up the stairs. I followed. At the second floor she stopped at a door behind which more music surged and throbbed in endless repetition.

'Now listen,' I said. 'I don't mind what you say to get him to the door, but the moment he starts to open it you're to run down those stairs – and I mean run – and lock yourself in your flat, is that clear?'

'What else did you think I was going to do, introduce you?'

She turned to the door and banged on it with her fist. The music was turned down a shade and a man's voice called out something in Arabic. The girl answered. I had no idea what was said but she seemed to know what she was doing. I only hoped I wasn't being set up and about to walk into a trap. Was racial solidarity stronger than the desire to even up a score?

The discussion, such as it was, bounced to and fro through the closed door. Finally, the man must have decided that he had best investigate. I heard a key being fitted into the lock.

'Right, down you go. And thanks.'

The girl took to her heels without a word. I prayed that the door wouldn't be on a chain, told myself that chains were for the embattled middle classes, huddling over their possessions. That might be nonsense, but on this occasion I was right. The door was pulled inwards and a man appeared, outlined against the harsh light from a single unshaded bulb which hung from the middle of the ceiling. I couldn't see anyone else.

I put my shoulder against the door, forcing it wide open, and brought my hand out of my pocket. I saw the man's eyes drop to the gun. Then they returned to my face. Now that I was inside the room I could see another man sitting on a low divan. They had been eating something and drinking what looked like tea.

'Get over there, next to him,' I said. The first man backed slowly across the room, his eyes on the gun. His friend fidgeted.

'You over there – if you move an inch I'll shoot you without even asking your name. What is your name, anyway?'

'Salek. Ali Salek.'

'And you're Ben Rifka.'

There was no answer, just a grunt. By now Ben Rifka had reached the divan and had sat down on it. He leaned forward as if to help himself to tea. 'If you move an inch I'll shoot you,' I said. 'You can see the silencer on the gun. I'm a very good shot. I shall shoot you from here, in the face. Both of you.'

They both sat back on the divan. Then Ben Rifka spoke.

'What the hell do you want? Who are you, anyway?'

'You know perfectly well who I am. You've been trying to kill me for long enough.'

'No idea who the hell you are. Must be some crazy nut, beating your way in here with a gun. We're peaceful workers. We don't know what you're talking about.'

I reached out for the record player with my left hand and turned the volume up. It must have been a gesture which was familiar to them in their profession. Only they were usually the ones to adjust the equipment. A look of abject terror came into the eyes of Salek.

'Before I deal with you both,' I said, 'I want to set your minds at rest, just in case you think I'm a ghost. The car bomb went off all right, only I wasn't in the car. It was a girl that you killed. She had never done you any harm. She had a lot to live for. So now you'd better start saying your prayers.'

My voice seemed to be coming from someone else. I knew what I was saying but I had no control over the fact of saying it. Is that how it is when people are under greater stress than they

can deal with? Never in a thousand years would I have bee
able to picture myself talking like this to two unshaven youn
men in torn jeans, the products of some North African slum, th
mindless, brutalised tools of men with ties and well-cut suit
who knew better and were not inclined to do their own dirt
work. I was about to kill the wrong people but, as I say, I wa
crazy at the time.

'Please don't shoot.' It was Ben Rifka, gulping out the words
'We can do a deal. What do you want? You want information
What do you want me to tell you? One can always do a deal.'

'There's nothing you know that I don't know too, but whil
you're about it you could tell me who gives you your orders.'

'It's Jules, Chavan's man.'

'What did they pay you?'

'Five thousand. And another five when the job's done.'

'You won't be getting the second five. Have you said you
prayers?'

The music was blaring and I was afraid the neighbour
might complain. And now I can only describe simply what wa
simply and calmly done. I brought up my left hand to grip m
right wrist in the approved style, steadying the gun. I fired on
shot at Ben Rifka and, immediately, another at Salek. Then
repeated what I had just done. In all it took maybe fou
seconds. I had hit them both in the face and both topple
forward with a choking sound – something like a whimper -
and fell in crumpled heaps across each other. I turned th
sound down and left the room, closing the door carefully behin
me. Neither the girl in the dressing gown nor anyone else sav
me leave the building.

As I walked fast up the rue St Denis I suddenly realised tha
I had started to cry again.

CHAPTER 25

13 rue des Saussaies

Baum had got himself a pot of coffee from somewhere and poured me a cup, very strong and black, heaping in a large portion of the Common Market sugar mountain. It was six thirty-five, still pitch dark outside and freezing hard. There had been snow again for most of the previous day and little of it had melted. The snowfall had brought a muffled peace to the city, wrapping her in a pure white blanket and filtering most of the noise out of the implacable Parisian traffic. It was the day before Christmas. Paris was still asleep, getting ready to live things up through the coming night – the *réveillon.* In the bleak corridors and the warren of grey offices at the DST there was a surprising degree of activity. Baum seemed to have mobilised half the staff in a grand gesture of defiance towards the absent Wavre.

'I am truly sorry,' he said. In a gesture of great tenderness he reached out his plump hand and patted my knee. 'You and she were – good friends.'

'We were.'

'You must have had a very bad day yesterday.'

'The press drove me mad, but in a sense it kept my mind off what had happened. I was able to be angry with the journalists. It was good for me.'

He nodded, sighed. 'The work must go on. It is all we can do.' He lit a cigarette to cover his embarrassment. 'I have six cars out with two men in each.' He passed me a sheet of paper. 'I don't know how many we'll find at home.'

There were nine names typed out:

Albert Marie Chavan
Simianski alias Radescu
Maurice Blanc
Mahmoud Ben Rifka
Mahmoud Ben Ballem
Ali Salek
Jules Roberton
Jean François Ravet
Luc Delahaye

I hesitated over Ben Ballem, my corpse from the Chemin de la Fosse, and the other two. A sense of delicacy had somehow prevented me from mentioning Ben Ballem's death to Baum. Nor was I going to say anything about the others.

'Ravet is your pseudo-Baum,' Baum said, 'and Blanc is one of the fellows who roughed you up. Delahaye is our best bet from the Auto Ecole Marceau. The three from Luna should yield something between them.'

I warmed my hands on the hot cup and wished I were elsewhere.

'They should start coming in soon, and we'll know any minute now how many we've got. We have radio contact with the cars.' He pressed a button on the office intercom. '*Charlot. Bonjour, mon vieux*. What news?'

'I've got reports from all cars. Five out of nine.'

'Who's missing?'

There was a pause. 'Two of the Africans have been found shot. Car No. three says it must have happened a day or two ago. The third African wasn't found.'

'Who else?'

'The man Roberton.'

Baum banged his fist onto the desk. '*Merde!* Listen, I want Jolivet to report to me the moment he gets back from Roberton's place. Immediately.'

'Right you are, *patron*.'

'It's just what I was afraid of,' Baum said to me. 'I'd take a bet on Roberton having disappeared. As for the others, it looks as if old scores are being settled. Or silence is being ensured. Now is the time for the opposition to shut some mouths.'

I said nothing at all, wondering if Baum's keen gaze carried any kind of message. I had the feeling you couldn't fool this strangely compelling little man.

By now there was plenty of noise in the building – tramping feet outside Baum's office and on the floor above and an indistinct babble of voices. Soon a knock on the door and Baum's gruff '*entrez*' brought a middle-aged swarthy man into the room. He was muffled to the chin in a heavy overcoat and knitted scarf. All of him looked apologetic.

'Well, Jolivet?'

'The Roberton apartment was empty. No reply to the bell, and we nearly beat the door down too. So I woke the concierge. She said the Robertons left for abroad yesterday. How did she know it was abroad? Labels on the luggage, she said. The Hilton Hotel in some city she couldn't recall, but she did remember the country: Brazil. She was sure of that.'

'Get back there right away,' Baum said, 'and get the concierge to let you in. If she won't do it, go in anyway. Take the place apart. Call me if you find anything you don't understand and get someone – Astruc perhaps – to do the same at Roberton's office at forty-eight boulevard des Italiens. He should question the staff, too. We're assuming Roberton was the cut-out between Brançon and the Soviets and that's all I can give you at the moment. I want to know his movements, what's in his address books – all the usual. And incidentally, check at both addresses to see if there's any notepaper to match a letter addressed to Brançon which they're looking at for me in the lab. And do the necessary at travel agents and airlines. I want to know where Mr Roberton has actually gone. You can forget Brazil. Did the concierge say who went with him?'

'His wife. There's just the two of them.'

'All right, off you go.'

The intercom buzzed. 'Yes?' Baum snapped at it.

'All five are in now, *patron*.'

Baum turned to me. 'I think I'll have a chat with Albert myself. I'd like you to stay.' He pressed a button. 'Bring in Chavan.'

Albert Chavan was unshaven and without a tie. A young assistant of some kind led him in and retreated before Baum's dismissive wave.

'Albert,' Baum said, shaking hands. 'How are you? You know our friend from England.'

Chavan gave me a quizzical smile and extended a hand. 'We meet in unfortunate circumstances, Mr Panmure. It's what I said – now on this side of the law, now on that.'

'So how are you keeping, Albert?' Baum's manner was relaxed, disarming.

'I'd be better for a bath and shave, *mon vieux*, but never mind. You have your job to do and no doubt our friend Wavre knows what he – or you – are up to.' The threat was delicately made.

'Never mind Wavre, Albert,' Baum said evenly. 'This time you're dealing with me.'

'You realise, Alfred, that I will have nothing to say this morning?'

'Then we shall have to await your remarks until this afternoon, this evening, tomorrow – I don't know . . .' Baum shrugged expressively.

'What is all this supposed to be about?'

'Well, let us make a start with incitement and conspiracy to murder, and we can move later to the security aspects of the case.'

Albert Chavan's laugh rumbled round the room. He made it sound genuine. 'And who was the intended victim?'

'Mr Panmure here, among others.'

Chavan swivelled his great frame in my direction. 'Has someone been trying to kill you, Mr Panmure?'

'Several people,' I said. 'Several times. By various methods. And they ended up killing the wrong person.'

'But after poor Avram's death, did I not warn you of precisely that?'

'You did. Perhaps you were well placed to do so.'

Chavan spread his big hands in an eloquently deprecatory gesture. 'Come now, Mr Panmure, would I risk my business and my liberty for such sordid ends?'

'I don't really know,' I said. 'You might.'

'Let me be as open with you, Albert, as this case permits,' Baum said. 'We are bringing in seven other people, mainly from Sofranal and the Luna outfit, and there will be more. You know as well as I do, my dear fellow, that the law of averages dictates that we will get some useful statements out of that lot. Now, I believe your role in all this has been a central one and that several of our customers will end by naming you and some of your people. So I propose to offer you a deal.'

Albert Chavan chuckled. 'Deals before eight am, with you in a tie and me without? Come, Alfred, that wouldn't be a deal, it would be an imposed solution.'

'With anyone else, maybe. But not with you, Albert. I have no doubt that necktie or no necktie, you are not the least bit intimidated.'

'That is correct.'

'So I am offering you a deal. You will tell me all you know about this business: who is employing you, what your instructions are, whom you are using, when it started, the lot. In return, you have my word that we will forget you have been here. We are after information, not prosecutions.'

Chavan shook his big head slowly from side to side in a theatrical gesture of pity. 'My poor Alfred,' he said, 'you must be in a hell of a difficulty to offer me a proposition like that. What I am required to deliver is clear enough. But what do you deliver in return? Precisely nothing. You say you will let me go home and will forget I was here. But, my dear fellow, that is exactly what you will have to do anyway, whether I talk to you or not. And if you say you plan to hold me here for I don't know how long, why then *I* say my lawyer is being instructed this morning to commence habeas corpus proceedings with a magistrate at precisely three this afternoon if I am not home by then.

No, no, you've got it all wrong. It is *I* who can offer *you* a deal.'

Baum's air of bonhomie had not deserted him. 'Let's hear it, Albert, for what it may be worth.'

'You send me home in one of your cars now – though I would take a cup of coffee with you first – and I will see that my friends in the Assembly don't raise hell about the lack of discipline and firm leadership at the DST. And that would only be the start.' He paused, then slowly: 'You may know that de Lannoy in the Minister's office owes me a favour. This would be his opportunity to discharge it.'

Baum looked up at Chavan from beneath his brows. Both men were immobile, silent. Chavan's head was wreathed in smoke from the cigarette hanging from the corner of his mouth. Across the plain metal desk Baum still wore his expression of faintly sardonic good nature. 'Albert,' he said, 'I am afraid you have misunderstood this rather complex situation. We are old friends, you and I, and I am not in the least offended by your remarks. As far as I am concerned, that little runt de Lannoy can bleat to the Minister about me as much as he chooses. Now listen to me carefully.'

He filled a cup with coffee, and pushed it towards Chavan and refilled his own cup and mine. Chavan lit another cigarette. The footsteps had died away in the corridors and only a distant murmur of voices could be heard.

'Behind your threat there is a mistaken assumption: that Wavre wants to paper over the Marchand affair while Panmure here and I want to make a cause célèbre out of it. In fact, we have no such interest. This affair has what I shall call a transatlantic dimension. That is what makes it delicate and what, in a sense, guarantees our discretion. But – and here is the heart of the matter – it also has what I shall call a European dimension. You are no longer in the service and so you will not expect me to spell it out. But it is that other dimension, and that only, which interests me and will interest Wavre when he gets back. And if de Lannoy or any of the deputies you have in your pocket starts making a fuss about what we are doing, he will eventually look very sick, I can assure you, and not all that patriotic.'

It was a good performance. Chavan shrugged his shoulders and laughed. 'Not bad, Alfred, not bad,' he said. 'But I know nothing of your dimensions – transatlantic, cisalpine or extra-European. And so I have nothing to contribute to this scenario of yours.'

Baum stroked his pink cheek with a forefinger. 'A pity, Albert,' he said. 'I would have thought you would prefer to keep your transatlantic connection off your dossier. But how can I guarantee you such a thing if you persist in your present course? What is more, Mr Hank Munthe will abandon you just as soon as it suits him. And when that happens, my dear Albert, you will need all the physical protection you can get.'

'I have all I can use, Alfred.'

Baum seemed to come to a quick decision. 'I think you need time to reflect, Albert,' he said, 'so I propose to ask you to leave us. You can tell one of my men to contact me whenever you decide to resume our little chat.'

When Chavan had been taken away, Baum said: 'Albert will talk. He can't afford to have "connected with the CIA" written all over his dossier.'

Baum had been right. The interrogations went on throughout the day, with weary DST men reporting from time to time, though there was little enough to report. No one was talking willingly and even the prospect of missing the Christmas festivities wasn't loosening any tongues. Late in the evening Baum called for Radescu, the dubious boss of Sofranal.

A few moments later Laurent, one of the DST men, ushered in a short, bald and puffy man in his sixties. He was loosely packed into a pale blue track suit with IR embroidered on the chest next to the *griffe* of Pierre Cardin. He managed to achieve a sort of unctuous authority despite the unlikely outfit.

'Ah, Monsieur Baum, precisely. I am honoured to meet

you, *Monsieur*. I know of your work, of course, which I much admire –'

'You do not know of my work, Simianski, so please save your breath, which you will need shortly, and sit in that chair.'

'My name is not Simianski, *Monsieur*, no. It is Radescu, Ion Radescu.' He pointed to the initials as if they constituted evidence.

'That is an opinion I do not share. To me you are Boris Simianski: to me and to our archives here at the DST.'

'My identity papers, *Monsieur*, are in order. Certainly. I must tell you that I am well-known at the Ministry of the Interior –'

'And at the DST and the Sûreté and, I fear, the Préfecture. But,' and here Baum held up a pudgy but imperious hand to dam the other's flow of words, 'but please do not allow yourself to be worried by the fact that I am fresh from reading your file. I am an open-minded man, and speaking as a sort of policeman I have to say that I am not allowed to hold the past against you. It is the present, Simianski, that concerns me, and it is the future which I believe should concern you.'

'I do assure you that you are quite mistaken as to my identity. Definitely mistaken, yes. My friends at the Interior and particularly my very good friends at the US Embassy – Mr Collet and Mr Hergesheimer and Ambassador Sherman (perhaps you know the Ambassador, a most charming man) – yes, these good friends of mine will be only too happy to vouch for me, I assure you. Then this unfortunate misunderstanding can be cleared up with the greatest speed, of course. And needless to say, my dear Sir, nothing whatever will be done by me to embarrass you and your men over the error, the inconvenience, you understand, the indignity –'

'There is no error, Simianski, and the inconvenience and indignity so far are as nothing to what will come if we don't start getting some sense out of you soon. Your men Ravet and Blanc are talking their heads off already and I have made a useful deal with Albert Chavan, who seems to have little affection for you.

So you, Simianski, are odd man out, which will make it very difficult for me to do anything for you.'

'My dear Baum,' Simianski-Radescu replied, trying the familiar mode, 'you and I know that such matters are not always what they appear to be. Definitely not. What importance can it have when underlings talk, my dear Baum? What credence can be given to loose talk provoked by pressure, I ask you most sincerely? Always remembering, my dear Sir, that it is talk about someone who has friends. Influential friends at many levels in the administration.' He paused, smiled, tapped the side of his nose twice with a thick forefinger and repeated, 'Friends'.

'Everyone in France has friends,' Baum said cheerfully. 'Any pimp on the street corner will tell you he can't be touched because he has an uncle licking stamps at the Mairie. My colleagues of the criminal police have a lot of trouble with our French system of having friends, but this is the DST, Simianski, not the Préfecture. And here the system works less well.' He paused and leant forward over his desk. 'As far as I can see, Simianski, you have stumbled into an area where you will not have a friend in the world – not when it is realised that we are dealing here with a question of espionage on behalf of the USSR.' His voice underlined the four initials.

The fat man in the pale blue track suit blinked twice and looked quickly from Baum to me as if one of us would tell him it was all a joke after all. 'You are bluffing,' he said. 'You are definitely bluffing. And you are infringing on my rights.'

'Shut up,' Baum said brusquely. 'Your rights here are what I choose to make them. Your prints are now being checked against those in the dossier of Boris Simianski, tried in March 1946 for collaboration with the enemy and theft of Jewish property and condemned to ten years in jail. We'll have the computer's opinion later. That will be time enough for you to complain.'

'I want my lawyer,' Simianski said weakly. 'I will say nothing without my lawyer, save to warn you of the consequences of your actions.' Small beads of sweat had formed on the top of his head and again he looked towards me as if he would somehow get better treatment from that quarter.

'Take him away,' Baum said wearily, 'and continue the interrogation. Let me know when he begins to see sense. And if he wants to make a deal, he'd better hurry because I don't make deals after the first day.' He was talking as if Radescu was no longer there.

'I don't believe –' Radescu was saying, but Baum interrupted him. 'Out with him,' he said, waving an arm, 'I'm busy.'

The DST man took Radescu firmly by the pale blue arm and propelled him out of the chair and through the door.

'That may help,' Baum said, 'but I do not have high hopes of that repellent creature. Let us turn to something else. Let us eat something.'

'I think,' Baum said a little later between mouthfuls of sauerkraut, sausage and boiled pork ribs, 'that as soon as we have disposed of our dinner we should play our ace with Albert.'

'Ace of diamonds – a red card?'

'Precisely.' We ate for a while in silence. 'You know,' he said, 'this entire circus can collapse on my head at any time.'

'I know,' I said. 'Your nerve amazes me.'

Baum smiled. 'Sometimes one has to take a risk or two. But please don't think I'm suffering from an attack of Anglo-French solidarity or even crusading zeal. I am running risks because I came to the conclusion that not running them would constitute a greater risk.'

'For you personally?'

'For the country, and therefore for me personally. I try not to separate the two in my thinking.'

'Your reasoning processes aren't my business so I won't ask you why you concluded you had best dig into all this. But I have to say I am grateful to you.'

'That's as may be,' Baum said, 'but believe me, my motives

are entirely selfish. If our interests can coincide with those of your country, that's fine. Splendid. But if they can't, then that's too bad. There's no room for romantic international gestures in these matters.'

Baum crossed his knife and fork on his plate, pushed it away and refilled his glass. Then he addressed the intercom. 'Bring Chavan in.' When Chavan arrived Baum waved him to a seat.

'I am sorry you are having such a day, Albert. I hope we can now bring matters to a head so that we can go home to our wives.'

Chavan shrugged. 'I doubt it,' he said.

Baum filled a glass and pushed it in Chavan's direction.

'I said this morning,' he continued quietly, 'that there was what I called a European dimension to this affair. You did not react to that – possibly because you didn't know about it and thought I was bluffing. But I wasn't bluffing, Albert. I now propose to take you into my confidence. The risk I take is that you will not respect that confidence. The risk you take is that if you decide to remain silent and unleash de Lannoy and the rest on me, you will find much later, at the end of the road, that you will all appear to have been working in the Soviet interest – an impression which your American friends will naturally do all they can to reinforce.'

He paused for effect but Albert Chavan said nothing. 'This case,' Baum continued, 'will not implicate Hank Munthe and the CIA. If it is a case at all it will be directed against the Soviets. And that is because Marchand, perhaps unwittingly, perhaps not, was working for both sides. You didn't know, of course. But *I* know, and you will see, therefore, that in lending yourself to the dirty work involved in covering up the Marchand affair, you have in fact been covering up an affair of Soviet intelligence, in which one of the principal characters has already decided that the best thing he could do was make himself scarce. That was late yesterday, and it wasn't such a foolish move on his part.'

'Who was that?'

'A man called Jules Roberton: the cut-out.'

'I never heard of him.'

'It doesn't surprise me. Nor does it make any difference. You know enough about such matters to know that the dirt will spread outwards from this Roberton to contaminate anyone who was in any way connected with this business. And when the press gets on to it there will be victims, my dear Albert, because the press always requires victims. But consider how many people are involved in our enquiries already. There are several dozen in this building right now. Someone, sooner or later, is bound to say: "Try Chavan and his outfit, only don't say I said so." It'll be someone, maybe one of my own men, who needs a favour from the press or has a debt to repay. You know how these things are.'

Chavan took a gulp of wine and held out his glass to be refilled. 'You are bluffing, Alfred. The last thing this Government wants is a case in which the name of André Marchand is mentioned.'

Baum sighed. 'If you work on that premise,' he said, 'you are taking a very big risk. Consider: the man Roberton has fled and we may or may not catch up with him. But catch him or not, *someone* will be found who can be pulled into court. The press will find out and the press will demand it. My guess is as good as yours, but I would say the Government hasn't the internal coherence to resist the kind of press campaign I can see here. And if my guess is right, you are at very great risk, Albert. Your men have been down to the Brançon/Bracony place. You yourself are now fully implicated with Luna and Sofranal. Our friend Panmure here has some damning evidence to give. And I cannot afford to appear less than scrupulous in my investigations.'

'You've nothing concrete. Only speculation.'

'What do I have? I have a photograph of you at the door of Sofranal and statements from Sofranal personnel which implicate you in the attempt on Panmure's life. I have statements from two of the Luna mob that you placed the contract on him.

I have Avram Artunian's death: we're far from being finished with that. I have your car sighted on the road to Conques. And I shall have what you will tell me before you leave here and what your people will tell me after being in our hands for a few days. That is what I will have, and whatever we may do with it in court, all of it will go into your dossier, Albert, and one day, one day . . .' He let his voice trail off. 'Unless,' he added quietly, 'you are interested in the deal I offered you this morning.'

Albert Chavan took another draught of wine and again held out the glass. Baum filled it and Chavan leant back in his chair, staring silently into the dull red liquid. 'All right,' he said, 'put me in a quiet room with some writing things. We'll see what we can do.'

When Chavan had been taken away, Baum said: 'Let's see how my men have been getting on with the Roberton enquiry.' He turned to the intercom: 'Send in Jolivet.'

The man on the Roberton assignment came in holding a tattered notebook. He consulted it as he spoke.

'Astruc reports that he interviewed the staff at Roberton's offices and found nothing suspicious. He and his men then went through Roberton's private office. They've brought a lot of stuff back for further examination – address books, engagement diary, files and so on.' He paused, but Baum waved him on. 'Together with two of my men I spent the day taking the Roberton apartment to pieces. There's a certain amount of stuff I brought back which may yield something. It's too soon to say.'

'Any luck with the writing paper?'

'Yes, there's a box of paper and envelopes in the apartment which match the letter in the lab.'

'And the travel agents?'

'We traced a booking through the Air France office near the Opéra. They flew to Zurich from Orly on single tickets yesterday afternoon. We're in touch with the Swiss police via Interpol. Nothing yet.'

'Nor will there be,' Baum said quietly. 'All right, thank you.'

The Chavan statement spelt most of it out but not quite all of it. It appeared that Hank's instructions had escalated in violence with startling rapidity. At first, Chavan was merely to head me off, and particularly to prevent me contacting Baum. Hence the elaborate kidnapping and the mayhem on the seventh floor. That served both to fool me and to fulfil the second instruction, which came hard on the heels of the first: to scare me off. And as I, in my foolishness, kept coming back for more, the instruction changed yet again. Now it was to dispose of me – Hank no doubt called it, in his sensitive way, creating a negative survival situation. Why he wanted both a fake car accident and the rubbing out by Algerian bandits, Chavan didn't know, though I could hazard the guess that the Algerians sounded like a safer bet.

So Chavan did what he was paid to do – arranged, via Sofranal, for the tricksy Marceau car, and fixed up the contract with the Luna mob. If one failed, the other would succeed. When both failed and I got to Bracony, Chavan was instructed to get his men down there to deal with me and then phone for further orders. Finding what they found, they were told to dispose of Bracony's corpse and of the transmitter. We would find the transmitter, Chavan wrote, in pieces in a shallow pit in the field immediately behind the house. It had been covered with hay, muck and debris. Bracony had been buried in the woods a kilometre away. Meanwhile, the contract with Luna stood: hence the *plastique* at Isabel's place and the car bomb.

Chavan had written it all out carefully, giving dates and organising his story in the way he knew the DST would want it. What he put in on his own behalf was a firm disclaimer: he knew nothing about an alleged Soviet connection and nothing about US espionage. What he left out altogether was how he had got into bed with Hank Munthe in the first place and what he'd done for him in the past. He had nothing to say about Avram Artunian and Anny Dupuy. Complicity in attempted murder was one thing: in actual murder, another.

'It's good as far as it goes,' Baum said, 'but it doesn't go very far. Consider: you speak to Avram and within twenty-four hours Chavan is briefed to have him killed and to deal with you in a specific and complicated fashion. That kind of speed is very neat and thoroughly implausible. It's almost as if he was *waiting* for you.'

'Which means a leak in London. Someone who was keeping Hank Munthe informed.'

'Who knew?'

'The top of the SIS and the Special Branch and probably half the Foreign Office, now I come to think of it.'

'With a list like that here in Paris, the Politburo in Moscow would have had the whole thing within twenty-four hours.'

'Not all that different where I come from,' I said. There was a silence. 'Spying for the Americans isn't called spying, for some reason.'

'The whole thing sounds about right the way we have it now,' Baum said.

'Sofranal,' I said, half to myself. 'A CIA front if ever I saw one.'

'If we had been as smart with the Americans as we think we are with the Soviets, it would have been on our files.'

'We all make mistakes,' I said.

Later we said goodbye to Albert Chavan, who had managed to retain his impressive poise.

'That was quite a useful statement, Albert,' Baum said. 'It gave me about fifty per cent of what I needed and what you could have supplied.'

Chavan managed a look of broad astonishment. 'You are hard to please, Alfred. What you have there is enough to destroy me. What more could you possibly want?'

'You know what I could want, Albert, so I will not bore you by repeating it. But never mind. I think you should go home now. I also think you should keep in touch with me on any little jobs you may find yourself doing for Mr Hank Munthe.'

'If all this hasn't blown me,' Chavan said.

'You'll know how to deal with that,' Baum said. 'I back you against the American any day of the week.'

'Thank you, Alfred,' Chavan said. He paused. 'And my dossier . . . ?'

'Unsullied,' Baum said. 'And if you keep in touch in the way I have suggested, why, we will be able to insert your CIA relationship in your dossier in a thoroughly praiseworthy form.'

Chavan grunted. 'I have to trust you, Alfred,' he said, 'because I have no choice in the matter.' He stretched out a great fist and took the statement, still lying in the centre of Baum's desk. He put it in his breast pocket.

'We don't want this as a *pièce* in my dossier at this stage, do we?'

Baum made no attempt to retrieve the sheets. He activated the intercom. 'I want a car and driver to take Monsieur Chavan home.'

When Chavan had left, Baum phoned the duty officer at the Quai d'Orsay. Had there been any movements of Soviet diplomats reported in the past forty-eight hours? The duty officer said he didn't know. He promised to phone back. An hour later he did so. One Teresvili, a Second Secretary, had left on the Aeroflot flight that morning. And a man named Vlassov from the Tass* office had left on the same flight. Both had indicated to the Ministry that they would not be returning. Baum asked if these departures were considered in any way odd by the Russian Desk.

'A bit precipitate,' the duty officer said, 'but not all that unusual.'

'They're cleaning out the stable,' Baum said to me. 'I know both those gentlemen as KGB. I'd have been astonished if no one had left when Roberton took off.'

'By the way,' I said, 'will you be able to hold the press at bay?'

* The official Soviet newsagency.

'I was bluffing, of course,' Baum replied. 'The Government will see to it that the press keeps away from the story.'

'Even *l'Humanité*?'

'They don't matter. They've cried treason too often for anyone to pay serious attention, and they know it themselves. It's why the PCF approached you.'

'What about all these types being interviewed? Are you likely to get anything out of them?'

'You can count it as window-dressing. I daresay we'll get something, but there isn't much point because we shan't be using it.' Baum shook his head sadly. 'It's good practice for my lads, that's all.'

'I must go,' I said. 'I could use some sleep.' We shook hands. 'Thank you,' I said.

'I am sure you would do the same for me,' Baum said. 'It has been a very pleasant co-operation. But you should have told me the truth about Brançon and Jules Roberton. We might have pulled off quite a coup, you and I.'

I slept till two next afternoon and at three I found Arthur slumped in the Scribe bar.

'It's all over,' I said. 'Wrapped up. *Finis*.'

'Got what you wanted?'

'I suppose so, if I ever really wanted anything out of all this. I leave seven corpses behind me and I doubt whether I have added to the sum total of human happiness. Also, it's not really how I like to treat the French.'

Arthur grunted and drank. 'They gave you a hiding for your pains,' he said. 'Maybe that makes the score even.'

We drank in silence for what seemed a long time.

'A lovely girl,' Arthur said, looking hard into his glass.

'A lovely girl.'

'Breeding.'

'To hell with breeding. Let's just say a lovely girl.'

'I know how you feel, Carey my old sport.'

'You don't. It was a monstrous piece of arrogance on my

part, kidding myself they couldn't get to me. I had no right to risk her life just because I was stupid enough to risk my own. And I thought I was a pro.'

'We all make mistakes.'

'Don't steal my clichés, Arthur.'

I finished my drink and gave him a thump on the shoulder. 'Thanks for your help,' I said. 'Sorry I never gave you a story.'

I went straight from there to Charles de Gaulle. Down in the shopping concourse I bought a card depicting, of all things, the Eiffel Tower and addressed it to Ariane Bontemps. 'I have finished my *reportage*,' I wrote, 'and I have all the answers you or I could need. I feel sure you do not want to be troubled with them now. Thank you both.' Then I made my way up the space-age walkways and out to Satellite 5 and aboard the flight.

CHAPTER 26

Leonid Vasilievich Serov

None of us, I suppose, is as tough as he likes to make out, or as he seems, or as he needs to be. Only the psychopaths have no chinks in their armour.

I moaned to Otto Feld, a man trained to hear about other people's anguish without showing embarrassment. 'It appears to me,' I said, 'that I am your authentic loser. Every success of the kind I chalk up is a loss. Can anyone possibly make what I've accomplished so brilliantly in France look like an achievement?'

Otto's cherubic face showed no emotion.

'Seven corpses,' I said. 'I left seven corpses behind me. Without exception, those deaths are meaningless. They served no purpose whatever.'

'Explain, please.'

'The French order these things better,' I said. 'They see a potential mess and what do they do? Smother it, to avoid a bigger mess. What do we do? Go after the facts, ferret about, stir up old sins and emotions, kill a few people and come up with the answers. *Then* what do we do? Look at the answers we've come up with, decide we're appalled at the consequences of acting on them, and probably end up doing what the French did in the first place.'

'You are cynical, my friend.'

'Why not? Cynics are better equipped to deal with the ironies of fate.'

'Explain, please.'

'Well, take André Marchand. A genuine hero of the Resistance. But he falls in love, and that's what destroys him and makes a crook out of him: just falling in love. Because if they hadn't got at him via Anny Dupuy he might well have held out against the Gestapo just like a lot of others. And he'd have ended either as a martyr to the cause – *mort pour la France* in Fresnes or Auschwitz – or as Prime Minister. Yet it would have been the same man who spent half a lifetime betraying his country. Not a better man or a worse man, but the same man. His mistake was falling in love.'

Otto shook his head. 'Not a mistake. An accident, if you like.'

'In Paris,' I said, 'I was somewhat accident-prone myself.'

'It is the profession,' he said. 'We are not really fit people to know.'

Later, I ploughed through the ten pages of NATO minutes which friend Danvers had provided. They were in reported speech and the waffle had been cut out. There wasn't enough heat in the proceedings of the Political Committee to boil a small egg. But in the Security Commission's minutes I found something:

> The Chairman stated that he had received a communication, via channels, from the Director of the US Federal Bureau of Investigation, Washington. It related to the defection on 9 November of Leonid Vasilievich Serov, a Third Secretary in the Soviet Embassy, Washington, and previously at the Paris Embassy for four years. Serov claimed to be a ranking officer in the KGB and to have important information regarding security risks at Cabinet level in France. His debriefing had commenced and was expected to take some time. The Director would keep the French Government and the Security Commission of the NATO Council informed.

According to the minutes, no discussion followed this statement and the Commission moved on to other business.

'That must have been the "game's up" signal which led Marchand to reach for the pill bottle,' I said to Pabjoy.

'Not quite,' he said. I waited for more but it didn't come.

'I suppose Marchand reckoned that if he was going to end it all he might as well do so in London because that somehow internationalised his action and would pull it onto the front pages outside France, which would make the French that much keener to smother the whole thing. You know: a very public death designed to obscure a private motive.'

'Very subtle, that,' Pabjoy said.

'And you can hardly blame him for not reckoning with our dogged pursuit of truth and justice – your authentic Anglo-Saxon urge to unearth, judge and ultimately punish.'

Pabjoy grunted. 'In Helsinki the other day,' he said suddenly, 'I was talking to Gennadi.'

I waited. He was at his silly game of peeling the facts off the onion one at a time. 'We finally agreed that no useful purpose would be served by mounting a posthumous *auto-da-fé* on André Marchand. But I made it plain that I might not be able to deliver because there were plenty of people here who wanted a big show. People like that shit Killigrew. And enthusiastic political types. And of course the press.'

'Did he buy that?'

'Of course he bought it. Doesn't he have the same problem in Moscow?'

Pabjoy was silent, hoping to make me sweat. So I said nothing. 'You know, Carey,' he said, 'I sometimes think we in this game are the only sane ones. We aren't mesmerised by political faith. We aren't subject to pressure from crazy ideologists who want to smash everything up in order to prove or disprove what Marx wrote in 1854. We're not excited or angry. And we're the only ones who will stay in touch with the opposition when all the other talking has to stop.'

'Menzies and Canaris stayed in touch in the war,' I said. 'It didn't achieve anything I ever heard of.'

'No one knows,' Pabjoy said darkly. 'Anyway, *I* keep in touch with Gennadi. Otherwise we'd arrest, expel and kill quite unnecessarily.' He lapsed into silence. 'You know,' he went on, 'he's given me the whole thing.'

'Couldn't you have got it from him in the first place?' I asked. 'And saved me a lot of aggravation?'

'Oh, yes,' Pabjoy said. 'But that would never do. I've told you before – the Section is like the fuzz – we have to be seen to be pursuing our enquiries. And if Gennadi ever got the impression that we don't do our homework, he'd be tempted to tell me stories. He only told me this because he knew you had the guts of it already.'

'Are you saying you two don't lie to each other?'

'That is what I'm saying. What would be the point of talking if we lied? The thing would be a farce. No, it's either the truth or "no comment". It could be vital *in extremis*, you know, for there to be *one*, just *one* channel of communication that is beyond propaganda or trickery. No bluff, no brinkmanship, no bullshit. The hotlines are all very well for day-to-day bickering. But how could a hot line be the slightest use to avert catastrophe when you had, say, a Nixon or a Reagan at one end and a KGB politico like Andropov at the other? Men you can't get too close to in case they steal your front teeth.'

If I tried to get Pabjoy away from playing at God and asked what he had learned in Helsinki about André Marchand I wouldn't get an answer. So I didn't ask.

'They had a hold on Bracony, of course,' he said. 'From his wartime activities. The Communist Party found him again a few years ago.'

'So the Party knew Marchand belonged to the Soviets as well as the Americans?'

'Not at all. The KGB has enough trouble with its own people without putting their trust in a lot of French Communists who have been pretty heavily infiltrated by the Sûreté and Wavre's lot anyway. No, they told the PCF they weren't interested. Forget it, they said. Then they got Bracony to pass them regular copies of the tapes once they'd done the mod on his equipment. No doubt they told him they'd make mincemeat of him if he talked. I suppose that was all done through the cut-out Roberton. Your man Baum had a sound hunch there. When Tallard contacted you for a meeting on behalf of the Party, he reckoned Marchand was only working for the Americans.'

Pabjoy was drawing boxes again. 'I will show you a memorandum which deals in rather more detail with the Serov case.'

He unlocked the steel-lined top drawer of his desk and drew out a single sheet of paper. It was US State Department stationery. A passage in the middle of the text had been marked with red felt-tip down the margin. 'Read the marked bit,' Pabjoy said. 'The thing's dated seventeenth November, just before the NATO meeting, but we only just got hold of it.'

I read:

> Serov stated in negotiating his defection that he would provide the name of a top-ranking political personality in France who had been under the control of the KGB for a number of years. He claimed that while in Paris he had personally acted as this man's case officer. The debriefing of Serov by FBI agents has been in process since 11 November and at this writing Serov is still seeking certain assurances on his future and is withholding the name as the most valuable material he has to offer. The Director takes the view that once this name has been obtained and processed, Serov will have to be pre-emptively neutralised. If what he asserts proves to be true, it is not considered expedient to have him released at any time. If it proves to be an attempt by the KGB at disinformation, the same view prevails. It is requested that the contents of this memorandum be verbally communicated to suitable person/s in Paris in view of the close relationship between France and the NATO Powers and the effect on NATO policy of any serious breach of security in France.

'"Pre-emptively neutralised" is good,' I said. 'It's what they nearly did to me. What's happened to Serov?'

Pabjoy looked at me and his pale eyes showed no discernible emotion. 'My personal estimate is that they've killed him, if I may avoid a euphemism for once. He may have given them the name. If so, the Director probably decided that was one can of worms *he* wasn't going to open. Whether he cleared that view with the White House or anyone else, I've no idea. But he won't have cleared it with Langley for fear the CIA would capture the whole thing. The Foreign Secretary thinks we have inter-service problems here but he doesn't know what the phrase *means*.' He pulled one of his yellow pads towards him and took great care in selecting a fresh pencil from the sealskin holder. He started to draw again. 'I don't actually *know* if Serov talked, but I'll take anyone's money on two things: he won't emerge alive and we'll never know what he had to say for himself.'

'I read about the Serov defection at the time, in a French newspaper. It didn't mention his four years in Paris and I never gave it another thought. I had other things on my mind.'

Pabjoy wasn't listening. 'Of course Serov was lying. It's true that they were getting stuff from Marchand, but I doubt if Marchand himself knew as much, though of course that's another thing we'll never know. It was Bracony they had on their payroll, not Marchand.'

'So what happened at the NATO meeting?'

'The Chairman must have taken Marchand aside, as the trustworthy envoy of the French Government, and shown him that State Department letter. After all, it was what he'd come to London to be shown. And that was that.'

Later, on our way over to the Foreign Office, Pabjoy was looking evasive. 'You realise, Carey,' he said out of the corner of his mouth as we walked up George IV Street, 'that none of all this is for the Foreign Secretary.'

'So no one will ever know of my heroic exploits?'

'You're paid for it,' Pabjoy said. 'There's no clause about your right to glory.'

We dodged the buses across Parliament Square and found our way up to the Foreign Secretary's room via the private door on the park side of the Foreign Office. The wizened and crusty Danvers was there, silent on a chair at the end of the Foreign Secretary's desk. Next to him sat pinstriped Vivian with a notepad on his knee. Neither Killigrew nor the pink and ginger type from the War Office was present. I felt I'd miss the sheer stimulus of Killigrew.

The Foreign Secretary emitted sparks of Celtic energy in his usual fashion. 'Well, well, gentlemen, I am very glad to see you again. Tell me, did you get the NATO minutes?'

'Yes, thank you, Foreign Secretary,' Pabjoy said.

'And were they worth the bloody trouble?'

'Very useful, Sir. They helped to eliminate certain hypotheses.'

'I took a look at them myself. I must say, the reference to a Soviet defector with a claim to have a name – a French name – that looked a bit disturbing, don't you think?'

'Not as much as might first appear.'

'I'm glad to hear you say that, Andrew. But to me it read disturbingly. Didn't you think so, Danvers?'

Danvers said 'Yes, Foreign Secretary,' on the principle that saying No would probably lead to more trouble than it was worth.

'You see,' the Foreign Secretary said, 'Danvers here agrees that it could be disturbing. Why do you say it is not disturbing, Andrew?'

'Because Carey's investigations in France show no link between André Marchand and any foreign intelligence service. We are at one with the French on that. Furthermore, it is now more than six weeks since this man Serov defected with his promise to reveal a name, and he hasn't revealed it. We get a lot like that, you know, offering titbits in order to get out.'

The Foreign Secretary screwed up his eyes and looked long and hard at Pabjoy. He didn't look as if he believed this facile stuff. 'Do the Americans confirm that the man Serov hasn't made good with his promise?'

'Yes, Sir,' Pabjoy said. He didn't blink.

'So why did Monsieur Marchand kill himself, Andrew? What shall I tell the Prime Minister?'

'A woman,' Pabjoy said crisply. 'A woman named Anny Dupuy. A long-standing affair. She has since been found dead in Paris. Carey here uncovered the relationship. He saw her in Paris before she died. What we do not know, and will probably never know, is why Marchand killed himself here in London, unless it was that he had news while he was here that brought on an immediate fit of clinical depression. I have taken advice on that point from our man Feld and I am advised it is medically possible.'

I swallowed hard and hoped the Foreign Secretary wouldn't turn to me next.

Relief and disbelief struggled across the shrewd features. He appeared to be hearing what he wanted to hear but also what his sharp mind told him was preposterously convenient and improbable. No sounds emerged from Danvers. Vivian was watching the Foreign Secretary like an eager puppy trying to guess which way the rubber ball would be thrown.

'Are you saying this woman sent him packing?'

'Yes, Sir.'

'That right, Carey?'

I took a grip on myself. 'Yes, Foreign Secretary.'

'What was she like, this *femme fatale* who rocks Governments?'

'A handsome woman,' I said. 'Forceful. I can see how the whole thing could have happened.'

'A case of *l'amour, toujours l'amour*,' the Foreign Secretary said.

Vivian sniggered. The Foreign Secretary was sinking in my estimation. His accent didn't help. 'Yes, Sir,' I said. 'It was a very stormy relationship. He had been in love with her for many years.'

There was silence in the room and I found it difficult to meet the Foreign Secretary's knowing brown eyes. My gaze wandered to Danvers and his withered arm with the white lisle glove. I wondered if there was a real hand or something in plastic inside it. He looked more than ever like a remnant from the KGB's bottom drawer. I wondered where they'd dug him up. *Why* they'd dug him up.

'Our recommendation,' Pabjoy was saying, 'is that we accept the assurance of the DST in Paris that they have no reason for concern about Mr Marchand and will inform us if they change that view. We will also keep in touch with Washington on the defector Serov, though with respect, Sir, I think that need not worry you or the Prime Minister.'

The Foreign Secretary seemed to come to a decision. 'Very well, Andrew,' he said, 'thank you for your efforts. Thank you, young man, for your work, too. I want nothing in writing, gentlemen. God forbid there should be anything in writing to plague our old age. I will make a personal report to the Prime Minister who, I hope, will be properly relieved, just as I hope to God nothing happens to make us all look silly. Can I take it, Andrew, that nothing will happen to make us all look silly?'

'You can, Foreign Secretary.' Pabjoy spoke with utter confidence.

'Good. Now, you will observe that the Commander is not here. I understand he has been unable to contribute to your enquiry, so I didn't want to waste his time. Danvers, you'll let him know right away, won't you, that the enquiry is closed.'

'Yes, Foreign Minister.' Danvers looked alarmed at the prospect of getting the awesome Killigrew to do something which he possibly didn't want to do.

'All right, then,' the Foreign Secretary said. 'Thank you all and good day.'

Next morning I told George Roberts and Harry what they had to be told. Harry was rude about it but George didn't seem to care one way or the other. He was working on something else. After lunch I looked in to Andrew Pabjoy's office to tie up the loose ends. I sat in the big chair where Hank Munthe had sprawled, asking me if I'd been busting broncos, Charlie.

'What about Hank?' I said. 'Is he to know how much we know?'

Pabjoy shook his head. 'Counter-productive,' he said. 'Not helpful if we wish to preserve an effective Anglo-American interface.'

Something else was bothering me – an untidy strand in the story. 'During the years that Marchand's stuff was going to the KGB as well, do you think Hank knew?'

'Of course he knew.'

'Then why didn't he do something about it?'

Pabjoy looked at me with pity. 'And risk the other side blowing the whole thing open? Don't be silly, Carey. Would Hank want every newspaper in the civilised world chortling over the CIA mole in the French cabinet who was a Soviet mole as well? And all organised by Hank C. Munthe, who would now have to explain why?'

I reflected on this latest piece of hard realism. 'There's something else,' I said. 'There were easier and less painful ways for Hank to abort our investigation. He didn't have to try to get me killed.'

'He never liked you,' Pabjoy said simply. 'And in any case, his tendency is always the same, you know. To kill. It's tidier. He'd call it a definitive outcome, as opposed to an as-of-now solution.'

'I've been thinking,' I said. 'What you told the Foreign Secretary wasn't really a fabrication at all.'

'It was,' Pabjoy said bluntly.

'Not if you look at it in a certain light. You said Marchand killed himself because of a woman. Well, you know, he did. All his political life was what it was because of a woman. And so was his death. Without Anny Dupuy none of it would have happened. You told a kind of truth, over there at the Foreign Office. A kind of truth . . .'

As real as today's headlines – and even more shocking . . .

ROBERT MOSS AND ARNAUD DE BORCHGRAVE

Bestselling authors of The Spike

July 1980: at a secret meeting in Monimbo, Nicaragua, Fidel Castro unveils a devastating Kremlin-backed masterplan to unleash bloodshed and chaos on the streets of America.

Among Washington's Press corps, only Robert Hockney dares to suspect Cuban intentions. But will he survive long enough to break the story? And can one man's warning voice halt America's countdown to doomsday?

From the violent underworld of Miami terrorism to the deadly realities of political terrorism, MONIMBO is a searing attack on Western complacency and a blockbusting novel of suspense, action and intrigue.

'Fast-paced and thought-provoking.' *Henry Kissinger.*

ADVENTURE THRILLER 0 7221 18651 £2.25

The explosive new thriller of World War II's most baffling enigma

THE JUDAS CODE

DEREK LAMBERT

Bestselling author of I, SAID THE SPY

A journalist advertises for information about the key to the Judas Code. An elderly gentleman turns up at his flat and threatens to kill him. But the journalist nevertheless manages to meet someone who tells him the story . . .

Hitler, Churchill and Stalin are all involved in a tale of intrigue and double-cross on an unrivalled scale. A young Czech in neutral Lisbon, a British intelligence agent operative of very divided loyalties and a beautiful Jewess are all manipulated by a master planner, in a breathtaking scheme to propel Russia and Germany into conflict, buying the Allies the most precious commodity of all: time.

'Mr. Lambert is .... very informed about the known facts of the war into which he weaves his fantasy.' *Daily Telegraph.*

'Lambert certainly keeps the action moving.' *Liverpool Daily Post*.

FICTION/ADVENTURE THRILLER 0 7221 5350 3 £2.25